Published by Stormy Night Publications and Design, LLC.
Hensley, Blake
Blake, Zoe
Hensley, Alta
The More I Hate

Cover Design by Deranged Doctor
Original Custom Illustration by the artist Yozart

INTRODUCING

BLAKE HENSLEY

**The sinfully decadent dream project
of best friends and USA TODAY Bestselling authors,
Zoe Blake and Alta Hensley.**

Alta Hensley, renowned for her hot, dark, and dirty romances, showcases her distinctive blend of alpha heroes, captivating love stories, and scorching eroticism.

Meanwhile, Zoe Blake brings a touch of darkness and glamour to the series, featuring her signature style of possessive billionaires, taboo scenes, and unexpected twists.

Together, as Blake Hensley, they combine their storytelling prowess to deliver "Twice the Darkness," promising sordid scandals, hidden secrets, and forbidden desires of New York's jaded high society in their new series,
Gilded Decadence.

THE MORE I HATE

A DARK BILLIONAIRE ENEMIES TO LOVERS ROMANCE

GILDED DECADENCE SERIES
BOOK ONE

BLAKE HENSLEY

with
ZOE BLAKE
with
ALTA HENSLEY

THE GILDED DECADENCE SERIES

BY BLAKE HENSLEY

A seductively dark tale of privilege and passion.

Ripping off the gilded veneer of elite privilege exposes the sordid scandals, dark secrets, and taboo desires of New York's jaded high society. Where the corrupt game is a seductive power struggle of old money, social prestige, and fragile fortunes… only the most ruthless survive.

The More I Hate
Book One
#arrangedmarriage

Then Hate Me
Book Two
#kidnapped/capture

My Only Hate
Book Three
#officeromance

Fair Love of Hate
Book Four
#bodyguard

A Hate at First
Book Five
#agegap

CONTENTS

CHAPTER 1

LUCIAN

*A*s I watched the bride dutifully walk down the aisle, I knew only a soulless bastard would ruin her day for his own selfish reasons.

Crushing the delicately strewn rose petal path under my shoes, I marched down the aisle in her wake, calling out in a clear, sharp tone, "I object to this wedding."

I kept my gaze trained on the altar.

To look at the guests would imply I gave a damn about their reaction to my outburst.

I was a Manwarring, heir to one of the largest fortunes in America.

Their opinions meant less than nothing to me.

The bride and groom turned at my approach.

The groom, Marksen Dubois, stepped forward, his brow lowered. "If this is your idea of a joke, Manwarring, I'm not laughing."

I cocked my head as I casually brushed nonexistent lint off the shoulder of his tuxedo. "No, old friend, this is *just business*." I leveled a cold stare at him as I used the same phrase he had used in my office last week when he informed me that by marrying Amelia Astrid, his family would have the leverage and financial backing to go after mine.

I could have warned him at the time that I would never allow such an alliance, but this way was much more fun.

He curled his right hand into a fist. "You have two seconds to get the hell out of here."

I quirked one eyebrow then raised my voice for the benefit of the rapacious guests shifting in their seats as they tried to overhear our exchange. "Why don't you ask the bride what she wants?"

Marksen whipped his head to the right.

For the first time, I allowed myself to look at her, to observe the woman whose not only day, but life, I was about to ruin.

She met my gaze with an unexpected, strange forthrightness.

Her vivid, emerald eyes seemed to stare through me.

There was no expression on her face, no anger, surprise, or even confusion. Just a rigid calm.

It was unsettling.

I could feel myself rise to the challenge. I wanted to spear my fingers through her perfect, shiny hair and pull all the pins out until her curls were a tangled, unruly mess. I wanted to smear her lipstick and bring a flush to that pristine, porcelain cheek.

Anything to shatter her icy demeanor.

It was nothing against her personally.

It wasn't her fault.

It was how all daughters of high society were raised.

Perfect ice maidens.

Precious little darlings to be auctioned off to the highest bidder.

Bred to have no personality or opinions or ambitions of their own.

The only thing I despised more than the idea of a society bride was the necessity of having to marry one.

But again, this was all *just business*.

If I had to marry an insipid debutante, I might as well fuck over the former friend who was trying to steal my family business out from under me in the process.

Of course, no one could know that.

As far as any of these horrible guests would be concerned, they had witnessed a tragically romantic moment.

Amelia looked between the two of us.

Before she could respond, her mother stormed the altar.

I was ready for this. Never go into a boardroom or battle without knowing your enemy.

Mary Astrid was infamous, for so many reasons.

She had the personality of a sucked lemon and resembled a plastic Barbie funhouse-mirror version of her daughter. The only outward indication of her rage was the way the ample strands of pearls heavily draped around her throat trembled and rattled. Otherwise, Botox and various fillers had frozen her face into suspended shock.

She lifted her bulbous lips in what I could only assume was a smile which she directed at the guests, not at me. Keeping her voice low, she hissed, "I know who you are, Mr. Lucian Manwarring."

I smirked. "I'd be disappointed if you didn't."

She snorted through her surgically pinched and pruned nose, then pushed the words out through her painfully plumped and pursed lips. "If you don't leave immediately, there will be severe consequences."

I leaned in close and whispered for her ears only. "Funny, I don't see your son's *real* father here."

Her pearls rattled.

I cleared my throat. "Right now, you're wondering how much

3

I know and are trying to calculate if you can take the risk and still have me thrown out. The answer is… I know it all…and I wouldn't if I were you."

The true foundation of power was knowing your enemy's secrets… and making damn sure they never learned yours.

She grabbed the pearls at her throat. "You're blackmailing me? What do you want? Money?"

"Don't be so middle class. I don't need your money. *I want your daughter.*"

The wedding guests murmured and shifted in their seats.

Marksen interrupted. "I am out of patience."

I regarded the mother of the bride. "So am I."

In order for my plan to work, I would need her to play along.

She swallowed, then nodded almost imperceptibly. "The wedding is off."

Marksen ground out, "Now see here—"

She whipped her head to face him. "I said it's off!"

I slapped Marksen on the back. "I'll let you two talk. Excuse me for a moment…"

I pushed him aside and ascended the altar steps to where Amelia stood watching the proceedings curiously, as if she were observing a dramatic play and not her own life. Once again, I had this passionate urge to shake her out of her calm complacency.

I snaked my hand around her waist and pulled her against me.

Before Amelia could fight me off, I wrapped my other hand around her neck and leaned down to claim her mouth.

Her lips were soft and sweet, and she tasted of spearmint and honey tea. Where I'd expected her to smell of some cloying, rose-scented perfume, she carried instead the fresh trace of lemongrass shampoo in her hair. Whereas everything about her mother and her world was fake, preening, and pretentious, holding her, *tasting her*, felt clean and innocent.

The wedding guests erupted in shocked gasps and exclamations.

Amelia looked up at me. "Why are you doing this?"

"Because I love you," I replied loudly.

"I've never even met you."

I ran the backs of my knuckles over the smoothness of her cheek. My smile was for the benefit of the wedding guests. "Don't spoil the moment for our audience. Your mother will explain everything later. Now be a good girl and smile...or I'll be forced to kiss you again."

She obliged with a smile. Through clenched teeth, she hissed, "I hate you."

CHAPTER 2

LUCIAN

I leaned back in the soft leather chair at my club and savored the taste of victory.

Like all the Manwarring men who came before me, I too had always held myself to certain superstitions and traditions.

When your family built its fortune on scandalous secrets, bald-faced lies, and ruthless tenacity, you understood the importance of ritual.

It could center you, focus you, and appease the spirits. Even if you didn't believe in that kind of thing, you knew better than to take unnecessary risks.

Did I believe the fair folk would turn against me if I didn't celebrate every victory like my father and his father did? No. I had no illusions that my Irish ancestors looked down at me from Heaven, or probably up at me from Hell, and thought less of me. I was living the life I knew they would envy.

My ancestors ran Dublin.

They lied, cheated, swindled, and racketeered their way out of the dirt.

Then when one stole and extorted a not-so-small fortune, he

moved here just after Prohibition ended. He pretended he was from the English aristocracy. No relation to *those* Manwarrings who were infamous crooks.

Then he took his modest fortune and showed these United States the glory that was good whisky.

The drink of gentlemen, refined and made in aged barrels, not some backwater bathtub gin that wasn't worth the gut rot and three-day hangover. He became an importer of fine liquors and sold an "elite" whisky that was just bottom-of-the-barrel Irish trash. Eventually, he used that to fund the first distillery.

If those bastards could see me here now, sitting among and being seen as above most of the wealthiest families in New York, having just defeated my enemy and then stolen his bride for my own just to add insult to injury, I liked to think they'd be proud.

Like them, I took what I wanted. It was what I was owed.

Anything that I wanted, it was my right to take.

If another man wasn't strong enough to keep what was his, then why shouldn't it be mine?

Marksen had stood in front of that altar, and that pretty little girl, and watched, speechless, as I stole her with the entire world watching.

Really, I did that poor girl a favor.

With my victory secure, it was in my ancestors' honor that I still sat beside the roaring fire in my favorite red-leather-uphol-stered club chair at The Empire Club. While drinking from a bottle of the oldest reserve whisky my family distilled, I toasted to the Manwarring empire.

As I did for each of my many wins.

For a little extra luck, I always made sure I tipped the wait-ress who brought me the drink. She would receive an outrageous half the value of the bottle—more if I decided to allow her to be generous with her other gifts.

I drank the good spirits to honor the dead ones.

After every victory, every foe defeated, I honored them with the celebration ritual.

The first time I sat here was with my father, when I celebrated graduating from the London School of Business. Not only because I'd studied hard—that was expected of me—but I'd put some snarky little fifteenth from the throne pissant on his ass for saying something about my sister Olivia. Then I'd discredited him, had him arrested for embezzlement, bought his family's holding, and had his entire line shunned.

All for looking at my baby sister a little too long.

So that was where I was after I successfully derailed Marksen's ill-fated match. I was enjoying the ritual while Emily, the waitress, was licking her lips and looking at me, letting me know she would be happy to take me to one of the back rooms and show me how grateful she was for the six-figure tip.

I was tempted. I'd had Emily a few times. She made the most amazing little panting noises when I took her roughly from behind. Her scent was like vanilla and coffee and her throat felt like velvet when it gripped my cock to the base. She would hungrily swallow me down, taking all of me, even though tears ran from her eyes as she struggled to suppress her gag reflex.

Emily was the perfect pet to celebrate with. She also knew that, to me at least, she would never be more than a waitress, and a quick fuck. It was okay with her. I was sure she had her eyes on a few other, older patrons who were looking for their fourth or fifth wives, someone loaded but feeble-minded and near death. That was the payday she was after, and I didn't fit the description nor was I willing to provide.

What I could give her was a good fuck that would leave her satisfied without the aid of pharmaceuticals.

No, Emily knew exactly where we stood, and I appreciated that. Her ambition was elsewhere, as was mine. Still, a few hours of unbridled fun was always a good way to celebrate a win.

The thought quickly fled when the man of the hour himself, Marksen Dubois, marched into the club, still wearing his black tuxedo.

He loosened his bow tie as he ordered a gin. Overpriced swill, but Marksen never understood the complexities of a good drink.

Bankers and real estate investors never did.

How could they? They traded in less-tangible assets, numbers on screens, buildings they rarely, if ever, set foot in, interest rates, and dividends. How could he understand the craftsmanship and history that went into a quality drink? All he understood was the result.

That was why men like him were arrogant in their ignorance, lacking in any creativity.

Was he a worthy opponent at times? Sure. He got a few wins on me.

But not this time.

"Marksen, I didn't expect to see you here," I remarked with a shit-eating grin. "You know, although the dress code is formal, tuxedos are not required during the day. A simple Italian suit will suffice, provided, of course, it is properly tailored."

He looked over his shoulder before taking a long sip of his cocktail. "Quite a stunt you just pulled, Manwarring, but I'd expect nothing less from an uncouth, classless Irish thug like yourself."

"Stunt? That was a dramatic display of my undying love *for your bride*—or so the papers will say." I blinked up at him before taking another sip of my drink and letting it warm my belly.

It was the weekend, but still early enough in the day that most of the men here were older, retired, and put out to pasture by their families.

They came here more out of habit, needing something to occupy their time since they had long since made their mark and handed the baton off to the next generation. They came here to read the paper and rehash the victories of their glory days as titans of industry, while they harassed the waitresses who tolerated them, thinking they could be the next Mrs. Whoever the IV once the current wives aged out at thirty-five.

It was pathetic, and I sincerely hoped someone put me out of my misery before I joined their wrinkled ranks.

Abandoning his crap drink at the bar, he took the seat across from me, uninvited, and poured himself a glass of my whisky. "You can't possibly imagine I'm going to let you get away with this...*stunt*."

He knocked back the whisky like it was some cheap vodka he drank on spring break back in university out of some delusional girl's belly button, proving yet again breeding wasn't everything.

"That drink you just wasted was a century old. At least pretend to show it the respect it deserves." I raised an eyebrow as I moved the bottle away from him.

He casually reached for the bottle and examined the label. Then, keeping his gaze trained on me, he threw it over his shoulder into the fireplace.

The blue flames jumped and licked the top of the brick hearth.

An attendant immediately came over to lower the gas flow and get the flames under control before something caught on fire.

I leaned back as I raised my glass to my lips. "That was a nearly full bottle and worth just shy of one point five million dollars last time it was appraised."

He raised his empty glass in a mock toast. "I'll write you a fucking check."

"Don't bother. I have another two cases in the vault, and then five more from the next year. Besides, I got something far more valuable today."

It may have been petty, but I loved rubbing salt in his wounds, especially if I was the one who had wounded him.

He rose again like he had too much anger running through his veins to sit still. He paced like a caged tiger in the circus, pretending he was still a predator and the ringmaster hadn't had his teeth pulled and his claws clipped.

Once he'd placed his empty glass on the mantel, he turned to me as he cupped his right hand over his left fist. "This *stunt* of yours was childish and beneath you, Manwarring. As my rival, I'm going to crush you now."

"Marksen, you have never been my rival," I partially lied. "To be a rival, you'd have to be at my level. Had you married the Astrid girl, maybe her connections would have made you more of an annoyance, but…well, I guess we all know how that went for you today." I grinned as I took another sip.

"You don't mean to actually marry the girl?" He continued pacing back and forth in front of the fireplace with his jacket open and his hands on his hips.

I shrugged. "And why not? Now my family's legacy is protected, and I have a beautiful new fiancée who will soon be my wife. Her brother will eat dinner at my table. Just think of all the influence that will give me. *Influence that would have been yours.* It really is great timing. We are looking at opening a few new warehouses and could use her brother the DA to help overlook a few details."

He rubbed his hand over his jaw. "We used to be friends."

"We did, so imagine my surprise when my *friend* openly went after my family's legacy. If we were such good friends, you should have known better than to get in between me and what is mine."

"It's not like the fucking whisky business even nets a worthwhile profit," he said, proving he knew nothing about anything.

This business was at the heart of everything my family had built.

"It's just fucking business."

I stood and met his aggression. He had forgotten who he was dealing with if he thought his insults would go unnoticed or unanswered.

"You're right, it's just business, *my business*. You thought you could take me out, you thought your balls were big enough to take me on, so you struck, and I struck back. Harder. I protect what is mine, and now that includes the pretty little girl your daddy bought and paid for."

He scoffed and turned away from me.

I grabbed his arm and yanked him back. I wasn't done.

"Now, because you weren't man enough, that pretty little girl is going to spend the rest of her life bouncing on my cock, grateful she got to marry a real man who doesn't need her family to make business deals on his behalf."

He smirked. "I was man enough for her last night. Good luck enjoying my seconds."

I bared my teeth at him, reminding him while I may be dressed as an aristocrat and educated as a gentleman, I could, and would, hold my own in a fight.

More importantly, he knew I didn't fight fair.

Now he knew that went for business as well as my personal life.

We were squaring off in one of the most exclusive clubs in the world, let alone New York City, and while fights were not a normal occurrence, you couldn't have so many world leaders, so many power-hungry men trying to screw each other over, and not have the occasional scuffle break out. After all, millions had been gained and lost in this room.

Fortunes rose as legacies died.

"Gentlemen, if your intent is violence, we ask that you please refrain from fighting in the lounge and instead move to take this outside." Jonathan, one of the hosts, came over to defuse any tension.

"That won't be necessary, Jonathan. We were just finishing up. Isn't that right, Marksen?" I straightened my tie and tipped more whisky into my mouth, taking a moment to savor the smooth-aged liquor.

The complexity of the vanilla, tobacco, and hint of spice always hit just right.

Marksen crossed his arms, pulling tight at his suit jacket. "I'm just getting started with you."

"There is just one insignificant problem with that, Marksen. Business 101, you have no leverage over me."

I drained my glass, turned it upside down, and slammed it on the table as I turned to leave. "Now, if you will excuse me, I have a wedding to plan."

As I crossed the threshold, he called out, "You've forgotten one thing in planning this revenge *stunt* of yours, Manwarring."

I stopped and turned my head, barely glancing over my shoulder, keeping my back to him. "And what is that?"

"Amelia Astrid isn't the only eligible society bride on the market."

My chest tightened.

He tilted his head to the side. "How is that *sweet little sister* of yours? What was her name? Olivia?"

My fingers curled into a fist, refusing to take the bait. *Fuck.*

As I stormed out of the club, I reached into my jacket pocket for my phone to call my security team and double Olivia's guard.

CHAPTER 3

AMELIA

Don't react.
Do not lose it in front of these people.
Their eyes are on you.
Do not further embarrass the family.
Do not show them you care.
For the love of God, don't let anyone know the only thing you feel is
relief.

With a shove, I pushed myself out of this stranger's grasp. Ignoring my sister holding my bouquet of soulless white lilies, I turned and marched back up the cathedral's aisle, away from my mother, who was still trying to make excuses for whatever had just happened.

Without a second thought, I left my fiancé, who was fuming with visible rage.

I also left Mr. Manwarring, a man I knew only by his reputation as a ruthless sociopath.

The whispers about him were all very mysterious. The only thing the gossip could agree on was that he was the heir to a multi-billion-dollar fortune that was built around whisky and, if rumors were to be believed, questionable practices.

If I wasn't getting married, there was no reason for me to be standing at the altar like a fool in front of so many of the most affluent people in New York City.

I didn't look back at Mr. Manwarring.

Or at Mr. Dubois, whom I was supposed to be marrying, and who had shockingly stood by and let the disruption happen.

Or even my mother, who had called off the wedding instead of demanding Mr. Manwarring leave.

The three of them created this mess; they could deal with it. I was already balancing on the knife's edge between a panic attack and a full-blown mental break.

The layers of tulle, silk, and God only knew what else the monstrosity of a wedding dress was constructed of swished obnoxiously as I forced my way past the guests, many of whom had risen to their feet to watch the commotion or try to offer aid in some way.

The cathedral's pews were filled with a few hundred people, all in their couture gowns and formal tuxedos. Everyone appeared to wear the same fashionable beige and seasonal pastels that were so muted it was as if they had sun bleached the life out of their clothes before they got dressed. Passing through that colorless hall was like being suffocated by a drab, untreated canvas.

I wanted to run. I wanted to hide, but that would make the scene worse, and add fuel to the Page Six fire that was going to engulf my reputation.

I knew better.

I was still a daughter of the Astrid family, and I had been taught to handle everything with dignity and grace. So, my head high, I ignored the murmurs and whispers, tamped down the warring emotions in my stomach, and made my way down the marble aisle, alone. My entire body was tensed to the point of pain so no one would see me shaking.

Well, not alone for long. The delicate clacking of the obscene number of pearls my mother wore followed me. She owed me an explanation, but I doubted I'd get one. Not one that would make up for this. I couldn't even imagine what was whispered in her ear for her to have allowed this to happen.

No, she would no doubt make whatever just happened here my fault. God forbid she ever took ownership of any problem or inconvenience.

She was the kind of woman who, if she dropped a fork at a table, had a server fired. If she missed an appointment, a maid was dismissed for altering her date book. And, if she had a single white hair or a wrinkle at her age, the world was against her, and she took it out on the nearest salesclerk or waitstaff.

She'd gone through ten hairdressers in a month before someone told her that silver hair was all the rage in Paris. Then it was a matter of dyeing her natural gray, which was more a snow white, to a distinguished sterling shade. No one had the nerve to point out she matched the silverware, and the shade was far too ashen to complement her warm skin tone.

It made her look like an evil queen in a child's fairy-tale book.

And now, her daughter's wedding was ruined.

Heads were going to roll.

Not out of some maternal instinct to protect or avenge me, her daughter, the bride.

No, this would be seen as an embarrassment to the family and a slight aimed at her.

My feelings about it were inconsequential.

For a moment, I wondered if I could be fired or dismissed or even let go from being her daughter, the perfect society woman.

She could fire me, replace me with a slimmer, chicer model, and I could be free to live my life. It was the perfect fantasy. She would enter my room one afternoon and tell me that biological daughters were so last season, and I was being replaced with a newer model from Tokyo.

If only. I didn't even let myself daydream about freedom anymore, no longer sure what I would do if my life were my own.

Finally, I burst through the heavy wooden doors leading outside and ran down the sidewalk as a summer shower started ruining my perfectly coiffed updo. It didn't even faze me at this point. I climbed into the waiting limo, hoping to leave before my mother got in. Sadly, the ridiculously cumbersome train with its lace appliques that matched the dress took too long to pull in after me.

God, I hated this dress.

I simply wanted a moment alone to process what had just happened and the swirling emotions running through my veins. Some were familiar. The relief at not marrying Marksen Dubois was palpable, but so was the fear of what my mother would do, and the disappointment of not leaving my childhood home.

Then there was something else, something less familiar, a gnawing need that I had felt when Manwarring had grabbed and kissed me.

His kiss hadn't been sweet like I'd expected Dubois's to be.

It hadn't been gentle or even indifferent. It hadn't been anything like what the other girls had described when they talked about kissing their boyfriends. His kiss had been controlling, his lips and tongue had devoured mine, and I'd felt a strange magnetism drawing me to him like I wanted more. I could still feel the way he made my entire body tingle.

I had felt nothing like it before.

That couldn't be it. I had to be misinterpreting my body's

reaction. A single kiss with a man I didn't know should not—could not—have had such a potent effect on my body. I should've been enraged that he had the audacity to kiss me, not wondering when he would do it again and if it would always feel like that.

Mother pushed her way into the limo and settled herself on the plush black leather seat directly across from me. Instantly, the limo was filled with the jasmine-and-rose stench of her Guerlain's Shalimar Eau de Parfum.

Her mouth was distorted in an odd, misshapen, duck-lipped expression, the closest she could come to pursing her lips since her latest Botox and filler injections.

"Well, do you have anything to say for yourself?" She drew the bottle of Dom Pérignon Rose 1959 out of its sterling silver ice bucket and poured herself a glass in one of the crystal flutes that had been chilled. It was a rare, expensive vintage I had meant to drink to celebrate my wedding and my escape from her drunken tyranny.

She drank like it was just another bottle.

"Please explain to me what just happened." I kept my tone as even as possible.

Manwarring had said something to her, something that had made my mother call off the wedding. I had no clue what could have been so important that she'd do that and not at least try to save face and continue the ceremony.

"You tell me. You are the whore whose lover just ruined a very lucrative merger." The word *whore* slapped me in the face, and cracks formed in my porcelain mask.

"I have never met Mr. Manwarring before. I was ready to let you and Mr. Dubious handle it until you said the wedding was off. What did he say to you?" I demanded.

If my mother noticed my slip in calling Mr. Dubois by the nickname I'd had for him since she'd informed me of my engagement, she said nothing.

19

She narrowed her eyes at me. I don't think I had ever talked back to her like that, at least not out loud.

"He has information that would embarrass the family. He'll keep our secret as long as he gets what he wants. For some reason, he wants you. You will marry him and make sure his fortune and reputation are tied to ours so he can never use what he knows against any of us. You did whatever it was you did to inspire him to find this information. It now falls to you to safeguard it."

"I don't think he cares about his reputation, Mother." I looked away so she couldn't see my eyes roll.

Even now, there was a limit to my bravery. "If he did, he would have brought this to your attention before the wedding. He wants a scandal, not a wife."

The dress she'd picked out for me was suffocating, and the lace was making my skin crawl. I pulled at the lace appliques, desperate for some relief. The lace practically disintegrated in my hands as I pulled one of the flowers off and tossed it aside.

"What are you doing?" I winced at her screech. "That is a couture gown!"

"I'm sorry. Were you going to want me to wear this dress to my next wedding?" I asked, already well aware of her response.

She had chosen this dress because it was the fashion at the exact moment I was being married. It would be out of date by tonight.

At least I hoped that was why she had forced me to wear this hideous thing.

She calmly set down her champagne glass then grabbed my arm. Her acrylic talons dug into my flesh hard enough that tears sprang to my eyes, and I had to bite back a cry of pain.

"Do not forget your place. You are an Astrid. This is clearly your fault. You flaunted yourself like a whore in front of Manwarring, and now he must have his little promiscuous slut on his arm." She leaned further forward, the pearls at her neck clacking and rattling.

"I didn't." Per usual, my words fell on deaf ears.

She dug her nails in harder as I tried to pull back my arm.

"There is no other reason he would want a woman like you, so uncouth. God knows, I tried to make a proper lady out of you, but your father had to let you go to that filthy school with all those common people. It's a wonder you didn't come back pregnant, addicted to drugs, and with an incurable venereal disease."

I ground my teeth and tried to hold back the words on the tip of my tongue.

It didn't matter that I was as pure as the driven snow.

Hell, the asshole who had just ruined my wedding had stolen my first kiss.

It didn't matter that I was proud of my art history degree from NYU and that it was one of the hardest programs to get into. She would hear none of it anyway, so I bit my tongue and took her verbal abuse.

If I stayed quiet, maybe she would finish the bottle and drink herself into a stupor.

Standing up for myself made her violent.

There were only so many ways to cover bruises in the New York summer heat.

"You're right, Mother."

The anger that had been building inside me since Manwarring stood up finally boiled over. "I am a prostitute. You made me one the second you sold me off to the highest bidder. That's my role in this family. To be whored out for the financial benefit of the Astrid name. Don't you dare look down on me for being what you demanded of me!"

I ripped the rest of the delicate lace from my neck.

Finally able to breathe, I met my mother's gaze.

Her eyes were filled with anger, her pearls rattling like a

snake about to strike. This time, her lips managed to twist into a scowl, probably ruining the Botox she had injected the other day so she could outshine me at my wedding. I would be blamed for that as well once she noticed.

Did she not know how transparent her vain attempts were?

"How dare you," she started. "Do you know what I have sacrificed for you, to raise you?"

"The hours you spent slaving over the pictures of nannies until you found one that you felt was ugly enough not to tempt Daddy, but pretty enough you could stand looking at?" I bit back. "It must have been harrowing."

"I don't know what has gotten into you." She grabbed my arm again, sinking those razor-sharp claws into my skin hard enough that I'd have to wear long sleeves for the next few days. "But you do not speak to me like that. I will not be spoken to like that by anyone, let alone some little slut who just embarrassed our family." Her nails sank in deeper, and I had to bite back a cry of pain.

"Let go of me!" I tried to pull my arm back, but she was strong.

"Here's what's going to happen. You are going to marry Mr. Manwarring. We are going to spin it like a star-crossed lovers' romance of the century. The papers will eat it up."

"No!" I wrenched on my arm again.

When she finally unhooked her claws, I fell into the side of the limo and struck my head on the window. My vision blurred for a moment, making my head spin.

"If you mess this up, it's not me that you will be hurting. You will take your brother down with you. Is that what you want?"

"How will who I marry impact the Manhattan District Attorney's Office?"

Her words had taken a lot of the power from my rage.

I loved Harrison. I respected him. He had worked for his

position. Daddy hadn't bought it like he'd bought Benjamin's—my other brother's—military career.

"That is none of your concern. You will do as you are told. Remember, you are not too old to be sent to a convent or locked in an asylum."

CHAPTER 4

LUC

"*H*ello, Amelia, darling." I gritted my teeth as the valet opened the door to Amelia's black Town Car.

I offered her my left arm to help her from the vehicle, which she gracefully took, as was expected of her.

At least she hadn't forgotten all her manners. "You look stunning tonight."

She really looked absolutely stunning, wearing a classic black, high-necked gown with a scintillating slit to her thigh that showed off enough skin to be mouthwatering, but not so much as to be indecent. She didn't wear any jewelry. She didn't need to. The dress itself seemed to sparkle like diamonds as she moved. The look was completed with her smoky eyes and red lips, the makeup painted onto her flawless, frozen face.

I had to give her mother credit.

The shrew knew what she was doing.

Amelia was everything a high society bride should be, perfect on the outside and hollow on the inside.

Pretty enough to be on my arm for events and to give me

children, but cold enough not to care when I inevitably went elsewhere for entertainment. A man could not be expected to live his life without a woman who was passion and fire. That was how they became soft in the head and married twenty-some-thing waitresses without prenups.

She smiled politely at me but didn't say a word, just took my arm and allowed me to escort her from the drop-off line to the gala.

The red carpet was, of course, rolled out for the event, and a few paparazzi snapped pictures as we walked arm in arm into the sculpture garden that led into the mansion.

We passed the fountains of cherubs pissing into the pools of water. I never understood why statues of pissing babies were the height of sophistication, but like so many older mansions such as this, there were statues of babies, or of women with their breasts exposed as they poured water.

Amelia remained silent on my arm.

Her gaze appeared to linger over the various statues, like she was assessing them, taking them in one by one as we approached the large open double doors of the Diederich mansion to attend yet another garish fundraiser for the New York Public Library. Apparently, they desperately needed funds so they could buy something important, and it hadn't occurred to anyone to just ask for the donations instead of spending half of them on this party.

Above us were several balconies, a few guests already mingling and watching the parade of wealthy narcissists. Prob-ably making bets on who would be featured on the society pages as the "best dressed" and "worst dressed." All while getting their asses kissed for being at a charitable event.

A few signs explained what it was they were raising money for exactly. I didn't even bother looking them over.

I didn't care.

No one at this event gave a damn about the library or what the money was being raised for. This event was to see and be seen.

Truth be told, I loathed charity galas.

They were never truly parties but networking events where men were forced to bring their wives so they could show off their arm candy. It was a waste of time, but expected of me, so I was here, with my reluctant soon-to-be-bride on my arm.

As we moved into the mansion, my senses were immediately assaulted with the cloying, heavy perfumes of the other women. Several were milling about, looking at the paintings, no doubt of the Diederich ancestors, or even commenting on the gilded frames. A double grand marble staircase dominated the foyer, its European ironwork a sharp contrast to the white stone steps. Other guests were headed up to look down at the party from the balconies, not only outside, but no doubt above the ballroom as well.

Grand mansions such as this always seemed to have several places where the owner could look down upon his guests. Any man who needed a balcony to look down on people wasn't much of a man at all. Though I supposed some members of the fairer sex would call the balconies "romantic," daydreaming about Romeo and Juliet like they were some great love story.

"I hate these events," I said under my breath.

"Don't enjoy giving money to charity?" Amelia asked, not looking at me.

"No, I appreciate the tax write-off. What I don't like are pompous men playing at being masters of the universe. They pretend to have worked for everything they have in their lives, then sit around congratulating each other on jobs well done. Enough of my time is spent around these crypt keepers. I don't want to spend my evenings meeting their wives and acting like I give a shit about their snot-nosed kids' achievements or the new horse, car, or humidor they just bought."

I flagged down a waiter wearing a white tux with white gloves. "Though I suppose you like them? You and Marksen attend any of these events?"

I didn't miss the bitterness in my tone. Marksen had been running through my mind all day, and it affected me more than I liked. It hadn't occurred to me to investigate how far he had gotten with my would-be bride. At the time, it didn't matter for my revenge.

It shouldn't matter now.

Except for some reason, it did.

"No." She didn't elaborate, and I didn't ask. I didn't want to think about what she'd done with other men, and I really didn't want to think about why that made me so irrationally mad.

The only good thing about these parties was the food, which was usually decent, and I hadn't had time to eat at work today.

"I find your attitude surprising," she said as she plucked a morsel off a silver tray.

"And why is that?"

"It seems a little hypocritical. Aren't you one of the men who just 'play at being a master of the universe,' as you put it, or am I mistaken?"

"You're mistaken and out of line," I said, reaching for my own stuffed mushroom cap.

She arched a perfectly shaped brow in challenge. "Then I apologize. I didn't realize you started your family business yourself. I thought your father handed it to you like his father handed it to him."

She had made her point, but she had no idea what she was starting.

"Tell me then, Ms. Astrid, what have you accomplished in your life that is so noteworthy?"

If she was already my wife, I would be looking forward to punishing her for the way she talked back to me.

She would learn her place at my feet soon enough.

"Nothing." She shrugged, unbothered by my observation. "I have the privilege of coming from generational wealth, but the misfortune of being a woman. No one will ever hand me a business or even give me the opportunity to pursue a fortune of my own. My passions are of little consequence and will never amount to more than hobbies. But I don't look down on those around me just because they are in a similar situation."

"Good, then when we are married you can do these insipid events in my stead."

"Fine." She didn't add to that, she just looked up at a painting of a man with ruddy cheeks against a pitch-black background. I was sure the mini spotlight and the hand-carved cross work on the frame, painted with gold leaf, made it appear darker than it was.

"You can't possibly like these events, being surrounded by brain-dead imbeciles too drunk on their own self-importance?" I asked.

"As you may have noticed when you interrupted my wedding by blackmailing my mother, I rarely get what I want." She tried to take a step away from me, unsuccessful when I pressed my hand on her arm in mine, not letting her leave.

"Was being Marksen's wife what you wanted?" Rancor laced my words, and I didn't bother hiding it.

"No."

The finality in her tone surprised me.

CHAPTER 5

LUC

We made our way into the grand ballroom, and I was right. The room was three stories high, and people milled about on the second-story balcony. The third, however, was empty. Probably roped off somewhere to keep the guests out of offices or even personal rooms.

The interior was dim enough to offer the illusion of a more intimate affair, and light reflecting off the glittering chandelier flitted around the space. I had the sudden urge to lead Amelia into the ballroom and dance with her, letting those errant beams of light hit her sparkling dress so it shimmered like stars.

The compulsion to show her off, to show everyone she was mine, was strong, even if Dubois had had her first.

Something about her was different, and I was determined to find out what it was.

Too bad I was not the type of man to dance. I knew how, of course; I chose not to. Most of the time.

"I heard the most interesting rumor," I whispered into Amelia's ear, again surprised by her refreshingly crisp, clean scent. I wanted to bury my nose in her hair so I could smell only her and none of the others.

"Is it the one about the barbarian who embarrassed the woman he had never met before by ruining her wedding and claiming her like she was livestock that strayed from its keep?"

Her face hardly moved as she spoke. Her soft, pleasant smile was still firmly in place despite the harshness of her tone. It took me a moment to process what she'd said.

"No, darling." I gritted my teeth. "It was the one about the vapid Upper East Side princess who didn't have the manners to wait where she was told so her husband could pick her up like a proper gentleman."

"No." She met my eye, and for a moment, I could have sworn I glimpsed a flash of genuine emotion.

It was rage or hatred, but still it was a crack in that porcelain face.

"I hadn't heard that. It must have been quite the scandal. After all, Upper East Side princesses only ever do what they are told. Our only real purpose in life is to look pretty, obey, and breed. Like purebred bitches."

That caught me off guard. My palm ached to warm her pert little ass for daring to speak to me like that. I scrambled for some reply when one of the old biddies approached us.

Not for the first time tonight, I wondered if I had misread Amelia.

Could she be more than just an ice queen?

"Amelia, darling, congratulations on your new engagement. I must say, we were all entirely shocked at the church. It was such a scandal." Her eyes actually lit up when she said "scandal." "But to have such an amazing love match between two families. It's a blessing." She took Amelia's hands, and Amelia graciously smiled down at the old woman.

"Thank you, ma'am. It has been quite the whirlwind that I never expected. I didn't even know it was possible."

Her insinuation was not lost on me.

Thankfully, the other woman didn't seem to pick up on her double meaning.

I was finding out my bride had more bite than I had expected. She was going to be a lot more fun than I'd assumed. Excitement bubbled up inside me. She was going to be a challenge.

I loved a good challenge.

There were so many ways I could tame her smart mouth.

"Oh, of that I am sure, dear." She looked at Amelia's gloved hands and her brow furrowed. "Oh, dear, don't you have a ring yet?"

"No, not yet. There are three other weddings this month, and he has to make sure none of the other brides are of better breeding stock before he invests in this merger."

"What?" The older lady looked taken aback, and I was forced to intervene.

"Pardon me. I'm so sorry, ma'am, I need to steal my bride away for a moment. Excuse us." Amelia's arm was relaxed under my grip as I pulled her away from the elderly woman who was still looking confused. "What do you think you are doing, telling people that? Do you understand how fast gossip spreads in these circles?"

She blinked up innocently at me. "I don't see how. According to you, everyone in here is a brain-dead imbecile whose minds have been clouded by their own self-importance."

I leaned down and whispered in her ear. "Be careful, little girl, or I will show you what happens to mouthy little brats who can't behave themselves."

"Well, how should I know why I don't have a ring or what your intentions are? We have never had a conversation before,

Mr. Manwarring. I can only guess what possible excuses you have for upending my life."

"We are getting married soon. Call me Luc."

"I don't engage in any informal conversation with people I'm not acquainted with. I'm sure you understand, Mr. Manwarring."

"You can call me Luc, or sir, your choice. There would be a ring on your finger now if you would have waited for me to pick you up," I said, talking over her.

Her lip curled in disgust as she spoke, giving me the first actual glimpse of the fire she had in her. "I don't need your trinkets. You don't have to buy me. You already embarrassed me and tarnished my reputation enough that you are the only viable suitor left."

It was buried deep under layers of makeup, breeding, and bullshit, but it was there.

I wanted to stoke those flames. I had the urge to taste her lips again, to see if what I'd felt at the wedding was a fluke, adrenaline from fucking with Marksen's plans, or if it was her.

"I don't care what you need. You will wear my ring."

"Oh Amelia. Mr. Manwarring." Another older lady, whose name escaped me, came up to us and pulled Amelia into a hug. "Congratulations, dear. You two are the talk of the party. Everyone is so excited about your wedding, or scandalized. Either way, it's all people can talk about." She looked Amelia and me up and down. "And look, you two make such a handsome couple. Your children will be simply stunning."

"Thank you." Amelia looked down at the older woman with the same softness as before. "You are too kind, Mrs. Cooper."

The woman grabbed Amelia's hands to hold them, her thumbs running over the backs of her fingers. "Where is your ring?" she asked, aghast, reaching up to clutch her double string of pearls.

I had to wonder if the first nosy old bat had told her about

Amelia's lack of an engagement ring or if that was all these women cared about.

Either way, I refused to be the talk of this party because my woman wasn't wearing my ring. I much preferred the women talk about how I'd swept her off her feet while the men talked about how much stronger the Manwarrings were going to be now with the Astrids and how I had taken her from Dubois.

No one was going to be saying that I was cheap or hard up. That would lead to speculation about financial trouble. And that was unacceptable.

"Oh, darling." I placed my hand on her lower back, for the first time noticing it was completely bare.

Her skin was impossibly soft and warm, and far too much of it was exposed.

The dress she wore had a plunging back that stopped just above the curve of her ass.

I gritted my teeth and held my smile. "That's right, I'm so sorry. I forgot I had picked it up from the jeweler earlier." I looked back at the older woman. "I had to get it sized."

She nodded like it was perfectly reasonable for a man not to know his intended's ring size. Like every woman here didn't have a file at Tiffany's with her size and style preferences.

I pulled the signature blue box from my breast pocket and opened it for her. Nestled in the white satin lining was a simple platinum band with a five-carat, emerald-cut diamond. It was stunning, elegant, and timeless.

I had to admit I'd been surprised when I found out this was where her personal tastes lay. I had seen the gaudy thing Marksen had made her wear. Since the Dubois family ring would go to his older brother's wife, I'd assumed she'd picked out the one she'd worn and was a "more is more" type.

After seeing her in her wedding dress, I was positive that was the case, preferring the expense to taste.

This ring said something a little different.

It was a little less Kardashian and a lot more Hepburn.

I had much to learn about this woman, and even more to teach her.

She looked down at the ring, her lips pursed slightly like she was trying not to let slip any response.

I knew, for a fact, this was the ring she wanted.

What I didn't know was why she didn't want to let me know I was right.

This stubborn little brat would learn her place soon enough.

The old woman reached up to grab my wrist and pull it down so she could have a better look.

"That's stunning. The clarity is incredible," she gushed.

I gently took back my hand, then lifted the ring from the box, which I tucked back in my pocket. Then I reached for Amelia's hand and slid the ring on over her glove. It was a little tight with the fabric, but the silk let it slide on easily enough. Then I leaned over and placed a kiss on her cheek like a good future husband should.

"It's so pretty," the older woman said.

"Isn't it?" Amelia admired the ring, and I had this strange, light feeling in my gut. Like I was proud to have her wearing my ring and pleased that she liked it. "I picked it out a few months ago at Tiffany's." She looked down at the other woman conspiratorially. "Isn't it so nice when men can follow directions?"

The older woman laughed, and I gritted my teeth, not enjoying being the butt of her little jokes. I was going to have to teach her some respect soon enough.

"If you will excuse us," I said as I grabbed Amelia's arm and pulled her away from the elderly woman.

"What is wrong with you?" I asked.

"I don't know what you mean." She opened her eyes wide to look innocent and blinked up at me.

"You should know better. Your dress is too revealing. You're actively trying to belittle me. I'm going to be your husband. You're mine. Act like it!"

"Am I?" she seethed. "Because the other day, I could have sworn I was going to marry another man. That didn't happen, so why should I think this engagement is any different?"

I grabbed her arm again, and she winced.

There was no way I grabbed her hard enough to cause any pain.

I was a bastard, but I wouldn't hurt her, at least not with so many witnesses. Even then, any time I caused her pain, it would be to further her pleasure.

With a quick yank, I pulled down the tops of her long gloves and revealed four long, thin bruises on one of her arms. A clear handprint that was topped with little half-moon scabs that were still healing.

"Who did this to you?"

"It's none of your concern." She yanked the gloves back in place.

"Tell me who dared put their hands on you."

"No," she said between clenched teeth.

"Tell me now, so I can handle it. If you don't, I swear I'll show you what happens to little girls who don't behave."

"What are you going to do?" she asked. "Look around. We are surrounded by people. People you do business with, and after ruining my wedding to Dubois, I doubt you want a scene here. I'm here playing the happy little bride. If you don't like my performance, fine. Call off the wedding."

"Little girl, you have no idea what I am going to do to you." I put my hand on her hip, holding her in place as I leaned in.

Anyone looking at us would assume I was whispering sweet nothings into her ear, telling her how beautiful she was, or all the things I'd rather do to her somewhere private.

"You already publicly humiliated me. You have people thinking I have been with you behind Dubois's back. I am being called a whore by my peers, and lecherous men are leering at me, wondering what kind of magic I can do in the bedroom to be worthy of such a public scene. What more could you possibly do to me? Lock me in a tower? Send me to a convent after we are married? But wait, all of that would reflect poorly on you."

She turned her back to me, and seeing her bare skin, I snapped.

I encircled her wrist, holding firmly but not tight enough to hurt in case she had more bruises that I hadn't seen yet. I pulled her out of the ballroom and down the hall.

"I think you and I need to have a *talk*."

CHAPTER 6

AMELIA

*S*everal men were playing billiards when we burst into the room.

Luc took one look at them and ordered, "Out."

Without any objection, the men dropped their pool cues and left.

Luc slammed the double doors shut after the last man... and locked them.

The cold, damning sound of the bolt sliding into place sent a chill up my spine.

I knew better than to call out for help. Not only would that cause an unforgiveable scene, but it would also be for nothing. They would take one look at Luc and not risk his wrath, or more accurately financial ruin, by helping me.

Crossing my arms over my middle, I tapped my foot. "Well, you wanted to talk. So talk."

He shrugged out of his tuxedo jacket and tossed it over the nearest oxblood leather chair. Raising his arm, he unhooked his cuff link and rolled up first one sleeve then the other. "I misspoke. *Talking* wasn't what I had in mind."

I frowned as I backed up, placing the billiards table between us. I answered in a frigid tone. "You forget yourself, sir."

"On the contrary, I'm reminding you precisely who I am in this relationship," he ground out as he stalked around the table toward me.

I scurried to the other side of the table. Forgetting my earlier conviction, I threatened him. "I'll scream."

He continued to relentlessly pursue me. "I don't mind an audience for what I'm about to do…but you might."

I blanched, tripping over my skirt in my momentary distraction.

Taking advantage, he lunged.

Before I could object, he snatched me around the waist and bent me over the billiards table. A rush of chilled air raised goosebumps on the exposed flesh of my thighs as he flipped the voluminous skirt of my dress over my hips to expose my silk panties.

"How dare you!" My words hissed from between my clenched teeth as I flattened my palms against the green felt and tried to force up my torso.

He placed a firm hand between my shoulder blades to keep me in place. "You are about to learn I will dare a great deal when it comes to you."

The retort died on my lips as he landed a sharp, stinging slap on my right ass cheek.

I cried out, more from shock than pain. "Are you mad? Unhand me!"

Luc responded by peppering my ass several more times, building in intensity with each connection of his palm against my silk-clad bottom.

I curled my hands into fists, pounding them on the billiards table. "Stop! It hurts!"

"It's supposed to hurt," he taunted. "It's a punishment."

I glared at him over my shoulder. "I'm not some little girl to be spanked over your knee!"

Fisting my hair, he leaned over me, his lips mere inches from mine. His gaze moved from my lips to my eyes.

My breath seized. Was he going to kiss me again? Did I want him to?

My toes curled inside my high heels as I clenched my inner thighs.

Everything about this was dark and twisted. It was as if the very air crackled with barely suppressed sexual violence, like the moment right before receiving a shock from an exposed wire. There was the spark. You knew the pain was coming. You could feel the rush of adrenaline as your body prepared for it. You knew there would be this sick rush of euphoria afterward, as if you just cheated death.

Then for some strange reason you couldn't explain, you found yourself stretching your fingertip out again...to touch the wire...one more time.

I should be enraged. I should be screaming for the authorities, and yet there was something arousing about having him looming over me, his body weight pinning me down, his punishing hand on my skin. How the pain made my body come alive in ways I hadn't felt before, my dull existence having tamped down all other forms of emotion.

Finally, he warned, "If you don't want to be punished like a misbehaving little girl, then next time don't behave like one."

I narrowed my eyes. "I hate you."

The corner of his mouth lifted. "Fortunately, love is not a prerequisite for a society marriage... or fucking."

My cheeks flushed scarlet at the crude word. It wasn't that I was so sheltered I'd never heard the word, I just wasn't used to it being uttered in my presence.

Rising to his full height, he spanked me several more times.

Heat spread through my body, a mixture of arousal and anger, the two emotions mingling in a way that left me confused and helpless.

"Do you like that?" His voice was low and husky as he continued to punish my ass.

I gritted my teeth, trying to fight back the moan that threatened to escape my lips. I didn't want to give him the satisfaction of knowing that he was turning me on, but at the same time, I couldn't help but feel my pussy growing wetter with each sharp smack.

"Answer me," he growled, punctuating his words with another hard slap to my ass.

I refused.

His chuckle sent shivers down my spine. "Still want to be stubborn? Good," he said. "Because we're just getting started." And with that, he pulled me up onto my feet and pinned me against the wall, his hard cock pressing against my thigh as he wrapped his fingers around my neck.

He squeezed my throat, and my body wanted to flee, fight, rage, and run as far away from this man as possible, all at once.

I gasped for breath, my eyes widening in both fear and desire.

His grip tightened further, his eyes piercing into mine. "I'm warning you once and only once. Test me, and there *will* be consequences."

He trailed his free hand down my body, and it came to rest on my hip.

I tried to shake my head, to deny that this twisted mixture of fear and arousal was anything but repulsive, but my body betrayed me. The heat between my legs grew more intense, and my back arched involuntarily.

His lips curled into a sinister smile, and he leaned in closer to me, his breath hot against my ear. "You're mine." His voice was possessive and commanding. "And I'm not letting you go."

He chuckled darkly and released my throat but did not move away from my body. Instead, he slid his hand down my curves, tracing the lines of my body with his fingers as if memorizing every inch.

My mind screamed at me to fight back, to push him away, but my body was already giving in.

I was the harlot my mother had always accused me of being.

He slipped his hand under the fabric of my bodice and cupped my breast, rubbing his fingers over my hardening nipple.

I bit my lower lip until I tasted blood, trying to suppress my reaction to his touch.

Without showing any mercy, he stroked my sensitive flesh, teasing and tormenting me. He bit my earlobe, hard, sending a stab of pain through my body that made me gasp.

When I finally worked up the courage to speak, my voice was shaking and soft. "Why?" My eyes watered as my body ached for his touch.

He pulled back, examining my face. "Because I can. Because like all beautiful things, you can be bought. Possessed."

I moaned as his hand slid down between my legs, where he cupped my dripping wet pussy through my thin panties.

"Owned," he finished viciously as he rubbed my clit through my panties, making me shudder and gasp with pleasure.

I tried to pull away from him, but the moment I did, he pressed his hand against my breasts, pinching my nipples as I whimpered with desire.

"Never pull away from me." He pinched my nipple harder.

This was just another punishment from a man who clearly would never hesitate to *correct* me.

"Spread your legs." His order was given as he lowered my panties.

I did as he commanded, and his hand came to rest between

my thighs. I gasped as two of his fingers pressed down on my clit.

My head fell back as he swirled his fingers against my sensitive flesh, his touch far more experienced than I would ever have imagined. I moaned, bucking my hips against him as he continued to play with me, his fingers moving with the expertise of a classical cellist.

"That's it, *my sweet bride*," he purred softly, pushing a single finger into me. "Come for me. Now."

I gasped and clawed at his upper arms. Whether I was still trying to push him away or pull him closer, I no longer knew.

He bit my neck, tracing the line of my throat teasingly with his tongue as he moved his finger inside me, his thumb finding my clit and brushing across it before coming to rest against my entrance.

I groaned, pressing my hips into him, wanting, but he pulled his hand away from me, leaving me aching for more.

This was wrong.

Scandalous.

Luc was a powerful man. He got whatever he wanted. Whatever he demanded would be his. But I had no idea just how much until now. He had the ability to control everything... even me.

He began to play with me again, his fingers dipping into my wet folds, spreading my arousal over my slit. He groaned as I fisted the expensive material of his shirt.

I hissed as he ruthlessly thrust his fingers into me.

My body writhed in pleasure, my hips thrusting into him, begging him to give me what I wanted, what my body needed.

He finally moved his fingers faster, and my begging turned into loud cries.

I was already shaking, quivering with need, my thighs soaked with my own arousal, when he brought his fingers—coated in my arousal—up and painted my lips with my come. His eyes locked with mine, filling my vision until my eyelids fluttered at the touch of his lips to mine in a kiss.

Pulling away just enough so he could lock eyes with me again, he said, "You are my property. My pawn in whatever game I choose to play. Don't ever forget that."

CHAPTER 7

LUC

"*M*r. Manwarring, so good of you to receive me this morning." Mary Quinn Astrid, my soon to be monster-in-law, offered her hand, wrist turned down, like I was supposed to kiss it or something ridiculous.

I ignored it.

"Well, after the way you harassed my concierge, I didn't see how I had a choice." I kept my tone pleasant enough, but the slight flaring of her nostrils told me my words hit home.

"We need to talk." She stalked into my entryway, her beige Birkin bag awkwardly swinging in one hand as she wrapped her arms around her middle, pressing her breasts together.

It was nine a.m., and she was in my penthouse wearing clothes that would be inappropriate for a woman half her age, trying to make her over-filled, fake tits seem appealing.

If she made a pass at me, I was throwing her off the balcony.

"Can I get you something to drink?" I asked out of habit, I supposed. Though I wasn't in the habit of letting women I wasn't fucking into my home. Even then, few made it here.

"Yes, thank you." She gave me a polite smile that never reached her eyes.

Would she even bother with the pretense of manners if she knew how I'd bent her daughter over that pool table last night?

Or how I'd made her come on my fingers just to prove I owned her body?

I spent a great deal of time last night thinking about how Amelia's body responded to my touch. There definitely was more to my ice princess than I'd first assumed. She'd had the audacity to tell me no, like I had given her a choice. It didn't matter. Her lips said one thing but her body another.

Amelia had enjoyed our little tiff as much as I had. Her pussy was soaked well before I started rubbing her clit, and she couldn't suppress all her little moans of pleasure or the way her lips parted in a beautiful, silent scream when she came on my command.

And to make it even sweeter, all of that had happened after I spanked the generous curves of her ass.

She could glare daggers at me all she liked.

She could tell me she hated every minute.

She could call me a brute and a savage beast.

That was all fine.

She could lie to herself all she liked, but she couldn't lie to me.

Not after I painted her lips with her own come then kissed them clean.

Would Mrs. Astrid be acting differently if she knew how close I'd been to fucking her precious little girl at one of the largest society events of the year?

Probably not. I very much doubted this shrew gave a fuck about her daughter's welfare. If she did, she wouldn't have been so amenable to giving her to me in the first place.

She pushed past me to enter further into my large penthouse as if she owned the place. "A cup of coffee would be wonderful."

I hated having guests in my home.

I barely tolerated having my father here. This was my space, my sanctuary where I could work without my father looking over my shoulder, without people interrupting me. I shouldn't have to host the overprivileged waste of plastic surgery that was Mrs. Astrid.

A small part of me wanted to tell her exactly what I did to her daughter last night, in excruciating detail, just to make her storm out. It wasn't like I had fucked the girl, but we'd still gotten far closer than women like Mrs. Astrid would believe was proper. But then again, it wasn't like this cheating trophy wife had any room to judge me.

"Unfortunately, my coffee maker isn't working at the moment." I lied. I wasn't about to give her a reason to linger.

"Tea, then."

"All out." I lied again.

"Water with lemon?" Her hands went to her hips, and she tried to purse her lips in disapproval.

"They're doing maintenance on the pipes, and the water has been shut off."

She stuck her nose in the air. "I'll wait in the parlor while you get whatever you have available. Thank you." She waved her hand like she was dismissing me in my own home.

The fucking nerve of this woman.

I gritted my teeth and made a mental note to inform Amelia she would not be seeing her mother often after the wedding. Then again, considering the bruises on my bride that this bitch must have left, I doubted Amelia would object.

With a deep breath, I got my anger under control. It was probably a good thing she was here. Mrs. Astrid and I needed to have a little chat in private.

She needed to know what would and wouldn't be tolerated and exactly what was going to happen if she fucking crossed me. Putting her hands on what was mine was crossing the fucking line.

She sauntered deeper into my apartment while continuing to wave me off. This bitch had lost her damn mind if she thought I would even think about leaving her unattended in my home. I didn't know if I was more worried about her snooping, stealing, or planting a camera.

None of those things were going to happen.

"If you insist." I led her to the sitting area, its rich leather furniture positioned to take full advantage of the stunning view.

I loved this room. It was perfect for receiving guests. The view was impressive, and the furniture looked inviting but was uncomfortable enough that it didn't encourage people to stay. The perfect balance between a show of power and telling people to get the fuck out.

"Aren't you going to make that refreshment, dear?" She perched on one of the armchairs.

"Unfortunately, I just remembered I ran out of everything. Had you called before showing up, I would have had time to prepare for your visit. So, why don't you tell me why you are here? I'm sure you must be in a hurry, other doorsteps to darken."

"Can't a woman just show up to her soon to be son-in-law's home?"

I remained standing. "No, actually, it's rude. You, like anyone else, can make an appointment with my assistant."

"We are going to be family," she huffed.

"That isn't what this is and pretending otherwise is a waste of both of our time. I'm a busy man with several far more important matters to attend to, so why don't you just tell me why you are here?"

I probably should have been more polite, but I didn't want to accidentally give her the impression she was welcome here, or anywhere I was, without calling ahead.

"Obviously, I'm here to discuss the wedding. The last one was a complete disaster, thanks to you." She looked down her nose at me, a brave move for a woman with so much to lose. "I paid for the last one. You will be covering all the expenses of this one."

"All the expenses? Like what?"

"You will pay for the dresses, flowers, and jewelry for the entire bridal party, of course. The venue, caterer, planner, band, and really anything else that we deem appropriate. I also expect to be reimbursed for the first wedding."

"Correct me if I am wrong, but you didn't pay for anything."

I sat across from her and leaned back on the sofa. "You don't have any claim to your family's money, not after you married into a wealthier one, and you have never made any real money. Your husband paid for everything."

"When it comes to the children, I make all the decisions on my husband's behalf. It would just be far simpler to give me your black card and I will take care of everything. I'm thinking if I hurry, I can get someone bumped at The Plaza in, say, two years."

"We will have this wedding by the end of the quarter," I said. "And by 'we,' you mean Amelia." I sat forward on my sofa, resting my elbows on my knees.

"Excuse me?"

"You said 'what we deem appropriate'. By *we* you mean Amelia. It's *her* wedding, after all. Not yours."

"I'm her mother. I know what she needs."

I sincerely doubted that.

"Right, and how much do you think Amelia's needs are going to cost?"

"At least forty million." She didn't even blink, asking for that outrageous sum. "My daughter is worth the best, and that is what she shall have. That, of course, does not cover the reimbursement for the last event. That we can settle by a transfer of bonds or even stocks from your portfolio to mine. Say around thirty million."

"That's funny. You don't treat your daughter like she is worth much at all," I countered. "You sold her to me for a secret. Yet you paid thirty million for a party."

"Sold her? You have a funny way of defining blackmail."

She had a point.

"Okay, this is what I'm willing to do. I'll give my future wife the wedding of her dreams. No expense spared." I watched the greed seep into her beady little eyes. "But she has to come to me with the bills for everything and tell me what they are. I'll cover absolutely everything *her heart* desires. Not yours."

Her lips pursed as she stood and looked down at me.

"I am her mother—" Her voice dripped with unearned indignation.

"You said that part already," I interrupted.

"She doesn't know what she wants. I do. There is also the matter of a proper engagement ring."

"She has her ring."

"That simple thing looks like a pauper's ring." She spat as she spoke.

I made a mental note to have the cleaner disinfect the rug... or maybe burn it.

"It's the ring she liked, and it's a five-carat Tiffany's ring, with one of the most exquisite diamonds available outside of the royal jewels. I assure you it is not a pauper's ring."

I could practically see the dollar signs, like a cartoon character's, light up her eyes, telling me she'd seen the ring but hadn't understood its worth.

"I expect Amelia to be wearing my ring and no others every single day."

"Yes, well. My daughter and I still need to plan the wedding, and the end of next quarter is September. That is far too soon to plan a wedding."

"Then that is what she can tell me. The second she tells me what kind of wedding she wants, I will hand over my black card. Or better yet…"

I stood, so I was looking down at the harpy. "Why don't I come with you both and make sure my future wife gets every-thing she wants? I'm sure it will be a splendid opportunity for us to spend some quality time together."

Before she could say anything else, my front door opened, and my assistant entered carrying his briefcase while looking over some documents.

"Henry. Good. Can you please make Mrs. Astrid and me some coffee? We were just going over wedding plans."

"Right away, sir." Henry didn't even blink, but I knew he read the tension in the room and understood how much I valued my privacy in the morning. Had she gone through the proper chan-nels for this meeting, he would have never let her through.

"I thought you were out?" She raised an eyebrow at me.

"Henry would know where more is," I said. "He is that good at his job, and I would appreciate it if you reach out to him next time you want to talk to me."

"Oh, surely that won't be necessary. After all, we'll be family soon." She brushed her hand over her shoulder, a move meant to display her many gaudy rings, no doubt.

"Still, I prefer that guests be announced."

"How is that going to work?" She tilted her head.

"How is *what* going to work?"

"Are you going to force my daughter to live in this bachelor pad? It's not suitable for a young woman. Anyone could look in these massive windows. The whole of New York could watch her."

We were sitting on the eightieth floor. No one could see in here.

"I hardly see how that is any of your concern. I don't give a flying fuck if you approve of me because your approval isn't important. What I'm after is your complete compliance, and the understanding that if Amelia and I aren't married, then you will have a lot to answer for. By the way, did you know your prenup has an adultery clause?"

Her eyes got big, and she shook a little. "How could you possibly know that?"

"Never mind how I know. I'm guessing you didn't know. Well, let me fill you in. You get nothing. Zero. You get tossed out on your ass, and Harrison would also get nothing. Something to consider before you ever think about trying to show up here unannounced again or think that you somehow hold some sway over me. You don't."

She started to say something, but I talked right over her.

"You will not be getting reimbursed for a single fucking flower from that last wedding. If you have a problem with that, I don't give a shit."

Her face flushed scarlet. She was clearly not used to being talked to like this. Honestly, it was high time someone put this shrew in her place.

Before she could say another word, Henry came in with the coffee service.

He handed me my cup, then accidentally tripped and poured Mrs. Astrid's cup all over her.

Shrieking, she sprang to her feet, hand raised to strike Henry.

I caught it before she let it fly. I was not about to lose a valued employee to an assault charge.

She really needed to learn not to touch what was mine.

"How dare you!" she screamed at Henry.

"My apologies, madam," Henry said, unfazed.

He was going to receive a rather agreeable Christmas bonus this year.

"I demand you fire him immediately." She stomped her foot in a manner not far off from a toddler throwing a tantrum.

"No, and before you ask, I won't be covering your dry-cleaning bill either."

"This is silk!" she screeched.

"Oh no, such a shame. And on a white dress. Too bad." I didn't bother hiding my sarcasm. "We must get you home so you can change immediately before that sets." I ushered her toward the front door.

"We aren't done talking," she complained.

"We are. It is very simple. Amelia is mine. I take care of what is mine. She will get what she wants, not what you want." I opened the door and all but pushed her out.

"You can't just—"

"You might want to be more careful, or just avoid wearing white dresses."

She narrowed her eyes at me.

Good, she was getting all my backhanded comments today.

But just in case, I wanted to make this next one crystal clear. I needed to leave absolutely no room for misunderstanding.

"This time, Amelia will get the wedding she wants, not you. If you insist on inserting yourself, we can just go down to the courthouse and take care of it during lunch. Then I'll release the photos to the society pages and make it clear we were forced to do that because the mother of the bride kept trying to upstage her daughter." I looked her up and down and let my lip curl in disgust. "As if that were even possible."

"You don't know who you're talking to." She raised a finger at me, visibly shaking with rage. "I can make your life very difficult."

"No, you don't know who you are dealing with. If I find another bruise on my future wife, you and I will talk again. And I promise it will be a far less pleasant conversation than this has been. I will rain so much hellfire on you that by the time I'm done, Harrison's parentage won't even be the least of your fucking problems."

The blood drained from her face, and I knew I had made my point and that I needed to get my PI on her immediately because there was more to find out.

Mrs. Astrid made to say something else, but I let the heavy wooden door fall into place.

"Sir, who was that awful woman?" Henry asked behind me.

"That is a woman who is determined to find out the hard way that no one touches what is mine."

CHAPTER 8

AMELIA

"$\mathscr{I}$ think I want to wear the green Vera Wang dress this evening," I told Sarah, my maid, as I sat at my vanity.

I had commissioned the dress on a whim after this year's fashion shows. Mother didn't know, of course. It had been my own little rebellious secret. Until now, I had kept it hidden in the back of my closet, lacking the courage to wear the daring dress out in public.

Sarah, who often assisted my sister Rose and me with getting ready for all the events we were required to attend, stared at me for a moment, as if waiting for me to change my mind before moving to retrieve the dress from its hiding place.

I sighed. One more endless event. Another boring night representing our family at a charity or some other function, playing dress-us-up like little dolls so the tabloids would take our picture.

"That dress isn't appropriate." Rose was perched on the edge of my bed, her green eyes getting big and round.

"Nonsense. It's a perfect gown that is chic and a modern classic."

I sat in front of my vanity and studied myself.

The girl in the mirror was the same girl who had always been there. Despite everything that happened with Luc, there was no change in my appearance. I wasn't sure what I expected, to look older maybe, wiser, somehow more mature? Or maybe I expected to have a glow after the most incredibly erotic experience of my life.

"Have you come up with a name for this one yet?" she asked.

"A name?"

"For Mr. Manwarring. I think you referred to Mr. Dubois as Mr. Dubious." Rose giggled and lay back on the blush pink all-season duvet.

My room was beautifully decorated for me. When I was six. The walls were a perfect porcelain white with pale pink trim and gold filigree accents. It was bright and light and even had details that fit the original beaux arts style. Everything in the room dripped over-the-top wealth and decadence that I had adored... when I was a child.

After taking classes at NYU, I had tried to convince my mother to allow me to tone it all down to something more appropriate for an adult woman, but she wouldn't hear of it. Trying to take a deep breath, my chest tightened instead; everything around me was cluttered and stifling.

"Mr. Manchild, because he acts like a spoiled, greedy child," I answered, and Rose snorted out her laughter.

"Is he the reason you want to wear such an inappropriate dress?"

I met her eyes in the mirror and smiled. "No, the dress is for me. I love the color and the fabric. Mother isn't here to police my clothing, and he doesn't get to tell me what to wear... at least not yet. I'm simply taking advantage of the little freedom I have while I have it."

I shifted my gaze back to myself in the mirror, trying to decide what to do with my makeup.

I thought back to the way Mr. Manchild had touched me in the billiards room, the way he had made my body burn for him. I was surprised the experience hadn't somehow altered me.

Maybe it had, just not on the outside.

Maybe that part was up to me.

His touch had changed me, and I could choose to hide it.

Put on a sensible dress like my sister and be the good girl I always was, sticking with cute, conservative, and pastel. Or I could embrace what he was turning me into.

A woman who deserved to be desired.

"The lining on the sheer corset matches your skin tone and makes it look like you are practically naked from the waist up!" Rose shrieked.

She had a point. The dress may push everything too far. If I dressed like that, it would anger Mother, who was using me to pay off her blackmail.

It would also anger Mr. Manchild, who wanted me under his thumb.

If this wedding happened, and I became his wife, he'd be entitled to force me to dress a certain way. I'd have to behave in a manner befitting the wife of one of the most powerful men in the city.

But I'm not his wife yet.

I regarded myself in the mirror. Who did I want to be?

I had a brief window of remaining a single woman.

Did I want to use it? What was the worst he could do?

Punish me again with another body-wracking orgasm? I was still buzzing from the high his last touch had given me, and a part of me deep down wanted more.

Maybe he needed to be shown I wasn't a woman he could order around.

That I was a person… or maybe I wanted to push him and see how far he would go to punish me.

My sister was still staring at my reflection in the mirror, as if my choice of dress was outrageous. As if choosing this dress was the same as wearing nothing but body paint.

"And?" I asked, making up my mind as I moved to my jewelry box to pick out the perfect necklace.

I wanted something bold, something daring that would draw the eye straight to my cleavage. I moved aside the innocent white pearls and the ladylike diamonds. There had to be something stronger, something with color that would complement my emerald-green dress.

"And the skirt! The slit is so high on one side that it's practically half of a miniskirt. You are too tall for that dress! One wrong move and everyone will know what color underwear you are wearing." Rose paced around my room, her hands fluttering around her as she talked.

It was how she always got when something unexpected happened, and my fighting back was out of character.

If I didn't push back a bit now, I would never get the chance to again.

Rose would get on board with the plan as soon as she calmed herself. In the meantime, it was a little amusing watching her work herself up.

"You're right," I said with a deep breath. "The last thing I want is for Page Six to be commenting on the color of my underwear."

Rose sat back down on my bed with a sigh. "Good, so you won't wear that dress."

"No, I won't be wearing any underwear," I said with a smile. Sometimes working her up and watching her go was just fun.

"Amelia." Rose gripped the pearls at her throat. "What will Mother say?"

Her face turned red in shock and embarrassment.

This was the girl who blushed with secondhand embarrassment reading young adult novels. Rose rebelled against Mother, too, of course, but in different ways. She did unladylike things like running and wearing yoga pants on her way to a yoga studio.

Soon she would find her voice, I was sure, and she would discover something big enough to go head-to-head with our parents over, but she hadn't yet.

"She lost the right to say anything after she let that man ruin my wedding and then sold me off to him." I applied a thick liquid cat eye to my eyelids and a pencil liner in blackest black to my waterline. I wanted my eyes to look intense, bold, and confident. The green of my eyes matched my dress, and tonight I was proving a point—that I was not a little house pet who would obey.

Mr. Manchild was going to learn that I couldn't be broken. I was a person, not a possession.

A woman, not his pet.

He did something to me.

The other night, he awakened something in me, and I had no intention of silencing it.

My entire life I had been asleep in a gilded cage, but maybe if I fought back, if I stopped being so damn agreeable, if I proved to be too much for him, then he would set me free.

"Don't exaggerate." Rose rolled her eyes. "She isn't selling you off. She must think Mr. Manwarring would be a better match. I'm sure all she really cares about is your happiness."

We met each other's eyes in the mirror, and we both started laughing.

"I doubt that. Earlier today she saw me eat an apple at breakfast and raged about carbs. It was an apple. I've been hiding from her the entire day so I didn't have to keep hearing how I'm not thin enough or pretty enough."

"You are absolutely pretty enough," Rose said. "And you have all the right curves in all the right places."

"And you are simply adorable and are quickly growing into stunning," I responded, making her smile. "I didn't see you earlier. Where have you been all day?" I studied her in the mirror.

Her cheeks were tinted pink, and she wasn't looking me in the eye anymore. That was very unlike Rose. We told each other everything. I put the eyeliner brush down and turned to look at her directly. "Rose, what is it?"

"Have you seen the new gardener Father hired? He was planting the loveliest rose bushes on the grounds today." A sweet smile stretched her lips. "He gave me one of the Princess Anne roses. He cut it fresh for me and said that its beauty was a pale comparison to mine."

"When were you in the gardens?" I asked.

Rose hardly ever spent time in the back gardens. She preferred to stay inside, where there weren't any bugs or risk of her porcelain skin burning. Unless, of course, she was going for a run around the block, but even then, she preferred gyms.

"I saw him planting it from my window and he looked so hot…" Her skin flushed a deep red as she realized what she'd said.

This girl was never going to be able to hide her embarrassment. Anyone could read her like a large neon sign. "I mean, he looked like he was working hard and overheating, and I brought him some water and we talked for a bit…"

"Be careful," I warned her. "Do not get too close to the staff. If Mother were to see, the best thing that could happen is she fires him."

"It's nothing like that. She wouldn't…"

When I raised my eyebrow at her, she nodded. "Okay, I won't talk to him again."

"Smart move," I said as Sarah brought out the dress and hung it on a valet hook by the wall. "It's perfect."

"It's salacious," Rose argued.

"We're seeing *Salome* at the opera. Scandal is kind of the theme of the night," I said, taking the dress behind the privacy screen in my room.

"What dress would you like to wear tonight, Ms. Rose?" Sarah asked.

"I think the pink Dior. One of us should look more like a lady of breeding." Her peals of laughter were light. Her laughter had always reminded me of bells, and I hoped she got to retain her youthful innocence. I hoped life didn't stomp it out of her.

The dress fit perfectly. The shiny green silk of the skirt felt cool and smooth against my legs, and the way it moved made it look almost liquid. The corseted bodice was lined with a soft beige fabric that really matched my skin perfectly. A single layer of soft, pale-green tulle covered the lining, and the piping over the boning of the corset was a green that matched the skirt.

Observing myself in the mirror, I could admit it was a tad much.

The slit was dangerously high. I would be able to feel the cold air between my thighs, and my ample breasts overfilled the corset's cups. It had probably been measured wrong and they had made it a size too small, or the orders had been mixed up and I'd received a more petite girl's dress.

That just made me love it more.

What would I see in Mr. Manchild's eyes when he looked at me?

Would he think I was stunning and want to show me off? Or would he hate it? From his reaction to my backless dress, I had an idea which reaction I was going to get.

Would he punish me with more pleasure?

Would he force me to pleasure him?

Even the thought of him taking me in hand made my blood heat. Why did he excite me the way he did? The filthy promises he'd made to me in the billiards room echoed in my mind, and part of me wondered if I was subconsciously calling his bluff.

The necklace I chose was a simple silver chain with a large emerald pendant. It would rest just above the neckline of the corset, drawing eyes to my breasts every time it caught the light.

My old college roommate had referred to it as "cleavage candy," and for tonight, that was exactly what I wanted.

It was perfect.

"That is really pretty," Rose said, "but Mother is going to kill you."

"No, she won't. If I don't marry Mr. Manchild, then he'll expose some deep dark secret, and I can't marry him if I am dead."

"Mr. Manchild!" Rose laughed again, doubling over in a very unladylike fashion. "I can't get over how good that is. It just fits."

Smiling back at Rose in the mirror, I wondered if I had ever laughed so uninhibitedly before. I refocused on getting my makeup just right.

I really did tell my sister everything. Well, everything except what had happened in that billiards room at the gala.

That, I would take to my grave.

I didn't think she would judge me for what he'd done. She might judge me if I admitted how much it turned me on. Or how I took a long hot bath when I got home and pictured what it would have been like if he had followed through on his threats and taken me right there.

Sarah brought in my sister's dress and she went to change. Motioning for me to take a seat in front of the vanity, Sarah asked, "What are we doing with your hair tonight? Maybe leaving it down in loose waves for a little modesty?" She fluffed it and draped the long, dark-brown locks over my chest.

"No, I think we should pin it up. I think a simple twist will work, or a sleek bun."

Sarah looked like she wanted to say something but didn't.

My mother had verbally beaten all opinions out of her.

That was probably why she had lasted so much longer than the others. She styled my hair as I asked, pulling it all back from my face and pinning it in an elegant twist. Then she took it a step further and secured it with silver hair sticks, emerald beads dangling from the ends, catching the light.

"Perfect. Thank you." I smiled at Sarah, and she nodded and went to help my sister while I finished my look with a nude lip and a pair of black Jimmy Choo stilettos. I was ready to go. Not that I didn't have every intention of making my date for the night wait.

Rose came out from behind the curtain looking just lovely and sweet in her light-pink dress, her curls loose around her shoulders. She looked like a slightly younger, more girlish version of me. The version, I was sure, my mother hoped I would look like tonight, and Mr. Manchild, too, no doubt.

"I can't tell," Rose said, looking at me. "Are you going to the opera or are you going to kill James Bond? Or maybe you're going to steal the throne from Thor?"

I couldn't help the snort of laughter that bubbled out of me at my sister's quip. "I haven't decided. It's early, it could still go either way."

Sarah left for a moment, and I helped Rose finish her look, completing the perfect picture of delicate femininity.

"You look like an elevated Shirley Temple if she was a brunette." I yanked on one of her curls, and she stuck her tongue out at me.

"Do you think he would like this dress?" she asked.

"Who?"

"The gardener." The way her eyes sparkled and her lips parted, I knew she was in trouble.

"Look at me." I grabbed her hands. "Who are we?"

"We are the Astrid daughters," she immediately answered, meeting my gaze.

This was something we did when one of us ever dared to dream of a life outside these walls.

"What does that mean?"

"It means we live a life of wealth and privilege."

"And what is the cost of that privilege?" I held her green eyes with mine as she took a deep breath.

"It means that we represent our families at all times until the time in which we are married to the husband that Mother chooses for us. Then we represent both families."

"What are dreams?" I asked.

"A fool's pastime," she recited.

"What is love?"

"A fairy tale meant for others."

A single tear ran down her cheek, and I pulled her into my arms, giving her a tight hug and just holding her for a second to comfort her but also myself.

"I know it hurts, but it will hurt far less if you end this brief infatuation now. It will hurt so much more if you allow yourself to let it grow into love. Trust me, I know it hurts, but end it now." I was lying to my sister.

I had no idea how it felt. I had never even let myself have a crush. What was the point?

"The best we can hope for is a good match with a man who eventually becomes a friend."

"That's not entirely true." Rose sniffed, then ran her fingers under her eyes, wiping away any smeared makeup. "We could also wish for our husbands to die in mysterious circumstances young enough so we can still marry again, maybe not for love,

but certainly for lust. I hear pool boys are the to-kill-for accessory for widows this season."

Her dark sense of humor caught me off guard, and I stared at
her for a moment before we both broke down in giggles.

Rose was on a roll. "You really are dressed like a femme
fatale, ready to kill a man if he dares forget to open a door.
Maybe you can save on the fee and be your own hit woman?"

We were both laughing when Sarah returned to inform us
that Mr. Manwarring was downstairs waiting with his sisters to
escort us to the opera.

"We will be down in a moment." I moved back to the vanity
to check my makeup.

Deciding my eyeliner wasn't dramatic enough, I lengthened
the wings until I really looked like a Bond girl trying to channel
Loki. What was that Taylor Swift line? Eyeliner sharp enough to
kill a man.

"Ready, Bitchy-Galore?"

"Alvays, dahling," I said in a terrible accent as I slipped my
shoes on and grabbed my purse.

I stopped for a moment. Watching Rose reapplying gloss, I
noticed how she matched my room. Whereas I was suffocating
under my mother's thumb, my sister seemed to flourish under it.
Or at least feign she was, better than I ever had.

I hoped she could forget her brief infatuation with this
gardener before it could change all of that. If she dared stray not
only before wedlock but with someone outside of our social
circle, the horror my mother would rain down on her would be
terrible. She would also go after the gardener, his family, and
anyone else in the household she could. It would be intense.

Maybe by that time I could convince Mr. Manchild to let us
have a spare room for Rose at our place, wherever that was
going to be.

He wasn't afraid of my mother.

If how he'd conducted himself at the cancelled wedding was any indication, he reveled in her indignation.

Maybe I could use that to provide my sister with a safe haven. Would she be safe under the same roof as him? Wealthy men did not have the same expectation of fidelity as women did. Could I keep her safe in my own home? I just wasn't sure yet.

"Okay, let's go. I don't actually want to be late," I said, not liking the direction my mind was taking.

"Yes, I can't wait for the show," Rose agreed, and then added, "The opera should be good, too."

"What show do you mean?"

"Mother's face when she sees you." She gave me an angelic smile and ran out the door.

I was more worried about *his* reaction.

With a deep breath, I followed her.

I saw him immediately. The black tuxedo he wore was perfectly tailored to his lean body. Combined with a black shirt underneath and a red tie, the effect was mouthwatering and sinful.

Even if I would never say it out loud, especially within his earshot, I had to admit he was strikingly handsome.

He looked up from where he stood inside the door to where I was still poised on the staircase, practically feeling his gaze as it traveled up and down my body slowly, then back up, meeting mine.

The heat from his regard burned my exposed skin, and there was much for him to fume over. His nostrils flared, and a little bit of red colored the tops of his cheeks, the muscles in his jaw all tightening.

I instantly knew I had pushed him too far.

"Mr. Manwarring, lovely to see you tonight. Shall we go?" I said, coming down the last few stairs and stopping in front of him.

I tried to usher him outside, where there would be more witnesses to keep me safe from the threats and dark promises dancing in his eyes.

He leaned in, and I could smell his cologne.

It was dark, spicy, and commanding, and did something to me that made me regret not wearing underwear. He brought his hand to my hip, then slid it down to where the slit in my dress exposed my upper thigh.

He whispered in my ear, "What the fuck do you think you're wearing?"

CHAPTER 9

LUC

*T*he fucking audacity of this woman!

She had no idea who she was messing with.

If Amelia fucking Astrid thought for a second that I'd let my future wife, my woman, go out in public looking like a common whore, she was about to learn a painful lesson.

She was supposed to be ready to go to the opera, not walk a red carpet like a trashy Hollywood starlet.

I was not a man to be tested or trifled with.

It had been years since I'd had to deal with people stupid enough to try my goddamned patience.

Now, in just a matter of days, this little girl and her bitch mother had gotten on every nerve I had.

Amelia Astrid was about to learn why she'd made an unfortunate decision.

She dared to stare me down, the expression of haughty importance on her face suggesting I should be grateful she was allowing me to look at her while she sauntered down the stairs.

When our eyes met, her confidence wavered for a moment,

just a flash of fear before her face froze in the emotionless mask ice queens like her put on to avoid wrinkles.

I drew a deep breath through my nose as I looked her up and down again. That dress was stunning. The color was vivid against her milky skin, and it showed off her perfectly honed hourglass figure. She was a Grecian goddess come to life.

That dress would never see the light of day again.

I didn't give a fuck if I had to burn it.

The only time I would ever permit her to wear something so revealing was if she was tied to my bed.

Even then, I thought I would prefer her to be naked, maybe just wearing a collar with my name on it. My cock swelled at the idea of this goddess of a woman tied to my bed like a damsel in distress in some fantasy movie.

In a moment, she was going to learn her place the hard way.

I turned toward her baby sister, who wore a boring but appropriate dress. She looked back and forth between Amelia and me, picking up on the tension.

I needed to get rid of her, now.

Amelia was in for a hard lesson, but there was no reason to scare her sister.

She would have to learn her own lessons when she entered her own arranged marriage.

"Rose, dear, my sisters Charlotte and Olivia are waiting in the limo. Why don't you join them? They're looking forward to meeting you. You ladies head to the opera and just send the limo back for your sister and me. We need to have a word before we join you."

There wasn't even a hint of the white-hot rage I felt in my voice, a skill I had spent years perfecting.

Still, Rose looked at me for a moment, a little unsure, then at her sister.

I glared darkly at Amelia in a way that promised a more

severe punishment if she didn't do as she was told. Her eyes widened slightly, and I knew she understood.

"It's okay." Amelia nodded at her sister. "We'll join you at the opera soon."

"Okay, well, hurry. Mother will be livid if you are late," she said, eyeing me warily.

"Your mother will be fine if we are a few moments late, as it seems Amelia forgot the rest of her dress." I leaned over and stage-whispered like it was a joke. "As soon as she changes into something more fitting, we will be there."

I gave Rose a gentle smile, and she nodded and smiled back before she looked at Amelia.

"I told you so." Rose stuck out her tongue.

"You told her what?" I asked.

"That her dress, while pretty, wasn't appropriate and was a size too small." Rose laughed.

"I think she looks lovely," I said, lying through my teeth. "I just need to have a word with my future wife."

Leaning down to whisper in her ear like I was going to let her in on a secret, I murmured, "I actually just want a moment alone with your sister to tell her how amazing I think she looks. Please don't tell your mother we were unsupervised for a few minutes."

"It's our little secret." She giggled and looked at me like I was a cute little schoolboy with a crush, not the big bad wolf here to devour her sister.

Good.

Let her think I was harmless as she headed out to the limo.

The second the door closed behind her, Amelia took a few steps backward.

She wasn't as confident now. Her green eyes dilated as they shifted around looking for something, someone, who could help her.

There was nothing and no one. She was trapped, and she knew it.

With each step she moved back, I took one forward, maintaining the distance between us.

"What the fuck do you think you are wearing?" I seethed.

"A Vera Wang gown." Her voice was steady, even if she was not.

She wobbled on her heels, having to reach out to the banister to keep herself upright. The top of that dress was so revealing her tits visibly jiggled as she righted herself.

Good, I wanted her off balance.

"That is not a dress that one wears in public unless they charge by the hour."

"Didn't you just say it looked pretty?" She clenched her jaw.

"You look beautiful, but entirely inappropriate. Take off that dress or I will rip it from you," I demanded.

My heart pounded, and I cracked my knuckles as I moved closer. I would never hit a woman out of anger. Striking her ass out of a need for discipline that led to mutual pleasure, though, was different, and something I reveled in.

But she didn't know yet what kind of man I was.

She'd had a taste, but she didn't know where my limits were. I was so angry right now, I wasn't sure if I knew where they were at the moment, either.

"No." Her voice was firm, but she was still taking steps back. "You do not get to dictate what I wear. I'm not your child. I'm supposed to be your fiancée."

"Exactly, you are my fiancée. Mine. Take it off now. You will change into an appropriate dress, one that doesn't show the world what is only for my eyes."

"Excuse me? No part of me is for your lecherous gaze."

Hatred lit her eyes, and my cock got hard for her.

It wasn't her undeniable beauty that turned me on, or her

dress showing far too much skin. It was her fire. The fucking audacity to willingly disobey me and then to stand up to me, even though her body language didn't match her words.

Most grown men didn't have the balls to face me like she was.

A tiny part of me respected her for that, but most of me was just enraged.

"Your back, your thighs, your tits, your ass, and your sweet little pussy are for me only. Do you understand? Maybe Marksen was okay showing you off like a fucking show pony. I am not."

"Do not speak to me like you would a whore."

"Then don't dress like one." I took another step toward her, cutting the short distance between us by half. "You're mine. If you want to dress in a way that shows off this much of your body, you will do it only while in my bed, or on your fucking knees."

"How dare you!" she screeched, clenching her fists like she was going to strike me.

Her eyes seemed to light with fury, and the tops of her cheeks grew bright red. She was breathing heavier, which just made her breasts heave like an old romance novel heroine. "No one has ever talked to me like that."

"You want my respect? You want me to treat you like a lady? I'll be happy to, as soon as you act like one. Once you stop behaving like a spoiled little princess and act like a woman worthy of wearing my ring and bearing my name, I will treat you as such." My palm twitched.

I ached to grab her and bend her over my goddamn knee, rip off the slip of fabric, and then spank her ass until it was bright red and her pussy was leaking, aching for me.

"We are going to go upstairs. You will take off that dress and show me how sorry you are for wasting my time. Then we will go to the opera, and you will look like a lady."

CHAPTER 10

LUC

"*I* don't know what the women you are used to dealing with find acceptable, but I will not be talked to in such a manner, especially by some brutish, classless asshole!" Her cheeks were flaming now, and the flushed color went down her neck all the way to the tops of her perfect breasts.

"I'm not just any brutish, classless asshole. I'm the brutish, classless asshole that just so happens to be your fucking husband." I was tempted to close the distance between us, grab the bodice of that dress, and rip it to shreds just so I could release those tits and see how far down the red of her blush went.

"Not yet, you're not," she bit back as she stepped out of her shoes, leaving them on the stairs.

We were about halfway up now, and she was panicking.

Her ribcage rose and fell with each agitated breath. Amelia looked around, gripping the wooden banister as she took a few more steps up, almost tripping over the train of her dress. "I like this dress, and this is what I'm going to wear."

I reached out and grabbed the skirt with both hands, yanking it hard enough to rip the seam holding the skirt to the front and sides of the corset and knock her on her ass.

I looked down at her perfectly pink, exposed pussy lips and saw red.

"You aren't even wearing fucking underwear. Tell me, are you trying to get pictures of your pussy all over Page Six?" I raged.

I brought my hand around her throat as I leaned down, getting in her face. I didn't squeeze hard enough to cut off her air supply, but hard enough she knew I could. "Explain yourself. Now."

Her eyes got bigger, and the blood drained from her face, giving her a pale, almost lifeless pallor when no one came to save her from me.

"No." Her eyes went wild as she strained to look around while she tried to scramble away from me. Her feet kept slipping on the fabric of the skirt, and she couldn't get any leverage.

"No one is coming to save you, little girl." I tightened my grip just a little. "It's just me and you here."

The staff had been given the rest of the night off, and the maid who'd opened the door left moments before Amelia deigned to grace us with her presence.

We were alone, and there was no one to protect her from me.

"Get your hands off of me," she said between gritted teeth.

I leaned down to kiss her, and she turned her head from me.

With a dark laugh, I placed a kiss on her neck just above where my hand was holding her down.

"Argue all you like. I can tell how aroused you are. Tell me, how many times did you pet this little pussy thinking about me the last few days?"

"None," she snapped, but she couldn't meet my gaze.

"Liar." I straightened back up and offered my hand to her.

She was sprawled out under me on the stairs, her long shapely legs on full display, from her toes to her rounded hips. If

I didn't know better, I would say she looked freshly fucked and hungry for round two.

Had Marksen been with her today?

Left her wanting because he wasn't man enough to get his girl, no, *my* girl, off. She was about to find out what it was like when a real man fucked her. I would leave her so fucking satisfied she wouldn't think of him again. If he ever showed up again, she would be far too sore to take him.

Maybe I should put her in a chastity belt just to be safe.

"Get up, unless you want to start your apology here on the fucking stairs?"

When she didn't move, I grabbed her arm, careful to avoid the places her mother had bruised her, and pulled her to her feet. Not even I was barbaric enough to fuck her on the stairs. Though her pussy was wet. I could see it glisten from here.

Did she enjoy making me angry, or did she like me taking control?

Either way was going to result in a far more eventful marriage than I had expected. I didn't know if that was a good or bad thing yet.

"Don't touch me." She pulled her arm from my grasp.

"Oh, I am going to do far more than just touch you, princess. You had your chance to behave. I may not have married you yet, but with what I have on your precious mother, you are mine to do with as I wish. I could drag you by your hair to the courthouse tomorrow and marry you there."

"Then why haven't you?" She bared her perfect teeth at me.

"The only reason I haven't is because I expect you to show some fucking respect and restraint. I don't care what you and Marksen used to have. I don't give a fuck if he liked when you dressed like a desperate slut. But now you represent the Manwarring family. Now you represent me. Take off that dress, or I will take it off of you myself. Then I will show you what it means to be an apologetic and well-behaved wife."

"No." Her eyes were wild, and her breath was heavier, her lips parted and color rising on her chest and neck. I could even see her pulse racing in the vein in her throat.

For a moment, I wondered how those intense green eyes would look staring up at me while her pretty pink lips were wrapped around my cock.

Would she glare up at me in hatred, or would she fall to her place? I wasn't sure. She had a fire in her, but her body betrayed how much it wanted to submit. I couldn't wait to find out.

As my wife, doing as I said would be her duty, using her body would be my right. I could have her on her knees every morning as I got ready for work. It would be part of my new morning routine. I'd wake up when she brought my first cup of coffee to me in bed. Then I could enjoy the feeling of her sucking my balls dry as I drank my coffee and read the news. Or maybe after the gym before my shower, I could fuck her throat until tears flowed down her cheeks and her lungs burned, needing air.

Then at night I'd take out the frustrations of my day in her sweet little pussy, and if her time with Marksen meant she wasn't tight enough, fine. As soon as I put a baby in her belly, I could just take her ass for my pleasure.

I hadn't intended to be such a savage husband, but I also hadn't counted on having such a willful bride.

A small part of me hoped that even then, she wouldn't lose this fire. I liked her mad. I liked her trying to fight what I knew she craved. She would break eventually, but I hoped she didn't break easily.

I wanted to revel in the fight.

"Take off that dress." I climbed the next two stairs. She was almost at the top.

"Fuck you." The fire in her eyes raged, and my cock was hard as steel.

"Keep testing me, little girl, and that is exactly what is going to happen." I clenched my jaw, eye level with her swollen, needy cunt.

"Go to hell," she said as she hit the top stair.

She turned and ran down the hall, the skirt of her green dress trailing after her, attached by only a few threads.

She ran from me.

No one had ever actually run from me. Usually, they backed away slowly, tail tucked firmly between their legs, or they turned and stormed out. But no one had physically run from me before.

Silly little girl. Hadn't her bitch mother ever told her not to run from a predator?

Because we like the chase.

I climbed up the rest of the stairs and ran after her, feeling truly alive.

My heart raced, my cock harder than ever before. I needed her under me now. I needed to make her submit to me.

There had never been a woman who had put up so much of a fight. Ever since I was a teenager, the second a woman heard my last name, she practically begged to suck me off, or she tripped over herself trying to open her legs for me.

Amelia was the first to ever tell me "no."

The first woman to fight me.

This chase was something new, and it was invigorating. She slammed the heavy white door in my face and slid the lock into place before I could grasp the delicate golden handle.

I slammed both palms against the door. "Amelia, open this door!" I raged, twisting the doorknob and beating the hand-carved wooden door panel with the side of my fist.

"No." Her scream was muffled by the door. She sounded

81

scared and panicked. I liked it. My cock had never been so hard. I could feel my pulse in my balls.

"Amelia, open this fucking door or I will break it down!"

It wasn't an idle threat. I had no idea how I would explain a broken door to her parents, but I didn't really care. She was mine, and nothing came between me and what was mine.

"No!"

"You will open this door and accept your punishment. Then you will change into a more appropriate dress that I will pick out since you have clearly lost your mind."

"You will never lay a hand on me," she yelled. "I want you to leave. I'm not going anywhere with you! Ever!" Her voice had escalated to a scream.

Time for a new tactic.

"Amelia, you're a smart girl. Let me lay out your choices for you. You will take off that dress and unlock this door, then you will get on your knees like a good girl and show me how sorry you are for making us late. Then you will be dressed and ready to leave and you will spend the rest of the night behaving."

"Pass!" she screamed back.

"Option two. You take off that fucking dress, open this door and take your punishment, then you dress, we go, and you have a sore ass the rest of the night."

"I said no!" she screamed again, and I lost my patience. This wasn't fun anymore. It was infuriating.

"The last fucking option is I break down this door, and I come in there and show you what happens to little girls who refuse to learn their fucking place."

"Fuck you!" she shouted.

"Fine, have it your way! Just remember, I tried to be reasonable." I took a few steps back and ran at the door, ramming it with my shoulder. It shook but didn't budge. Pain erupted through my shoulder as I hit some ridiculous ribbons and flowers that had been carved out of wood and attached to the door.

The pain was good. It focused my rage and fueled it.

"Leave now or I will call the police."

"I own the fucking police!"

Not entirely true, but close enough, and she knew it.

There was nothing she could do to me, even if her brother was the DA and she got a cop that wasn't on my payroll. The charges would never be filed, and I would never make it as far as even having a mugshot taken.

I rammed into the door again, and this time the wood gave a satisfying crack along the hinges.

"When I get this door open, that dress better be in the fucking trash, and you better be on your knees ready to beg like the good girl I paid for."

"You don't pay for ladies!" she fired at me. "You pay for whores. That's what you treated me like the other day, so that is what I dressed like."

"If you keep talking like that, I will find a much better use for your mouth," I warned.

Without waiting for another reply, I ran into the door again, and this time the wood splintered, and the door collapsed to the floor.

Amelia was still in that torn green dress, her pussy exposed, mouth open, eyes wide.

My breath was billowing in and out in rapid pants, and I could only imagine the beast I looked like to her right now.

I stalked into the room, stepping on top of what was her door and taking off my jacket.

"Now, little girl, are you going to find out what it's like to be punished, or are you going to beg for mercy?"

CHAPTER 11

AMELIA

"Get out!" I screamed, hoping there was no quiver in my voice as I did so.

He took another menacing step toward me. "I'm not going to tell you again. Take off the dress, or I will take it off for you."

"You have no right," I bit back.

"You're my future wife. I have every right."

"You can't just come here and demand that I—"

"Act and dress in ways befitting my wife. I most certainly can. And I have." He cleared the distance between us and took hold of the dress's fabric. The sound of material ripping blended with my screams of protest.

I fought to keep standing, but my knees buckled.

He caught me and yanked me back up.

"Please," I whimpered.

"Please what?"

"Please," I repeated.

"Please what?"

"Please don't hurt me," I whispered.

"Take off what's left of the dress," he demanded.

"No," I cried.

I prayed he didn't make me, but I knew he would.

My hands trembled as I reached behind my back and grabbed the fabric. I pulled the ends apart and let the dress fall to the floor around me. The cool air hit my skin, sending a shiver down my spine.

I cradled myself, arms wrapping around my chest. I had never felt so vulnerable before in my life. I refused to meet his gaze. I couldn't.

"Do you like the way this feels?" His slid his hand down my body, brushing my arms aside and palmed one of my breasts.

"No."

"Do you like the way I'm touching you?" He slid his hand lower, between my legs.

"No, I do not." But I was lying, and if he felt the wetness forming on my pussy, he'd know the answer for himself.

"Where's my brave and defiant bride now?" He leaned in and inhaled deeply. "I can smell the fear on you."

He pulled back just enough for me to see a spark of mischief glimmer in his eyes, and a wicked smile form on his face. "Good. Because you should be very afraid of what I'm about to do to you, and just how much you are going to enjoy it."

As I clung to the remnants of my modesty, he reached for his buckle, unfastened his belt, and swooped it free from the loops.

"Time for your punishment, darling. Bend over."

My eyes widened at the command, and I began to tremble. I tried to fight it, but I couldn't. "Naughty girls get punished in this marriage. Best you learn that now." He gave me another smile, his belt still clenched in his fist. "But I promise to kiss it all better at the end."

I couldn't tell if he was taunting me or making a delicious

promise. Either way, I couldn't move. My body remained frozen in place.

Then, with a firm tug, he yanked me by my arm and pulled me over to my vanity. With a sweep of his arm, he sent the small bottles of perfume and makeup brushes scattering to the carpet.

I tried to keep my feet, but his strength overpowered mine.

He bent me over the table, and he pushed my face into the wood. The smell of freshly polished mahogany was strong and comforting but not nearly as comforting as the feel of his hands between my shoulder blades and his breath on the back of my neck.

"How long has it been since someone took you in hand and spanked this perfect ass of yours? Was I your first the other night?"

"N-never," I stuttered. "Only you dared—"

"Well, let's make up for lost time, shall we?" He continued to caress my body. "I'm going to whip this ass of yours, and it's going to hurt. It's not going to be like before. I'm not going to stop after a few light swats."

A few light swats—was that what he called my punishment from the other night?

Oh God, what did that mean for this punishment?

With one harsh, swift swoosh of the belt, I felt the sting of leather against flesh.

I cried out at the contact, but the vanity table muffled the sound.

Even so, I could hear him straighten and take a step back.

Two, three, four, five.

Each smack was harder than the last.

I tried to be silent, my head lifting but my jaw clenched so hard I thought my teeth would shatter.

I didn't want to give the man the pleasure of hearing my cries.

87

The pain was intense, but there was something else. Something deeper. Something dark and forbidden. Something I couldn't name.

My head fell forward, and my vision blurred as hot, fresh tears spilled down my cheeks. I bit my lip, hoping to restrain the shrieks that threatened to escape from me.

When I thought the stinging would subside, he gave me another hard crack of the belt. I struggled for air as my lungs filled with cries of agony.

Maybe that soft touch on my backside was his hand? I was ready to feel a soothing caress.

Instead, his hand came down with a hard slap.

I screamed, and he spanked me again.

When I thought I couldn't take any more, he stopped. The weight of his body pressed down on me, and he gave my ass a hard squeeze.

"You're mine, and I'm going to fuck you tonight. I'm going to make you come over and over again. You're going to beg me for more."

I was on the verge of begging for mercy. I was a rag doll, hanging limp over the table.

I couldn't control my body. He had taken complete control of me.

Cool air hit my exposed skin when he stood up, and I began to quake. I couldn't contain my shivers, my skin breaking out in goosebumps as my overheated body reacted to the air's coolness.

I let my head fall forward, resting it on the table.

A finger traced from the top of my back down to the center of my ass. The skin there was red and hot. I ached for his touch.

"You did well, my bride. You are a good girl when you want to be. I didn't think you would behave so perfectly. I'm very proud of you."

I hung there helplessly, the tears free-falling down my face.

I felt myself slipping away, even as he let me up and pulled me back against him. His erection pressed against my ass. The feel of it made me wet and weak in the knees. My skin was still on fire from his spanking. I could feel the heat in my backside, and his hands running up and down my legs.

"I may not be the first to fuck this pussy of yours," he said as he began to stroke the delicate flesh. "But I'm going to be the last."

I shook my head, too stunned and breathless by the spanking to tell him how wrong he was. I'd never had sex with Marksen like he clearly assumed I had.

I was a virgin.

But as he shoved his finger into my pussy, I realized I wouldn't be a virgin for long.

He pulled his finger out of me and turned me around to face him. Reaching in, he spread my lips with his fingers, opening me up wide.

"Let me get a good look at this pussy before I completely destroy it."

His voice was deep and hypnotic. It made me feel like I was being drawn in by some kind of spell.

That's when he leaned in, holding my chin in his hand, and claimed my mouth. It wasn't a kiss, it was a show of power, of domination.

I didn't fight him. I couldn't. I was too weak, and my body wasn't my own. His hand was in my hair, grabbing fistfuls like he was claiming me.

I shuddered as he released my mouth.

He wrapped his hands around my waist and lifted me onto the vanity with my back against the mirror. My heart skipped as he knelt before me, placing his strong hands against my inner thighs, forcing them open.

I grasped his hair. "Wait. No. What are you doing?"

He raised an eyebrow. "Keeping my promise and kissing it to make it better first."

The tip of his tongue pierced the folds of my pussy, sending a shock wave straight up my spine. My back arched. If he hadn't been holding my thighs, I would have slid right off the vanity top.

"Oh God!" I called out, no longer even trying to hide my reaction.

He swirled his tongue around my clit, taunting and teasing me. Over and over again, applying just the right amount of pressure. It was nothing like the illicit pleasure from my own fingertips. This was darker, more intense. Dangerous.

He increased the pace as he flicked my sensitive nub before adding his fingers, thrusting them inside me.

Our bodies rocked so violently together we dislodged the mirror.

It slid behind the vanity, crashed to the floor, and shattered.

I came undone. It was too much. The pain. The pleasure. Every nerve in my body was firing sparks as bursts of light exploded behind my closed eyelids while the air in my lungs seized.

Before I had a chance to recover, he rose to his full height, towering over me. He stood between my still outstretched legs, pressing them painfully apart, until my muscles screamed from the tension. The soft metallic clicks of his trouser zipper followed.

Then the head of his cock slipped by my opening.

I felt the nudge of it, but I was powerless to protest.

He was too strong.

The head of his cock pressed against my entrance.

I knew what was about to happen and couldn't stop it...didn't want to stop it.

He slid in an inch. The width of him stretched me to my limits, and I cried out.

"I know it hurts, but I'll make it better," he said as he leaned over me and kissed my neck. "I'm not a small man, but you'll take me like a good girl."

I clenched the sides of the table with my hands. Sweat stung my eyes. I was so scared my body tensed, making it hurt even more.

"I'm going to fill you up, and you're going to like it."

His cock slid in another inch.

The biting pain was too much, and I cried out.

He stopped.

Clasping my jaw in his hands, he glared down at me. "You're a virgin."

As if I had somehow deceived him.

I blinked up at him, uncertain what to say.

The air was thick with tension. I couldn't breathe.

Then, without warning, he seized my mouth for another searing kiss. This one was different from the last. As if he didn't want to dominate, but rather, somehow fuse us...as one. His tongue swept inside, dueling with mine. Tasting me.

His dark gaze intensified. "There is no escaping me now, babygirl."

It was all too much, too overwhelming. I could deal with the overbearing version of him. I couldn't deal with the version of him that wanted to steal my soul. I tried to turn my head. I was going to pass out. The pain was too much.

Relief washed through me as he slid his cock out of me.

And yet... I'd never felt so empty before.

He wrapped his arms tightly around me and lifted me off the table. After swinging to the right, he carried me the few steps to the bed before he tossed me across the bottom half, pinning me down with his body.

He then slid back in, and I gritted my teeth at the new pain and pleasure.

I tried to move, but he held me in place, his hands wrapping around my wrists, stretching them over my head as he stared down at me.

He pulled out again, and then thrust back in, but further this time.

I felt my body stretching to take him.

He pushed most of the way in this time.

My back arched as a deep throated, keening moan slipped past my lips. I didn't know why I was crying out, but it felt too good. I didn't want the pain to go away.

He thrust forward suddenly, and the entire length of his cock filled me.

I was certain his cock was going to rip me in two as he stretched my insides.

He pulled out slowly and thrust back in.

I moaned again as he increased his pace, pounding into me without mercy.

His cock was so deep. The pressure was overwhelming.

I wanted him to fuck me. I wanted him to take me.

I wanted it to last forever.

In and out. In and out.

Each thrust sent pleasure through me. Each plunge made my pussy ache.

He was so big and hard. I wasn't sure I would ever get used to the feeling.

The weight of his body held me in place. I was helpless. I couldn't move if I wanted to.

"Be a good girl and come for me."

I managed to nod.

He thrust into me hard and fast as his hips ground into me.

I whimpered as he hit my special spot.

I was so full of him. So full and aching. I pushed back against him.

"Tell me," he ordered. "Tell me you're a good girl and will obey," he breathed against my neck as he released one of my wrists and reached between our bodies to tease my still sensitive clit.

I didn't want to admit it. I didn't want to say it. But I wanted him to keep fucking me. I needed him to keep fucking me.

My body was on fire. I let out a breathless moan.

He pulled out of me. "Say it," he commanded.

I felt empty and cold. I wanted him back inside me.

"I'll be your good girl."

He thrust in deep, and I was lost.

CHAPTER 12

LUC

*T*he whole of New York, the most powerful city in the world, was at my feet, as I stood in my father's corner office.

This was the view meant only for gods and the men who played at being them.

That was what we were, and these offices were meant not to remind us, but to intimidate every person who entered them.

We were above all. We looked down upon our kingdom that we merely allowed others to inhabit. I had been raised to rule my empire with an iron fist, and any less would mean the downfall of me and my family.

Failure was not an option.

The pressure had scared the shit out of me when I was a kid, but now the challenge excited me.

I loved looking at this view. Soon, very soon, it would be mine. I reveled in the challenge of rising to the level of a titan of industry and taking my place. Every time I looked out this window, that was the future I envisioned.

Though since the engagement, the mental pictures had some-what shifted.

I was no longer alone at the head of my family.

A wife stood next to me—well, below me—but still above everyone else.

Then there were the children who would inherit not only the family business as it was now, but what I grew it into. I no longer saw this as my empire, but one I was meant to strengthen and grow for the next generation of Manwarring men.

I just had a few things to do first, mainly, dispose of my father before his recklessness became a liability we couldn't mitigate.

That wasn't where my mind was this morning. I wasn't studying the buildings or the lights in the skyline, or even my future as the head of the family.

I was thinking about Amelia.

More specifically, the way I had left her the night before.

The struggle in her eyes as I left her, in her bed, alone to clean herself up, handle the fallout, and deal with the fact she was no longer a virgin.

I had been rash and fucking stupid.

Marksen had tried to get into my head with his lies, and I had let him.

The idea that he had been with her, that she wanted him and every time I fucked her she would think about him, had utterly consumed me. Or worse, that she'd go to him whenever she could.

He'd never had her. The more I thought about it, the more I doubted they'd ever had more than a few passing conversations, let alone some love connection or bond that united them as lovers.

No, he had bluffed, and though I hadn't given him what he wanted, I had let him get into my head, and I had taken my future wife's innocence by force.

Not that I would have made her first time on our honeymoon sweet or gentle.

God no. I would have at least been easier on her, though.

I would have done a better job making sure she was more prepared before I stretched her wide. She would have been ready, and I would have at least taught her what I like. Given her an opportunity to learn my body and discover what felt good for me and her.

Though she hadn't fought me for long.

When I'd agreed to this scheme, I'd known there was a good chance that every time I lay with my wife, she would merely lie there like a cold, dead fish. Just there to fulfill her obligations. I had expected sex with her to be a fight, then a chore.

She was nothing like I had expected.

Her body had responded to mine. She had leaned into my kiss, purred under my touch, and her hips rocked into mine, racing toward her own glorious release.

Once she'd let go, once she'd accepted what was happening, she'd become something unexpected. She was hot, wild, and hungry for me.

She'd been possessed by an exquisite, wild abandon, like she'd stopped thinking. She'd stopped analyzing everything and had given in to it. She gave in to me.

Every time I'd demanded more from her, she'd met the challenge.

It was the most unexpected, satisfying thing that had ever happened. Until I got out of her bed and got dressed. The look of a well-fucked, contented woman had melted off her face as she realized what had just happened. Like an idiot, I had left her there alone.

She was probably terrified of me now.

There were lines a man of society shouldn't cross, and I had crossed each of them. I had entered her house, destroyed an ornate antique door and ruined priceless furniture, and I had taken my bride before our wedding night.

We'd fucked like wild animals.

No, I'd fucked her like a whore, expecting that was what she really was.

I'd told myself that once we were married, I'd lock her away so she could never cuckold me like her mother had her father.

Any time I had to travel, I'd lock her in a chastity belt and keep her in my hotel room waiting for me. Even then, I would have every child she bore DNA tested. The second one of them wasn't mine, she would be penniless and out on her ass.

Those were the promises I'd made to myself until I pushed inside her tight little body and felt her innocence break at my intrusion.

No man had ever had her before.

I was the first to penetrate her, and so help me, I would be the last.

My cock stirred to life again as I thought about the way Amelia's body had bent to me, how the fear in her eyes had turned to pain and then pleasure as I coaxed the orgasm from her body.

Perhaps there was a way to fix this.

Maybe there was some hope for us to find a modicum of pleasure in this farce of a marriage. Not much, but some.

God knew she was a spoiled little bitch, but unlike the other women of our caliber, she wasn't an ice queen, not at her core.

She pretended, of course, but it had never fully seeped into her soul. Could I coax that small spark into a raging inferno of passion and lust?

She was all fire, rage, and hate.

A fine line existed between love and hate. I wasn't naïve enough to think I could make her love me, but surely I could make her crave me. Really, that was all I needed. I could make her associate me with pleasure, train her to crave my touch.

Maybe tonight I would have to go back to the club for another celebratory drink. Not only had my soon-to-be wife been a virgin, touched only by me, but when I had her mewing and panting under me, she was the best fuck I'd ever had.

The way her tight little body gripped me, sucking me in further, begging for my come. The way she'd lost herself once she allowed herself to feel the pleasure only I would ever bring her.

I had a little virgin who was aching to be turned into a wanton little slut, and she would only ever know my touch. Surely that called for a drink.

Or maybe I should have Amelia meet me somewhere after, and I could show her a few other things she would be expected to do as my wife.

Maybe I wouldn't touch her but force her to touch herself, wearing nothing but green silk while I watched. I could instruct her on how to bring pleasure to herself so she could do that each night, thinking of me until our wedding night.

Now that was an idea.

Have her bring herself pleasure each night thinking of me, learning that her own fingers might take the edge off in the short term, but only I could give her the release she really needed. By the time we got to our honeymoon suite, she would be the perfect, docile kitten begging for a treat.

I had planned to skip a honeymoon, but now I considered staying off work for a few days. Just long enough to have my new little wife properly trained in the ways to please me.

The door closed behind me and pulled me from my thoughts of Amelia.

CHAPTER 13

LUC

"*L*uc," my father said, taking a seat at his desk and motioning for me to sit across from him. This was a man who exuded power and prestige. He aged well. Very well. I only hoped to be blessed with the same genes.

"Father." I unbuttoned my suit jacket so I could sit. "You asked me to meet you up here."

"Yes, I wanted to go over some plans with you. Now that you have rid us of the Dubois problem, for the moment, we have to take full advantage of this marriage."

"Oh, I intend to," I said, not meaning it as a double entendre, at least not until I had said it out loud.

"Yes, yes. Have fun with the girl, let her give you powerful heirs and pretty daughters, but that isn't what I want to talk to you about." My father sat back at his massive mahogany table, his fingers steepled in front of him and elbows resting on the hardwood.

"Then what did you call me in here for?" I should have brought my coffee with me. Had I known my father was just planning on wasting my time, I could at least be enjoying my caffeine.

"We have more enemies that need to be handled."

"Who did you have in mind?" I asked.

"Who don't I have in mind?" He laughed. "But let's start with the Astrids."

"I hardly think my wife's family is going to be a problem for us." I made sure my tone was flat, and I didn't show my annoyance.

Work was piling up on my own desk. I didn't have time to play his little games.

"Her mother and father, no. Her mother has been tamed for our purposes, and her father seems to think this is a love match. He's just happy his daughter will be provided for and loved, or some such nonsense. The Astrid I am more concerned about is her brother. Will the young Harrison be a problem for us?"

"Harrison is busy with his own world. As long as we don't push anything too outrageous, I don't think he will notice."

"Too outrageous, like breaking down his sister's door?" He arched one eyebrow at me.

I stared back, daring him to say more.

"What did you hear?" I asked when it was clear he wasn't going to volunteer any further information.

"Just that Ms. Astrid's room was broken into by a few of the staff. That they had broken the door. Thankfully, it seems like Amelia wasn't there, since she was with you at the opera last night. Funny, though, I don't seem to recall seeing you there."

"I was busy with my fiancée, but if you ask, several of the staff will confirm I was there." Because they were paid to say that. "If there is nothing else…" I stood to head back to my desk.

"I'm sure, but we do have to get some other things handled." He rose and went to one of the large conference tables covered in several sheets of paper and blueprints.

"Who else do we need to have taken care of today, Father?"

"My son, the blood-thirsty businessman." He laughed to himself. "Don't worry. I'm sure we'll be sending those associates of ours after people again soon, but I'm thinking we should start with more legal avenues first."

He'd incorrectly assumed I had been implying we should have the Irish mob handle our affairs. "Come look over these plans for the new distillery, and let's get to work."

He took more plans out of cardboard tubes and flattened them out on the table, using little leather beanbags to hold down the corners.

That hadn't been what I meant.

I loathed having to use the mob. It was too much risk and not enough reward. I also believed a man should do his own dirty work—hiring it out was a sign of a coward—but I'd learned a long time ago not to correct my father. It simply wasn't worth the hassle. He wouldn't let me talk much, anyway. It was fine. I would listen to him, learn from his experience and wisdom, then do whatever I thought best.

He was only angered if my disobedience didn't prove to bring better results, which rarely happened. I knew this business inside and out, and as soon as I married, it would be handed over to me by his choice or my force. Then the thugs my father dealt with would be out the door right behind him.

A truly powerful man didn't need an attack dog.

He was the attack dog.

What I could do to anyone who faced me was far more painful than a beating from a brute.

"I want to look at how we can use this marriage for our gain," he said.

"What did you have in mind?"

"A lot. I know this initially prevented a loss, but we can gain quite a bit here as well. With that Astrid bastard being the district attorney. We can use that to our advantage and expand faster. I'm thinking Harrison can pave the way for us to go around a few city officials and a handful of laws and get the new divisions up and running by spring."

"What if he doesn't agree to help us?" I looked over the blue-prints. They were for another distillery with an attached ware-house. The permits on this were going to take months.

"He will. Astrid is a pushover. He lets his fucking whore wife run everything." He waved me off dismissively. "If she can't get senior to do what we need, she will get junior to handle it."

"Astrid senior may be easily manipulated by his wife, but I would bet good money that Harrison is not."

"How would you know that?" he scoffed.

"We went to boarding school together. Harrison isn't a weak man, and to approach him while underestimating him would be a mistake."

"Then what do you suggest?" My father cracked his knuckles, a sure sign he was losing patience.

"I'm sure we can browbeat Phillip Astrid to do as we please. More to the point, I don't think we will need to. The joining of our whisky with his tobacco can make for an extremely lucrative venture. I'm worried that if we approach in bad faith, Harrison may not be as amenable to working with us as he was with Dubois. Especially if he finds out about some of the less-than-legal methods used by some of our less-cultured associates," I said.

"If that Astrid bitch doesn't want her secrets out, she'll make her son see reason." My father cracked his knuckles again, and I wondered, not for the first time, if he knew he had so many tells, he was easy to read and therefore easy to manage.

"I don't think Mrs. Astrid controls her son as easily as she does her husband," I said. "Besides, we have already used that leverage on Mrs. Astrid."

"So? We can use it again."

"No. We can't." How could this man be so shortsighted?

"Says who? Does marrying the slut's daughter somehow undo the fact that the Astrid boy, the Manhattan district attorney, is a bastard?"

"No, but…"

"This is leverage. I have no intention of giving up anytime soon. He's a public official with a very dirty secret. If we just pull on a few strings, I'm sure more secrets will come to light that I, for one, have no problem letting the world in on if the Astrid whore doesn't do as she is told."

"Once I am married, we are linked to the Astrids."

I couldn't believe I had to spell this out. "Hurting them would hurt us. We got what we needed from Mary Quinn Astrid. Now, I intend on being around her as infrequently as possible."

"But this merger—"

"Has merit on its own. Why not take these plans to Astrid senior and Harrison, let them see the value, and create a merger based on my marriage and merit?"

"Because they can say no. They can choose to impede our progress or ask questions I'm less inclined to answer."

His face started turning ruddy around his temples. Lucian Manwarring did not like being questioned. Not even by his son. "Blackmail here is simpler and more efficient."

"Respectfully, Father, I disagree. It means we are operating in bad faith."

I held up my hand at his protest, something that would have gotten lesser men tossed out on their asses. "I agree, using black-mail was best to end the Dubois merger, but now I think we should make these deals aboveboard, get both Astrids to agree. It would be far easier and create a better relationship for the long run."

"You are being shortsighted. We can just blackmail the slut and ensure that we never have to compromise."

"Astrid is not a fool, a cuckold maybe, but in business, he is almost as savvy and clever as we are. If we make this deal in good faith, we can hold back the blackmail as leverage for when we need it," I argued.

This didn't sit right with me. I'd gotten what we bargained for. The threat of exposing Harrison's true father shouldn't be hovering over his mother anymore.

At least not from us.

"We have more resources to use if the blackmail ever becomes ineffective," he said, as he pulled out another chair and took a seat.

"No." I raised my voice. "She is to be my wife, which means our families are tied together. We will not resort to using those thugs on any of the Astrids. I know enough about Harrison to know he will burn the world to the ground to protect his sisters. They can never know our Irish mob ties are involved. I'm sure he will help us clear the way for them, but only so long as he thinks his sisters will never be close enough to them to be hurt."

"Sit down, boy." My father rolled his eyes.

"Not until you hear me on this. We can do this deal legitimately. The more dealings we have aboveboard, the easier it is to conceal the ones below. To be truly effective, we need Harrison to look as clean as possible for as long as possible."

"Maybe." He stroked his chin, his dark brown eyes contemplative. "Let's see what the Astrids think of this deal. If they are amenable, fine. But if they are less than accommodating, I will use this leverage to get what I want."

"Of course." I shrugged as if it didn't bother me. "This is business. We will get done what we need to, but I think we should save the leverage for something bigger. Unfortunately, our get-out-of-jail-free card can't be waved around wildly. A smarter man would save it for a rainy day," I said as I turned and left my father's office for mine. I had plans to make.

There had to be a way to stop my father from using this leverage, or at the very least, to protect Amelia from the fallout.

I would not have my wife's name dragged through the dirt with her mother.

It would reflect poorly upon my interests as well, since we were now aligned.

It would also hurt Amelia, and for some reason, that thought made my stomach twist, and I didn't like it.

She was mine, to fuck, to argue with, and to control.

That also meant she was mine to protect.

From her mother and my father.

My sins would always impact her, but I refused to let the ill-advised lunacy take any toll on her well-being.

CHAPTER 14

AMELIA

I've never liked yachts.

I've always been one to get terribly seasick, but at least tonight's party was on a yacht docked in the harbor.

Although there was another reason my stomach was flipping and churning inside.

Luc Manwarring was approaching me.

His piercing eyes locked with mine.

I hadn't seen him since *that* night.

The night he took my virginity.

And I'd be lying if I said I hadn't thought about every second of that night since.

Every. Single. Second.

"Care to dance?" he asked, extending his hand as any gentleman would.

Although I knew his secret. There was nothing gentlemanly about him.

I hesitated for a moment, but his intense gaze was too hard to resist.

I placed my hand in his, and he led me to the dance floor.

As he pulled me closer, I could feel the heat radiating off his body.

His hands were strong and firm on my waist. The music of the waltz swirled around us, and I could feel the tension building between us.

"You look stunning tonight." His voice was deep, seductive. "I'm pleased to see you've chosen something appropriate to wear this time."

My heart stuttered at his words.

At his subtle reminder of what had happened after my most recent attempt to test his patience with my scandalous dress.

Memories of that night, never far from my mind, came flooding back.

The way he'd punished me, the way he'd touched me, the way he'd demanded my submission and my body, the way he'd made me feel... and then the way he'd left without a word. Something about the way he'd looked at me before leaving made me want to forget all of that. And I had tried hard to forget about him, but it was impossible. Luc had left an indelible mark on my body and my soul.

I could smell his cologne mixed with the salt of the sea.

"I've missed your body," he whispered in my ear, his lips brushing against the sensitive skin there.

My heart raced, and my cheeks burned as I focused on the waltz, not sure how to respond. His touch was electric, and I tried to suppress a rush of desire.

He moved his hand to my bare back and caressed me below my shoulder blades.

Heat flooded my body as he traced his fingers down to my backside. He pulled me closer and pressed his body against mine. I wanted to push him away and slap him but couldn't.

His hardness pressed against my inner thigh, and it took every ounce of self-control not to reach down and stroke him.

He pressed his lips against my ear. "Do you remember how it felt when I fucked you? The way I made you come again and again?"

The heat surged through me as he continued to whisper in my ear, his words driving me wild. I couldn't deny the way he made me feel.

I wanted him, craved him.

I was a fool for not coming up with any witty banter.

The man rendered me speechless.

"Try not to squirm so much," he said as he pulled me even closer. "It's a waltz, not a tango."

I bit my lip and squeezed my legs together in an attempt to stop my body from reacting to him. There was no way I could hide my own arousal.

It was getting harder and harder to ignore my feelings for him.

I glanced around the room, and a small contingent of onlookers was watching us dance.

If they thought we had already consummated the marriage, they didn't show with scowls of disapproval or anything that hinted they believed we were acting inappropriately in any way.

If only they knew the truth.

I froze in his arms when I noticed my mother watching me intently from across the room. Her eyes bored into me with a gaze that sent a shiver down my spine. Clearly, she didn't approve of Luc's and my relationship, and yet she was allowing it for some unknown reason.

Luc pulled me forward as the music increased in tempo, and I struggled to keep my footing in my attempt to keep up with his quick, fluid movements. His dancing was effortless, as if he was doing nothing at all, and when he turned, he brought me so close to his body there wasn't a part of his firm, strong frame I couldn't feel. He slid his hand down to the small of my back while every inch of us touched.

"You feel that?" Luc whispered into my ear.

I nodded.

"That cock's for you, baby."

His warm breath gave me a rush of chills, and my sex throbbed with desire.

"But you have to ask me for it. Beg for it. I want to watch those pretty lips of yours plead for mercy right before I fuck your mouth as your perfect mascara runs down your face."

I cursed myself for the intensity of my desire for him. He was playing me. He knew I was aching for him, even though I had yet to say a word.

"Say it," he hissed in my ear. "Say you want me to fuck that pretty mouth of yours."

I swallowed past the lump in my throat.

"Say it now, or I'll spank your ass right here on the dance floor for all to see. You think you're blushing now? Just wait." He paused. "Say it."

"Please fuck my mouth," I whispered, barely audible.

"Louder," he growled. "I want to hear you beg for my cock."

I looked around the room, feeling the flush spreading across my cheeks. I didn't want to do this. I didn't want to humiliate myself like this.

I looked up into his eyes, his amusement clear in his gaze.

He was daring me to submit. Daring me to do what I knew deep down I wanted.

"Fuck my mouth," I whispered, louder this time but still hesitant.

"Louder," he said. "I didn't catch that."

"I want your cock in my mouth." The blush was creeping deeper and deeper as the other couples danced around us.

His eyes smoldered with desire, and I wanted to feel those eyes burning into me as he took me.

"There you go," he said as he spun me around. "Now we can go home and finish what we started."

"You're incorrigible."

"Oh, I'm far worse than that, my dear." His eyes searched mine. "I'm dangerous."

I wanted to tell him to stop talking. I wanted to close my eyes and pretend this was all a dream. It had to be a dream, right?

He couldn't really be so cruel. He couldn't really be that much of a bastard.

But he was, and I knew it.

"And you're going to love every minute of it."

He leaned down and kissed me on the lips, gently at first and then with more passion.

I closed my eyes and lost myself in the kiss, savoring the softness of his lips.

The dance ended, and Luc stepped back.

My breath caught.

He knew exactly how to push my buttons.

This was a game, and he was winning.

I was soaking wet, and my knees were shaking as the music faded.

"I think it's time we leave," he said as his strong hand clasped mine.

I nodded, although I knew he wasn't asking for my permission.

CHAPTER 15

LUC

*T*he smell of her arousal made my dick so hard, I couldn't stand another minute not being inside her.

Leading her off the yacht and down the gangplank to the limo, I felt her tug on my hand.

"Shouldn't we say our goodbyes? It isn't proper and—"

"Fuck proper."

"Luc..."

"Amelia, get in the limo, now." I assisted her inside, but it was the last gentle act I had planned for the evening.

Once I shut the door behind her, I stalked around the front of the limo to slide into the back seat. "Get on all fours," I ordered.

"Luc, I—" She turned to look at the driver. Her eyes were wide with shock.

"Drive," I commanded the driver, lifting the privacy glass as I did so.

Still, Amelia sat there.

Reaching under her dress, I hooked my finger in the waistband of her panties and slid them down her long, toned legs.

Lifting her ankles, I removed them completely before

spreading her thighs to give me a good look at her dripping pussy. "You're fucking soaked," I groaned.

Not waiting for her to follow my command, I flipped her over and adjusted her body so her ass was on full display. My perfect little bride was waiting... even if I wasn't quite sure if she truly was willing.

Her smooth skin was flushed, making her look even more radiant. Placing a hand on her back, I felt her resistance as I unzipped my pants with my free hand.

"Luc," she said, her voice shaking. "Someone could see us. We're driving down the street. I just don't think this is appropriate."

"I don't always do appropriate. It's best you learn that now, just like you're learning I don't take no for an answer."

"Luc—"

"Spread your legs," I ordered.

I gripped her waist and slapped her right cheek hard enough to make a loud smack, rewarded by her soft moan.

She stiffened, but her cunt grew even wetter, now dripping on the leather seat.

I could only imagine the show we would be giving to every person on the street if we weren't behind the tinted windows.

Curling my fingers into her hips, I pulled her back on my cock, savoring the sensation as I thrust into her.

She was tight, but so wet. I pulled my cock out and slid it back in.

Amelia cried out as my cock stretched her, but I didn't stop.

I pulled out and thrust into her again, and again. Each time, pounding into her a little harder than before.

I reached underneath her to pinch her clit, feeling her body jolt up and her cunt tightening around my cock.

"Luc, it hurts. You're too big," she whimpered, trying to wriggle away from my thrusts.

"Are you going to tell me no again?"

"No, but—"

"Good," I commended, before thrusting into her again, even harder this time.

Blood filled my ears as I pounded into her. My balls slapped against her as I used her to satisfy my lust.

I fucked her harder, pressing a hand to her back and my teeth to the base of her neck to keep her from moving.

"You like the pain. Don't you, dirty girl? You like the hurt. Are you going to come for me, Amelia?" I groaned into her ear. "Come for me now. Do it. Show me how much you want my cock. Be my little whore."

"Go to hell," she whimpered. "But oh God, yes."

Immediately, I pushed my thumb against her hard clit. She froze for a second, then came so hard on my cock I suspect she would have squirted if she wasn't already so fucking wet.

"That's right, babygirl," I growled as I took hold of her hair and yanked. "Come all over my cock."

I stilled the hand on her back and ran it down her silky skin to the base of her spine so I could hold her tightly as she came. Her pussy clenched around my cock as she moved her ass against my hand.

I looked down as she writhed in ecstasy.

"Christ," I groaned, pumping my cock into her a few more times before my release overtook me.

Fucking her from behind like this was the hottest thing I had ever experienced.

Once I'd come, we stayed locked together for a few minutes, letting our breathing calm. Then, I took a deep breath, withdrew my cock, and zipped my pants.

She gasped when I turned her around and drew her onto my lap. Her dress was still bunched up around her waist, and I pulled it back down around her legs as I kissed her. Running my fingers through her tangled hair, I held her head still so I could savor the sweetness of her lips opening helplessly beneath mine, the warmth of her body heat radiating against me.

Her bottom half under the skirt of her dress was still bare, vulnerable... used.

This moment was soft. Gentle. Not me. I didn't want her to get used to this.

"You fuck like a whore," I said as I nipped her lip. "You had me so worked up I forgot I was going to abuse this pretty mouth of yours. Next time."

She pulled away, eyes wide. She slipped off my lap and then slapped me across the face with as much force as she could, given the awkward angle she was still at. "You're a bastard."

I touched the sting on my face. "No question about it. I am."

"I'm not a whore!" She blushed deeply as we faced the front. "I can't believe you just—"

"I want my woman to be a whore in the bedroom but a lady on the street."

She positioned herself as far away from me as she could, leaning up against the door. The moment she noticed her panties crumpled up on the limo floor, she snatched them up as quickly as I had removed them. "Every day, I hate you more."

I chuckled. "Your pussy doesn't."

CHAPTER 16

AMELIA

*H*ow dare he!

I had never been so angry, felt so degraded in my life, and I had to deal with my mother daily. Not even Mother could make me feel so worthless, so complicit in my own degradation.

After he dropped me off at home, I ran to my room and let out the warring emotions that boiled up inside of me by screaming in fury into my pillow.

After, when I lay exhausted on my bed, my fingers running over the smooth fabric of my duvet, I thought about what had happened and how he had made me feel unencumbered, wild.

The way he'd grabbed and pulled my hair as he fucked me, the noises I'd made. The driver had probably heard us, and I didn't care. I wanted more of Luc. The carnal brutality of him and the way I'd chased that release as viciously as he had. I hadn't even known sex could be like that.

Which I could live with. I was upset and ashamed by my lack of reason, but that was all biology. I could forgive myself for a moment of weakness with an attractive man because he was going to be my husband.

What I couldn't contend with were the dirty things he whispered in my ear. How he'd seduced me to the darker side, made me burn with just a look and a few words. How my core ached for him before he even touched me.

That was unforgivable.

I was not some airheaded child who could be so easily seduced by pretty words, or in my case, vulgar words, which just made it worse. At least the words were his own and not some poorly recited Shakespeare.

* * *

I WOKE up the next morning sore and angry.

How dare he fuck me like a whore, again.

I was to be his wife, and he had the nerve to treat me like any other woman he picked up off the streets. He hadn't even bothered to take me to a bed. He had just fucked me in the back of the limo and then dropped me off at my family's estate.

The worst part, the part I could never forgive him for, was he'd made me like it.

He had done something that turned me into some kind of primal beast that enjoyed getting put on my knees, that reveled in the power, the ferocity of his thrusts behind me.

In that moment, I'd loved it, and I hadn't wanted him to stop.

I wanted more. I wanted him to ravage me, mark me, claim me.

I wanted him to show the world that I belonged only to him.

Even now, thinking about it—the sensation of his fingers digging into my hips, his teeth at my neck, and his cock slamming into me—my heart raced, my cheeks heated, and my core, even sore as it was, pulsed with need.

I had so much emotion, anger, shame, and need, I required an outlet. Maybe this was the inspiration I needed to create something worthwhile. I went to Rose's studio. She loved art as much as I did, but unlike me, she had talent, so Daddy kept it well stocked for her.

Occasionally, I would get it in my head that it wasn't that I had no talent, it was only I had yet to find the right medium for my talent to express itself. It was ridiculous. Nevertheless, what was it they said, hope springs eternal?

Rose had all types of tools and supplies in her studio, everything from watercolors to ceramics. Whereas I had not found a medium I was even passable with, she had yet to find one where she didn't excel. I loved her, but sometimes I loathed her a little, too.

The soft pink walls were covered with her watercolors of Central Park in the spring, pen and ink still life studies, even a few oil-painted sunsets over the New York skyline that were just breathtaking.

My favorite was when she did a whole series of paintings of random people she saw in the park or from her window. The way she portrayed each figure with so much personality, they felt real. Rose also kept a bottle of turpentine uncapped in this room. Just enough that it permeated the room with a permanent odor that our mother couldn't stand. She never came in here, and the studio became our refuge, the best place to hide, paint, read, or just be unbothered.

Scavenging through the drawers of pencils, brushes, and markers, I came across charcoals. The resulting thick dark lines and gradient shading I could get might be exactly what I needed to express my swirling negative emotions. I grabbed the set and a fresh sketchbook and set to work.

There was only one image in my mind, only one thing I could

picture, the only thing I had thought about since the night of the opera.

Luc Manwarring's sexy, smug, infuriating face.

His strong chiseled jaw, regal Roman nose, and serious brow. I tried to draw the intensity of his eyes. They were dark, but more than that—there was something behind them, a strength that went beyond that of money or breeding, a possessiveness that was primal in a way I couldn't quite capture. Several tries later, I was surrounded by piles of balled-up paper, and I gave up on capturing his eyes.

Frustrated, I threw down the paper and the charcoal and collapsed on the chaise lounge.

Closing my eyes, I visualized my subject.

I pictured his intense cobalt eyes and how they seemed to stare into my soul like he could read every impure thought in my mind. I thought of that sexy smirk, then I thought about how he looked up at me from between my thighs.

His lips were painted with mischief from the sinful smirk he gave me as I tried to catch my breath. He looked like the Devil, smug and satisfied, knowing he had me thoroughly entangled in his trap.

I wasn't going anywhere. I couldn't run, and what was worse, he made me question if I even wanted to.

Just recalling the way he looked was enough to make my blood heat and my core ache for more.

I pictured Luc sitting next to me on this couch. His hand would be on my thigh, trailing up my inner thigh, and slipping under my dress. The room was suddenly stifling.

"You have been such a good girl for me," he would whisper in my ear. "I'm going to give you a little treat for behaving."

His hand would move to my panties, and he wouldn't even take them off, just push them to the side so his fingers could slide between my lips, searching for my clit. He would run small circles over it, gently, not enough to make me come, but enough to make me ache for his cock.

I brought my own hand to my thigh and pushed my skirt up a bit.

My eyes fluttered open, glimpsing the cloudless blue sky visible through the windows as I bent one of my knees and trailed my fingers over my clothed core, simply enjoying the little shivers that flowed over my skin. My panties were damp. Those things he'd whispered in my ear while we danced... had the way my hand brushed against his cock been an accident?

He was doing something to me, changing me in some profound way that made me yearn for things I didn't know I should even want. I had been taught sex was for men to enjoy and for women to tolerate.

For the first time, I understood why women did such stupid things for the men they wanted.

I slid my fingers into my underwear and tried to mimic the way he touched me. It felt good, but not electric, like when he did it. I wanted it. I wanted him, but at what cost?

My eyes slid closed again as I focused on how it felt when he touched me. When I touched myself, I was always gentle, soothing as I coaxed my body to its release.

Luc didn't coax anything; he demanded my pleasure. He moved my body, then manipulated it to give him exactly what he wanted, and I hated it.

Almost as much as I loved it.

He made me burn for him. I became not just complicit in my demise, but actively took part in it. He made me want him in ways that were concerning to feminism.

I moved my fingers over my clit in fast circles, pressing so hard it almost hurt.

I had never known riding the line between pain and pleasure was where the most exquisite ecstasy could be found. My breath caught as my back arched, and the pressure built in my core.

Thoughts of his clean spicy scent, the way his body felt pressed on top of mine, the sound of his voice whispering demands, filled my mind. *Come for me now. Do it. Show me how much you want my cock. Be my little whore.*

As I bit down on my lip to stifle my moan, my core clenched around nothing as I came in an intense orgasm made all the stronger for the tinge of pain from my still-sore muscles.

I caught my breath, lying back on the chaise lounge, waiting for the sense of satisfaction and the blissful high that came after an orgasm.

It never came.

Instead, I was hungry for more.

My fingers hadn't taken the edge off, and I was suddenly worried the only way I could ever be satisfied again was if he was the one to give me pleasure.

My sister's voice came from just outside the door. I pulled my hand away from my body, quickly straightened my dress, and picked up the sketchbook and charcoals again, looking at what I had drawn before.

The eyes still weren't perfect.

I moved down the page and tried to draw the second-most alluring part of his face. His lips, full, with a perfectly defined cupid's bow that was just sexy when he gave that cocky smirk. That smirk that said he owned the world and knew it. There was nothing he couldn't get, no woman who wouldn't willingly open their legs for him.

I pushed away that thought. There was no need to add petty jealousy to the mix of emotions swirling in my gut. Did I even have the right to be jealous? I was expected to remain faithful to my husband, but men didn't always have the same expectations of themselves.

Did he have a girlfriend or partner?

I had no idea, and now that thought was stuck in my head.

Did he spend his nights pleasuring another woman? Was I one among many, or the trophy wife to cover his true love?

With an aggravated scream, I scribbled over the sketch I was struggling with, then ripped the paper out of the book and balled it up, clenching it tightly.

How could one man have me this frustrated?

I shouldn't want him.

The only things I should feel for this man were hate and contempt. I did hate him, but there was something more, too. Did he intrigue me? Did the man who could so calmly put my mother in her place fascinate me?

Luc was full of bewildering and captivating contradictions.

People said he was one of the most powerful men in society, but then still referred to him by his first name, saving the more formal greetings for his father. He made himself and his partners billions, but few went into business with him. He knew everyone but hated networking. The rumor mill talked about him constantly but had no actual information about him.

People called him a gentleman, but when it was just the two of us, he was anything but gentle. I wanted to loathe him, to scratch out his eyes with my freshly manicured fingers, but I also wanted him to possess me in a way I didn't think was possible.

I threw the balled-up sketch I was holding across the room, further than the other discarded papers.

CHAPTER 17

AMELIA

"What are you doing in here?" Rose asked, coming into the room.

"I just had the itch to remind myself how little talent I actually have." I slouched further down into the soft chaise lounge. "And Mother is on the warpath."

"Stay right there," she said. "Don't move a muscle." She grabbed an easel and put a canvas on it, positioning it across the room so she faced me.

"Please don't. I'm not in the mood today." I closed my eyes and prayed for it to all go away.

"You are in my studio, so you are fair game. Now bend your knees up and balance the sketchbook on your legs."

I groaned in annoyance but did as she asked.

"Yes, just like that." She started sketching lines on the canvas. "Go ahead and go back to whatever you were drawing. Just try not to get charcoal on that silk damask upholstery. It's antique and hard to remove stains."

"So where did you sneak off to this morning?" I settled into the chaise and started sketching lines again. "I didn't see you at breakfast."

"Nowhere important." Something about her tone was off.

I glanced at her and raised my brow, waiting for her to expand on that.

"Please keep looking at your paper and try not to move too much." Her hand was flying over the canvas. No doubt she already had my form appearing. God did I envy that ability.

"Then, dear sister, tell me where you were this morning."

"I was with Raul."

"Raul who?" I asked, thinking about the different men in our circles. There was a Ronaldo and a Richard, but I couldn't think of a Raul.

She stepped behind the easel and mumbled something I wasn't quite able to hear.

"I'm sorry. Can you say that again?"

"Raul is the new gardener."

"Rose, I thought we agreed you weren't going to talk to the gardener again."

I sounded harsh and judgmental, and it wasn't that I thought the gardener was beneath her.

I was worried about the repercussions of her actions.

Mother would destroy him.

There was no telling how far she would go. She would have him deported even if he was a naturalized citizen. She would accuse him of theft or, if he touched Rose, of worse, and have him locked away.

Not to mention Rose had grown up used to a specific lifestyle that I doubted the gardener would be able to give her.

Was an infatuation going to be enough to keep her happy?

"I know, I know," she said from behind her easel. "I didn't plan on it, but the morning light was so pretty. I took my break-fast on my balcony, and he was working on the plants directly under my window. He called out to me, and we got to talking, and he makes me feel…" She paused like she was looking for the right word.

"Makes you feel what?"

Could this man make her feel the way Mr. Manchild made me feel?

Was he manhandling her the way Mr. Manchild handled me?

That was a very serious offense.

I could do nothing about my fiancé touching me. He had the power, but if this Raul had laid a hand on my baby sister, and if it got out, she would be ruined.

"He made me feel seen and heard. When I spoke, he listened to what I said, hung on every word. Talking with him made me feel like I was important and not because of my family, but because I had something to say that was worth listening to."

"That must have been nice."

"It was. He was so sweet." She peeked her head around her easel, and for the first time, I saw the morning glory pinned behind her ear.

"Is that from him?" I nodded toward the pale pink flower behind her ear.

"It is." She disappeared behind her easel again. "I promise I am being careful. We haven't done anything more than talk. There was nothing inappropriate. We talked mostly about flowers, but Amelia, I really like him. I don't know what to do."

"I wish I could tell you." I sighed. "If I had the right answer, I would happily give it to you. It must feel great to be seen as a person and not just a name or net worth, but you know he isn't a viable option for you."

"I know." She put down her pencil and moved to gather the paints she wanted to use.

We worked in complete silence for a while, both lost in thought about the men who made us feel different than anyone else had made us feel before. Rose felt acknowledged and seen, and I felt desire and passion mixed with a distinct and intense loathing.

Why did Mr. Manchild have to have such a powerful effect on my sanity, on my body? That wasn't the marriage I was meant to have.

I was meant to have a marriage of cold detachment.

We were to be polite and show a united front in public. I was supposed to run my husband's social calendar, give him heirs, raise those heirs, and have polite conversations over dinner.

A marriage made as a business deal meant that, for all intents and purposes, we would live separate lives that just intersected with the children and social functions.

No one ever said anything about being with a man who made my blood boil with his fucking overbearing bullshit, or who could turn my body into a lustful traitor.

I scribbled through another sheet of paper then tossed it to the side as well, trying my best to stay in the same position for my sister.

On the next page, I decided to work on his eyes first.

If I couldn't get those right, there was no use in even trying with the rest of the portrait. Starting again, I dragged the charcoal in the thick lines of his low brow, then his wide almond eyes that were always a bit shaded. Getting the intensity in them with charcoal was near impossible. I would have better luck with another medium, but charcoal was what I currently had to work with.

His high, chiseled cheekbones and firm jaw came next, and back to the full, lush lips he used to whisper the filthiest things to me before kissing me like I was the only woman in the world.

A man who could kiss a woman like that, like he was claiming her body and soul, was a man from whom women should run. No one should have that much power over another.

He had the power to destroy me, and we weren't even married yet.

I had to find a way to break this engagement.

The risk with him was too great.

It would just be a matter of time before he took me apart, before he broke my heart, and I would never be able to recover.

I was destined to be one of those women who were rarely seen outside of high-end rehabs and "recovery resorts," trying to mend my broken heart and the inevitable addiction to painkillers and alcohol.

That was what happened to women in our world.

Divorce was shameful and did not happen. It didn't matter if your husband beat you, broke the law, or cheated and had a dozen bastards. The only excuse a woman could use to divorce was if he lost everything. If he was suddenly poor, it was understandable, but that was the only reason a woman could ask for a divorce. For men, of course, that didn't apply either.

The only option I had was to harden my heart to his presence. I would be the cold, well-mannered woman I was bred to be until I found my way out. Frigid women didn't love, their blood didn't boil, they didn't feel. That was what I had to do.

He was the villain in my story, no more, no less.

I hadn't realized until this moment how much I wished that wasn't true. The way he touched me made me feel alive. It made me want.

A knock on the door startled us both.

Rose went to answer it and spoke to someone on the other side for a moment. I stayed where I was and studied the sketch I held. It looked a little like him if I squinted. The features were close-ish, but their placement wasn't quite right and the proportions were off.

Charcoal was going on the list of things I was horrible with.

"Looks like you are being summoned," Rose said as she closed the door behind her. She had a piece of paper with the Astrid letterhead at the top, a note from the memo pad the maids used.

"Joy. What does Mother want from me now?"

"Your obedience, subjugation, and if it makes her look ten years younger, your soul." She handed me the paper. "But this message isn't from her, it's from the man who you seem to be a little obsessed with."

"I don't know what you mean." I snatched the note she held out to me.

"Tell that to your sketchbook," she said with a laugh then moved back to her easel.

She was right. The picture looked like it had been drawn by a little girl infatuated with a man she saw one time in passing, a vague likeness that was too kind.

I took the charcoal and drew horns on him.

If I couldn't capture his intensity, I could at least capture his essence.

CHAPTER 18

LUC

"*I* am so fucking stupid," I said to myself as I leaned back in my chair.

"Is there anything I may help with, sir?" Henry entered my office with a fresh cup of coffee.

"Yes, I need you to find out everything you can about Amelia Mae Astrid."

"Your intended, sir?" He raised an eyebrow. "*That* Amelia Mae Astrid?"

"Yes, Henry, I need all her records, financial, health, school, everything you can get."

"Are we treating this like an investigation of a company before a merger or like she is an actual person?"

"Like a person, Henry." I did not appreciate his tone.

"Have you tried having a conversation with her, sir?" he asked.

Henry had been my assistant for years, and he was fantastic. That was why I paid him an obscene amount of money, to keep him incentivized and to make sure he wasn't easily poached.

Unfortunately, he knew his worth and allowed it to make himself a little too comfortable.

"Henry, when you have a wife, then I will come to you for marriage advice."

"I have been happily married for three years. I have a two-year-old son and another on the way."

"Did I know that?" I honestly hadn't thought he had a family. When had I given him enough time to go home and have a family?

"Yes," he deadpanned, and I felt a little like an asshole. "I will have the files drawn up by the end of business today. In the meantime, I have already taken the liberty of looking into some of her likes and dislikes so I could pick out the appropriate birthday, Valentines, and anniversary gifts when the time comes."

"When did you do that?" I asked.

"About twenty seconds after you had me announce your engagement in the Times."

He wrote a few things out in his notebook. "My preliminary report is filed in your desk now, in your personal folder. I will have the more thorough report filed there as well."

"Thank you, and congratulations on the baby. Be sure to get yourself a baby shower gift."

"Already done, sir. The diaper genie is much appreciated." He pushed his square glasses up on his face.

"Is that all?" I asked, moving to the files that were tucked in a drawer.

At first glance, I was surprised how detailed his research was. The first page was her birthday, eye color, clothing size, and brand preferences, and the second began listing information about her likes and dislikes. This was a good start.

"No, sir, unfortunately, I got several calls from your father's less-reputable associates. It seems they are not convinced the

Dubois issue has been properly handled and they have some... concerns they would like addressed. I tried to brush them off, but they expressed that they feel it may be in their best interest to address the issues themselves."

Fuck! This was why working in bad faith at all times was a horrible idea.

My father had dealt with these thugs in bad faith one too many times, and now there was no trust. Now I had to talk to them myself to ensure they didn't put a hit out on the man. I wanted my old friend destroyed, not dead. How was I going to enjoy the look of utter devastation on his face if he was dead?

"Okay, thank you, Henry. I'll deal with them. Please get started on that report. And just in case they get any ideas, put a security detail on her. I want eyes on her any time she isn't at home or with me but have them be discreet."

"Already done, sir." He turned and went back to his desk a few feet beyond my office door.

I sat back in my chair and flipped through the pages of the report. She apparently had a love of art. That seemed like a good place to start.

"Henry," I called, and he was back at my door in a moment.

"Yes, sir?"

"Get my father's associates on the line for me, then call the Met and see if we can arrange a romantic private lunch for me and my fiancée in one of the wings. Call Amelia and make sure she is there at the appropriate time, then clear the rest of my day."

"Right away, sir."

"Oh, and Henry?" I said, stopping him from leaving. "Does that sound like something she would like? At this point, I think you know her better than I do."

"It checks all the boxes, sir. It's romantic, takes time and effort, and it's personalized to her tastes. The Met has a special exhibit on a few Impressionists. It opens in a few weeks, but I believe the paintings arrived last week. I'll try to arrange something there."

"Thank you." I sat back, wondering if this was going to be enough.

In the car last night, I had been too rough with a girl so inexperienced. I couldn't even imagine what she thought of me. She probably saw me the same way I saw certain associates of my father.

Barbaric, uncivilized, and violently immoral.

After last night, she might have a point.

It was time I showed my fiancée a different side of me.

"Sir, these gentlemen decided to make a face-to-face visit," Henry said, standing at my door again. "I'm afraid the idea of calling to schedule something slipped their minds. Should I show them in?"

"Yes, thank you." I rolled my eyes. Of course, my father's associates came all the way here to meet face to face. They were under the illusion that a bunch of unwashed gangsters from the "old country" was going to intimidate me.

They were sorely mistaken.

"Gentlemen, please have a seat." I didn't stand.

Which was a sign of disrespect, but if the three men in ill-fitting cheap suits took offense, they didn't show it. The O'Leary clan was an Irish mob from Belfast, small but well-known and, thanks in no small part to my father, well-funded and connected.

"Mr. Manwarring, that meeting has been set for 12:30. You'll need to leave in the next five minutes to arrive on time," Henry said, as if he was reminding me of an important business meeting and not lunch with my future wife. He really earned every cent I paid him.

"I'm sorry you came all the way here when I don't have the time for a proper sit-down, but how can I help you?"

"How do we know Dubois won't be a problem no more?" the middle one said.

He was a fat man with ruddy, pockmarked skin, crooked yellow teeth, and stark white hair. I didn't remember his name. I made a point to never remember their names. I didn't even like them in my office. My father wanted to bring them in. He should be the one dealing with him.

"Because the only power he had was going to come from marrying the district attorney's sister." I spoke as if I was explaining this to a small child because that was about the intelligence level I was dealing with. "She's close with her brother, and her husband would have the ear of the DA. Dubois will no longer be in a position where the DA will listen to him. The DA will listen to his sister's husband. That is going to be me."

"Why would the DA listen to you, just because you are shaggin' his baby sister?" one of the others said. His thick accent made me stop and take a moment to mentally decode his words.

"Because he wants to keep his sister happy. His family also made their fortune in tobacco. What's a better merger than whisky and tobacco?" I stood and grabbed my suit jacket from the hook, hoping the men took the hint.

They didn't; they remained seated.

"That still doesn't make sense. Why wouldn't he still listen to Dubois? It's not like he can't make an appointment."

"No, he can't. He has tried several times over the years. DA Astrid won't see them. He has refused every appointment, and marrying Ms. Astrid was his way in. My father and I are already working on the contracts for a few joint ventures that will link our fortune with the Astrid fortune. Which will incentivize Mr. Astrid to help with our endeavors."

"How so?" They still didn't move.

"Because if we go down, then so do they. It means that the district attorney has reasons to keep all of us safe, and if he doesn't, we have other leverage. I assure you, gentlemen, it is well in hand. Now if you don't mind, I have a meeting across town I must get to."

The three men rose and looked me up and down. It took everything I had not to roll my eyes at them again.

"Aight, we'll go, but don't go forgetting his fortune isn't the only one yours is tied to."

"Right, if you need further information, I suggest going to see my father. I believe he is in his office just down the way. He just got a fresh box of Regius Double Corona cigars in. I'm sure he would love a reason to break it open."

I lifted my arm and directed the men to my father's office before turning and locking mine.

Henry, the godsend that he was, stood at the elevator, holding it open for me.

"Did you really just send a bunch of Irish mobsters to your father's office to smoke fifty-thousand-dollar cigars?"

"Did he send a bunch of thugs to my office because he thought he could pawn the consequences of his poor choices off on me?" I shot back.

Henry didn't bother hiding his chuckle.

Truth be told, I wasn't sure my father hadn't sent them down just to convince me we didn't need to play nice with my in-laws.

"What all were you able to manage for this afternoon?" I asked, adjusting my shirtsleeves.

Surprisingly, this lunch was making me a little nervous.

It was the first time I was meeting Amelia that wasn't for some function we could be seen at. For all intents and purposes, this was our first date. Why did that thought make my stomach clench with nerves? I had already had her. I knew her body.

Why was getting to know her less carnally so intimidating?

Maybe this'd be easier if I convinced her to let me fuck her in the bathroom first.

"I called in a favor to the curator at the Met. The Impressionist exhibit hasn't been opened to the public, but we have the room, and a romantic lunch has been planned. The food will be there about thirty minutes after you both arrive, but there will be strawberries and chilled champagne waiting for you."

"Excellent work," I said, impressed by how quickly he was able to throw a catered museum lunch date together.

"Thank you , sir. Assuming traffic is normal, you should arrive just before she does."

"Are we sure she is actually going to show up?"

"I called her staff myself and told them you had arranged a special lunch and sent the car. I have no reason to think she won't be there. They said she would be excited when I mentioned the Met."

"Henry, what would I do without you?" I asked, stepping out of the elevator.

"Entertain the Irish mob and go home to a wife that despised you," he said as we went out the front door.

He wasn't wrong.

CHAPTER 19

LUC

We got to the Met, and Amelia's car pulled up right behind mine.

I went to open her door, and she stepped out, stunning in a bright red sundress.

Its longer skirt hit just above her knees and the top was modest enough to be appropriate, but the elastic neck begged for someone to yank it down to expose her generous tits. I had been mostly joking with myself about fucking her in the bathroom. The idea of someone else being able to walk in made that a non-starter.

Maybe if today went well, I would get the chance to take her somewhere more private.

Not in the limo.

This time I would bring her back to my place and take my time worshiping her body.

She knew how I fucked when I was angry and ravenous.

This date was about showing her a different side of me.

I offered my arm, and she linked hers with mine while we headed up the steps.

"How did you get us a private showing of the Manet/Degas exhibit?" she asked. "It doesn't open to the public for another week."

I had no idea how Henry had managed any of this.

"Darling, you are no longer the 'general public,'" I said as we entered the large stone building. Henry was waiting just inside the door to give us a moment of privacy.

"Right, this way miss, sir." He led us past several exhibits and through the European art room to a special exhibit room.

It had been cordoned off with a velvet rope and a large tarp, explaining the exhibit was under construction.

Henry unclipped the rope and pushed the tarp aside to let us step in.

Amelia gasped, taking in the room, and even I had to admit that Henry had outdone himself.

The exhibit had been finished, and the art was all displayed. A small table had been set up on one side of the room with an ice bucket and a bottle of champagne, as well as a display of perfectly red strawberries.

A man in a tuxedo stood next to the table with a white cloth over his arm. He poured the two champagne flutes and brought them to Amelia and me. She didn't even notice. She was trans-fixed by a painting of a naked young woman lounging on a chaise, with her maid offering flowers and a little black cat by her feet.

"*Olympia*," she said. "This painting has never been displayed in the US before. Isn't it incredible?"

"Stunning," I said, looking at her more than the art.

The way her lips parted as she was transfixed was one of the sexiest things I had ever seen. There was more than just an appreciation for something beautiful, or expensive. Most of the women I had known would love this because it would make them feel special and cultured.

Amelia was different. She looked like she was in awe of the art.

Not the special access, not the waitstaff here to serve her, not even the Dom and strawberries. Not even me taking time from my work to indulge her. The rest of this could disappear, and she would still have that expression of wonder.

I handed her the champagne flute which she took and just held while taking in the Impressionist masterpieces.

While she examined the art, I examined her.

There was a lot more to this girl than I had given her credit for, and I worried that if I wasn't careful, the damage I had already done would become a permanent crack between us.

When Henry signaled to me that lunch was served at the small table, I pulled her away from the paintings and guided her to the table and chairs. I even pulled her seat out for her and lifted the silver dome to reveal a light lunch of poached salmon with butter, roasted asparagus, and rice pilaf.

"Tell me which painting is your favorite?" I asked, taking the side across from her and removing the dome off my plate.

"I don't know," she said, stabbing a spear of asparagus. "They are all so beautiful."

"Surely you have a preference between Degas and Manet?"

"Not really." She gave me a dreamy smile. "Do you have a favorite?"

"Honestly, I haven't really looked," I admitted with a shrug.

"What do you mean? What have you been doing all this time?"

"Watching you take in the art." I took a bite of my salmon. "I enjoy watching you look at things you admire. I hope one day I can be counted among them."

"Why would you care?" Her question was abrupt and caught me off guard.

"What do you mean?"

"I mean, why would you care if I admired you? You bought me or blackmailed my mother to get me, all to get to my father and brother, and to keep Mr. Dubois from them. The way you have treated me has made it very clear what my role will be in our marriage."

Her words cut into my chest.

She was right.

If she had said all of this before the night we attended the opera, I would have been relieved. There would have been an understanding and no need to pretend in each other's company what our union meant. But after knowing the fire and passion that flowed just beneath her skin, after seeing the awe on her face as she came apart for me, and the admiration when she saw something she thought was truly remarkable, I needed more from her. If I was going to get it, I needed to fix this now.

"Ms. Astrid. Amelia." That was the first time I had said her name out loud, and the intimacy of it felt strange.

How messed up was it that I had been inside this woman?

I had made her come on my cock, but saying her first name felt too intimate?

"I'm afraid I have made a grave error in judgment about how I have treated you the last several days. Admittedly, I have acted brutish and rashly, and if you will allow me, I'd like the opportunity to make it up to you. We are getting married, for better or worse, and I'd at least like our union to have a chance at being a happy one."

"So you think buying your way into a closed exhibit is the way to do that?" She didn't trust me yet, and I didn't blame her.

"No, I think making time for you in the middle of the day for a date, at a location you love, and talking without our families or society or the paparazzi interrupting us, is a start. Let me get to know you." I reached out and took her hand in mine. Her hands were so soft and delicate, her French manicure perfectly done.

"What do you want to know?" She still sounded a little skeptical, but that was fine. It was a start.

"Everything." I let the word hang in the air between us for a moment. "But why don't you start with art? Tell me why you love it?"

"I love how a painting can capture so much and how a single portrait can make people feel different things." The way her eyes lit up and a soft smile graced her lips as she spoke had me captivated. "It can tell a story and you can learn the history behind it and try to guess what the artist was trying to say, or you can let your mind run wild and create your own fiction."

"What do you mean?"

"Well, look at that painting there." She pointed to a painting of two men in a park sitting with a nude woman. *"The Luncheon in the Grass.* It actually created quite the scandal."

"Because the woman is nude?" I asked.

She tilted her head from side to side. "In a way. It wasn't that he painted a nude woman. It's that she is so casually lying in the park next to two men who are fully clothed. It was supposed to be a nod to the sex workers who often worked their trade in parks. It was apparently a fact that everyone knew but it was not commented on or even acknowledged in society."

"And what do you see when you look at it? What fiction is in your head?"

"It feels free." She gazed longingly at the painting.

"Please, explain."

"In our world, women are expected to do certain things, act a certain way, dress a certain way. It can feel like a prison. In this painting, the woman is naked, unburdened from societal expectations. The way she is painted, staring so boldly at her audience, totally comfortable in her own skin. With her body, she isn't trying to be someone she isn't. She has a casual confidence that I don't think I would ever be able to embody."

145

"The casual confidence of a prostitute?"

"When I see it, I don't see a prostitute. I see a woman free to live how she chooses." She lifted her shoulders in a casual shrug.

I thought back to the night of the opera.

That dress had been a plea for some control in her life.

It hadn't been just a dismissal of my order; it had been a fight not to lose herself.

I couldn't help but wonder what could have happened if I had allowed her some freedom for a single night.

"You know, I went to art school. My mother thinks I did it just to spite her, and although I admit that was a nice benefit, it was probably one of the few things I have ever done for me."

"What did you want to do with your degree?"

"I always dreamed about teaching art. Working in some school somewhere teaching kids how to appreciate art and create it."

"So do you paint like this?" I motioned around the room.

She would never have a genuine job like that, but I didn't want to dwell on the negatives of marrying me. I wanted her to open up so she could start seeing the benefits.

"Like…"

"Impressionism," I clarified.

"No. I may have the love of art, but sadly Rose has all the talent. What is it they say? Those who can't do, teach." Her smile turned a little sad as she sat back in her chair and admired the art surrounding us.

"I don't believe that for a moment. You got into a prestigious program at NYU. There has to be some talent. Maybe you are too much of a critic when it comes to your own work."

"Maybe." She looked down at her hands, a touch of pink on her cheeks.

I was about to say more when Henry placed a hand on my shoulder and whispered, "Sir, there has been an incident at the office regarding your father's acquaintances. It requires your immediate attention."

"Thank you, Henry." I turned back to Amelia, who was studying the painting of the naked woman in the park again. "I want to see your work."

"I have nothing worth showing, and I don't keep my failures," she said without looking up at me.

I looked back at Henry and motioned for him to bring me my briefcase. I pulled out a notebook and my Montblanc fountain pen.

"Take these and draw something for me." I handed her the pen and paper. "An issue that I need to handle has come up. I will be only a moment."

She looked back and nodded, taking the pen and paper.

"Watch her," I said to my personal security that was always around the perimeter.

The chances I was being followed by those thugs were slim, but there was no telling what they would do to get at me, and I wouldn't put Amelia in danger.

CHAPTER 20

AMELIA

I didn't understand what was happening.

I stared after his retreating back as he stepped out to handle some business.

Being with a powerful man, interruptions like that were bound to happen.

That didn't bother me. I knew to expect it.

What had my brain reeling and butterflies fluttering in my stomach was how Luc had gone from treating me like a woman he had paid for to a woman he was trying to court. He was acting as if he wanted to woo me, to seduce me, as if I had a say in any of this.

Did he maybe feel something for me, too?

Could he be just as confused by our situation and our chemistry as I was? I pushed that thought from my head. It was ridiculous, and hope would only make it hurt worse when he returned to his brutish, womanizing ways. There was no way I could let my guard down around this man. He had far too much power over my body.

I refused to let him have my soul, too.

When I considered how Rose had spoken about the gardener this morning in the studio, about being seen and heard, I now realized it hadn't even occurred to me to want something like that. Everything about Luc told me that was never going to happen. Then he had listened to me babble about Manet. He had asked thoughtful questions that showed me that not only was he paying attention, he at least pretended he was interested.

He had planned a dream date, and had been present, physically and mentally.

Without even realizing it, I had let my guard down and been comfortable with him. It didn't hurt that the Met was probably one of my favorite places in the city. It was even the charity for which my family had chosen to act as patron.

My mother, of course, did it to be seen as charitable and cultured, but I didn't care. I loved it here, how there was always a small crowd speaking in hushed tones, just staring at the art in wonder. It was somewhere where it did not matter where you came from, what you looked like. We were all here for the same reason: to feel something magical, to get lost in a piece of art that could transcend even the most insurmountable differences.

Lunch was amazing. He had ordered my favorite dish from my favorite restaurant. I hadn't even been aware they catered. The thought and effort he had put into this... I had never heard of a man doing something like this, not outside of a romance novel. Even then, it was for the love of his life, not his arranged-marriage bride.

I had hoped this impromptu outing would help clear my mind about what I was feeling. That he would prove himself to be ignorant, selfish, and a narcissist who should never be tolerated for longer than absolutely necessary. Or better yet, he would be stupid, and therefore easily managed.

Instead, he was smart, considerate, quick-witted and, although not knowledgeable about art, quick to learn. There was no way I, or any other woman, could manage him any more than he would allow. It made him so much more irresistible, which in turn made it so much worse.

I was even more confused now.

Not only because I wanted him physically, and I enjoyed his company, but I didn't understand why he was doing any of this. None of it made any sense. He already had me. I didn't have a choice. My mother was going to force me to marry him regardless of whether I wanted to. I couldn't figure out what his game was. No matter how I looked at it, there was no real reason to put in this much effort other than it made me happy.

The way he had broken down my door hadn't been about making me happy. I had been terrified. Then he made sure I came before he did. Even in the limo, he had demanded my pleasure before he had taken his.

Still, this lunch didn't make sense, with all the attention to detail. He must have been paying attention while we spoke, when he was in my room, or even talking to my sister. To know that I liked art was one thing but he even got lunch from one of my favorite restaurants. He took me to an exhibit I had been looking forward to for months. We were sitting in front of my favorite painting in the entire world.

It couldn't all have been a coincidence.

He was trying to get to know me.

Maybe I should give him the same courtesy.

Planning a date like this would be inappropriate, but maybe I could find some things that he liked, discover what he did in his spare time. The dossiers my mother had drawn up those months ago had all this information on the other men, but his were blank.

I would ask him more about his goals, aspirations, and hobbies when he got back. In the meantime, I could do as he asked and attempt to draw something for him.

I started drawing on the paper he had given me, trying to sketch out the woman Manet had painted so beautifully.

His Montblanc fountain pen was thick, heavy, meant for hands bigger than mine, making it hard to control. The gold nib was honed perfectly, but not for my handwriting.

I was used to my lighter, slimmer S.T. Dupont fountain pen. Still, I tried to make it work while my thoughts raced and I tried to sort through them to figure out how I was going to get him to talk about himself.

Luc was the man I was going to marry.

He and I needed a civil relationship at least, but a small part of me wondered if there could be more.

Could we move to a genuine friendship, then maybe beyond that? I'd heard stories of arranged couples finding love.

Maybe there was hope?

I didn't even know what to ask him about. Did I try asking about his favorite artist? Would he even have one? Or should I try sports?

My pen scratched over the rough paper as I traced out lines and tried a little shading with the smooth nib. I let my mind wander to all the things I already knew about him, which wasn't much. His family had made their fortune in whisky. He'd gone to school with Harrison, but he and my brother weren't close. He had younger sisters, but I didn't even know if they were close.

What I didn't know was endless. Did he like sports? Did he want kids? What did he do for fun? Was he a ladies' man? Was he a workaholic?

He had surprised me with all of this, showing me he knew me better than I thought, and I hadn't been paying attention to him at all. I hadn't picked up on any of this.

Did that mean that between the two of us, I was the bad spouse?

Was I like my mother, more consumed with how everything affected me?

My stomach rolled at that thought.

I refused to treat Luc like my mother treated my father.

Even if it was never a love match, I didn't want to be the kind of person who did that to anyone.

When Luc returned, I would ask about him, and apologize for being so in my head, and focused on myself. Though, it was not like it was my fault.

The things he did to my body, the things he made me feel even when I didn't want to, were incredible. The way he touched me, kissed me. He was brutish, but I liked it. His touch matched his overbearing personality. At least, I thought it did.

It had matched how we had been together before, but now he was being sweet, considerate, and gentle. Did he have this other side in bed, too?

Was this man capable of being a gentle, caring lover?

He had always made me come, which if the maids were to be believed, was rare in a man, but he didn't give me pleasure. No, he took my pleasure for himself. He made me come because he liked it. Could he give me pleasure for the sake of making me feel good?

Would I even want that?

So far, having him bend me to his will and take me in a moment of raw passion and need felt... incredible.

Did liking that make me a bad feminist? I guessed it was just good that I was sketching a Manet and not a Frida Kahlo or Georgia O'Keeffe.

I was lost in thought when my hand stilled the eighteen karat gold nib still touching the paper, causing a glob of ink to ooze onto the sheet. It ruined the already graceless lines I had been attempting to mimic.

Frustrated, I tore the paper from the pad, along with the three under it into which ink had seeped.

I set them to the side and studied the pen.

It was a stunning testament to Montblanc refinement and beauty, but far too large for my dainty hands. Something better had to be in his briefcase. A ballpoint pen or a pencil would be ideal. It might not improve my lines, but it would at least not make a mess.

I opened the brass buckles and was rifling through the pen loops and compartments in the top looking for a pen when a folder with my name clearly printed on the manila tab caught my eye. It was sticking out of a leather portfolio in which a few more folders were tucked away.

The staff in the room weren't looking at me. Even if they were, they wouldn't stop me. I was pretty sure they worked for the museum or the restaurant, all except the large man, who was clearly private security. As such, he wasn't concerned with what I was doing, but who was around me.

I pulled out the manila folder and opened it.

There was an entirely invasive report on me.

The things I liked, didn't like, where I had attended school, where I ate and with whom and where I liked to shop. It even had a list of my measurements.

I dropped the pad of paper and pen to the floor as I looked through the contents of the folder, my hand pressed to my lips, nausea rolling through my stomach.

I was such a fucking idiot.

He wasn't paying attention at all.

He just wanted me to think he was.

This entire thing had been about making me complacent.

The file was filled with notes and surveillance from the past several weeks before he ruined my engagement with Dubois. He'd had me followed and studied.

The part that brought tears to my eyes wasn't even the surveillance photos. I hated that he'd had me followed, but not as much as I hated seeing the note attached to the front of the file.

Mr. Manwarring, this is just the preliminary report on your bride. I will have a more detailed account sent to you by the end of the day.

Henry

Mr. Manchild hadn't been paying attention.

He had paid someone else to do it.

He had delegated our relationship to his assistant.

Was this Henry the one I needed to thank for this afternoon? Had this all been his idea?

Hot angry tears gathered in the corners of my eyes.

I forced myself to draw a few deep breaths to slow my heart rate and maintain my composure.

Don't make a scene, Amelia.

Don't give people another reason to gossip about you.

They had plenty as it was.

I wasn't even mad at him, not really.

I was mad at myself for falling for it.

Here I was, sitting here like a stupid little girl believing his lies, falling for his faux charm hook, line, and sinker. Just daydreaming about what our lives could be and thinking I had been the inconsiderate one because I didn't know all these personal things about him.

Of course I didn't know. I wasn't having him followed!

This shouldn't have surprised me.

I should've known better.

I did know better.

The fairy tale he was spinning had just been too tempting.

I wanted it to be true. I wanted the things I had heard about him to be some façade he put on for the world, and the way he'd treated me before to be just one side of him. The idea that he could be more gave me hope, so I had chosen to believe it.

Or maybe he had intentionally deceived me. He had wanted me to be the good little girl and thought he could use a reward system like this to manipulate me. If I behaved as I had at the yacht, and in the limo, then he could reward me with a bit of attention and I would keep behaving, giving in to his depravity and letting him use my body as he saw fit.

He didn't care; he hadn't been paying attention.

Henry, his assistant, had been spying on me, or his security. Someone had been watching me for weeks. Weeks! If he had known this was what he was going to do, why wait until I was at the altar?

Calling off the wedding in the days leading up to it would have been just as effective to embarrass Mr. Dubois. Then it dawned on me, and I had to swallow the lump forming in my throat. It would have been just as embarrassing for Mr. Dubois, but not me.

By waiting until the last minute, when I was standing in front of all of New York, he had ensured I was damaged goods. He had ensured my reputation would be in tatters, and I would have no choice but to marry him.

Maybe it was time to give him a taste of his own medicine. Show him what it was like to be engaged to someone who ran hot and cold, who had more than one face.

Footsteps were approaching down the hall toward me, and he'd be back within moments.

Carefully, I put everything back the way I'd found it then grabbed a ballpoint pen from a pocket in his briefcase.

I picked up the paper from the floor, leaving his fountain pen, and started drawing. Just a few quick fast lines that looked like they could have taken time. I didn't want him to think anything was off.

A time would come, soon, when I confronted him about what I'd found, but I needed to think first.

He entered the gallery. His suit jacket had been re-buttoned, and he looked a little annoyed. I knew the feeling.

"I'm so sorry about that, Amelia." He undid his jacket button again and sat next to me on the bench. "I promise no more interruptions."

He leaned over my shoulder, his hand going to my waist as he peered at the paper I was working on and then the papers balled up on the wooden bench next to me. "Not able to find inspiration in Manet's work?"

"I've found plenty of inspiration." Not for drawing, but that was fine.

He brought his arm around me, and for the first time, his touch made my skin crawl. Not able to take it for a moment further, I stood.

"Thank you for lunch, Mr. Manwarring—"

"I asked you to call me Luc," he interrupted.

"Be that as it may, Mr. Manwarring, lunch was wonderful, but I have other engagements I must see to. And I'm sure you have to get back to work as well."

"I cleared the rest of my afternoon to spend time with you."

"How nice, but that is not a luxury I have today. I do have other appointments to attend."

I didn't look at him, I couldn't. If I met his gaze, he'd be able to see the warring emotions behind my eyes. My carefully honed mask hadn't slid into place as effortlessly as it usually did, and I wasn't about to let him see me cry.

"Let me escort you back then." He stood.

"That's okay, I have business not too far from here, and I'll just take the subway back."

"The subway." I could feel him start to get angry. "Why would you ever take the subway?"

"Because I'm a New Yorker," I said like it was obvious.

"What business do you have? I could give you a ride and go with—"

"Really, that won't be necessary. I'm perfectly capable of handling my affairs on my own."

"Amelia, you are testing my patience. Just once, can you behave?"

"Have a pleasant rest of your day, Mr. Manwarring." I smiled and left the gallery.

He called after me, but the second I rounded the corner, I sprinted out of the museum and found a spot behind one of the columns, where I didn't think I would be easily spotted, and waited.

Fewer than ten minutes passed before he stormed out of the building, his assistant trailing behind him. They got into his Town Car and left.

Now all I had to do was figure out what I would do to get even.

CHAPTER 21

AMELIA

Once I saw Mr. Manchild leave, I saw no reason not to go back into the museum to enjoy the best art collection in the country.

It would give me something to do while I tried to come up with a plan that would let me get back at him. At least I could try to level the playing field.

No, that wasn't what this was about. We would never be even.

That wasn't something a woman in this world could manage, but I could demand respect. I wanted to be seen as an individual, not as a decoration or a toy.

Who better to draw inspiration from than the greatest artists the world had ever known?

Honestly, I didn't want to go back home until I had to.

So far, I had avoided my mother's wedding plan conversations that were full of thinly veiled barbs. I was lost in thought, wandering around the Islamic art wing, marveling at the intricacies in the art, when a gold girdle clasp caught my eye. It was beautiful and inlaid with precious stones and intricate delicate carvings.

The little plaque said it was used not only as an accessory but as a safety net for the women who wore it. It was part of their dowry, but it didn't go to the husband. It was meant to protect the woman who owned it. If she were to lose, or be left by, her husband, or was to leave, she could sell it and provide for herself and her children.

Wealthy women born more than three hundred years ago had been given more options than I was now, assuming the plaque was true. Would a wealthy woman three hundred years ago have been free to leave her husband? Or had they lived in the same gilded cage I did? With the illusion of freedom.

Most people looking at me from the outside would say I had options, choices. I didn't, not really. Yes, I could theoretically sell off my jewelry and run away like the women who had worn this clasp might have, but what would I be left with?

How long would that money last? How long would a single piece of jewelry allow me to survive? What would happen to that woman if her husband came after her? How far away would she be able to get?

How far would a controlling man like Manwarring let me run before he hunted me down? Would I make it out of the country, or even the state? I doubted he would let me leave the city before he dragged me back kicking and screaming.

I was lost in thought considering what that meant when arms encircled my waist, and for a brief second, I was excited he had returned. Then I kicked myself for that instant reaction.

"Hey, little miss, you are supposed to be admiring the art, not shopping," someone with a deep, friendly voice whispered in my ear. I recognized him immediately. It wasn't Luc, and I should have been happy, but instead I felt a deep pang of disappointment.

"Marco." I turned in his arms and returned his hug. "How are you? It's been too long!"

"First you, why are there three big dudes all packing heat watching you? Does the Met have you on some kind of watch list?"

I wasn't even surprised I was still being watched. Though I was surprised Luc didn't march back in here and demand to know why I was trying to get rid of him.

Marco was a friend from art school. He had recently separated from his partner, and was always a lot of fun. More importantly, he was always up for a little mischief. Since he was six-four, classically handsome and from "new money," as my grandmother would say, he was the perfect partner in crime.

Marco had the benefit of being close enough to my world to see it clearly but separate enough to not be under its influence. His parents had meant it when they said he could date who he liked. They just wanted him to be happy.

"Marco, would you like to help me with a little project?"

He narrowed his eyes at me. "What kind of project, and why are you smiling like a super villain?"

"How are your acting skills?"

CHAPTER 22

AMELIA

"So, tell me again," Marco said, putting his arm around me as we headed down the street to a little bistro off Central Park, not too far from the museum. "What are you hoping to gain from this?"

"A little payback." I rested my head on his shoulder. "And maybe a little clarity."

"You are playing with fire but slay queen. Slay."

We went to put on a show for my uninvited, unwanted security detail at a little café on the Upper West Side.

We walked in the park holding hands while we caught up on our day to day. He had attended my wedding but had been too busy with his own relationship drama to reach out and check on me.

After the park, we went for coffee, walking with his arm wrapped around my waist to this cute café which was one of the most beautiful ones in New York. We sat outside on the street where anyone could see us, drinking coffee and laughing under a trellis full of fresh spring florals.

Several people stopped to take photos, some of the stunning, unique café and others who whispered my name or his to each other and would, without a doubt, be sending the photos to the gossip columns. To make the most of this, I made sure to constantly be touching Marco, a hand on his arm or caressing his face.

"What exactly did this man do, that you want to make him jealous?" Marco asked, taking a sip of his coffee.

"He thought I would be content, no, *flattered* with crumbs of his attention. And that he could delegate aspects of our relationship to his assistant."

"Kinky."

"Not like that, though at this point, I wouldn't be surprised if he asked Henry to knock me up if he had a more important meeting."

Marco choked on his coffee and took a moment to regain his composure. "You are kidding, right?"

"Maybe." I shrugged. "I don't even know him enough to know what he is capable of. He led me to believe he was paying attention and interested in what I like. He even arranged this incredible lunch for us at the Met and was asking all the right questions. I thought he cared. Then I found out that he had his assistant make a file on me and is having me followed and under surveillance. He didn't do any of it, his assistant did."

"Is that normal in your world?" he asked.

"No, having your intended stalked is not okay. When I found the dossier on me, I was livid, and when he sees the next report on me, I want him to be just as angry."

"You are intentionally pissing off one of the most powerful men in the country. A man you are going to be legally bound to till expensive lawyers do you part?" He raised an eyebrow at me.

"Yes."

"And you are putting me in his crosshairs, too," he pointed out.

I felt a little guilty about that, but I was pretty sure that once Mr. Manchild did his digging into Marco and found out I wasn't his preferred body type, he would leave Marco alone.

"I want to see if he will care." I sat back and took a sip of my coffee.

"Then let's turn this fire up a bit, shall we?"

"What do you have in mind?"

"I'm going to use everything I have learned in every acting class I have slept through. I will channel my inner straight man, and we're going to be disgustingly cute and in love."

He made a face, and I couldn't help the giggles that poured out of me. He grabbed my chair and pulled it around the small table so I was sitting next to him so he could lean and whisper into my ear, "This is so weird."

I laughed again as he put his arm around me and pulled me in closer.

"Is pretending to find me attractive that much of a struggle?" I teased.

"Shhh, in my mind you are six-two with broad shoulders, a great ass, and a gigantic cock."

I shook with laughter as I leaned into his embrace.

His body was warm and comforting, and Marco was very handsome, but I didn't feel the same undeniable pull I did with Mr. Manchild.

Marco's touch didn't cause a fire to race through my veins or heat to flood my core. My body didn't ache for him. Instead, he made me feel safe, protected, but the same way Harrison made me feel when he hugged me when I was little. It was a brotherly embrace, which was good, but not what I felt with Luc.

I hated that Luc was the only man who had ever made me feel like that.

"My friend," he said under his breath, all but whispering in my ear. "If we are going to sell this, you have to look like you are at least enjoying my extremely awkward and unpracticed displays of affection."

I turned to face him, pressing my forehead to his. "Sorry, I just thought of him for a second, but now I am back in this moment with you."

"Good, because I need you to answer a very important question for me." His hand reached up to caress my cheek before moving down to my leg. He slid his fingers under the hem of my dress, not inappropriately high, but high enough to imply intimacy.

"Anything."

"What is the point of a man touching a woman's thigh? If you were a dude, I'd be trying to figure out how big your dick is... but..."

I laughed so hard I had to sit back in my chair.

"There, that's the smile we need to sell this." He grinned at me, and I could feel my face heating as I turned a little red. "Now hold on to that and tell me what's the real reason we are doing this. This can't be just to make him mad. What do you want to happen here?"

That question hit harder than I expected.

I grabbed my coffee and took a sip to give myself a moment to think.

What did I want to happen? Did I want to make him jealous?

Would he even be jealous? He would be mad.

What I didn't know was if he would be mad because another man had his hands on me, or just territorial because another man was touching what he thought was his.

Or did I just want to show him I had options, or maybe prove to myself I had some power over him?

Honestly, I wasn't sure. Maybe if he thought I was with other men, he wouldn't want to marry me.

He knew he was the first to have sex with me, but maybe if he thought my heart belonged to another or if he thought I was willing to let another man inside me since my virginity was now long gone, maybe I could get him to call off the wedding.

Mother would have a fit. It would be embarrassing, and my reputation may never fully recover, but it was something.

"I need to know if he really cares or if he is going through the motions. This isn't a love match. I know that, and he knows that. It's a business arrangement, but sometimes he makes me feel… something. Right now, I have to know if there is a possibility for a genuine marriage or if it truly is just a business arrangement. Hopefully, how he reacts to this will tell me what I need to know."

"Explain something to me," Marco said, moving my legs to his lap.

This actually felt more like us. It was casual and friendly, but not sexual.

It was how we would sit in the dorms while studying at NYU. When I could pretend to be just Amelia, not Amelia Mae Astrid.

"My family is rich, but only two generations of having money rich, not old, 'we came over on the Mayflower and we give God loans with ridiculous interest rates,' money rich. So I don't know everything."

"What do you need me to explain?"

"What would happen if you just left?"

"What do you mean?"

"I mean, you're an adult. I know you probably don't have your trust fund yet, but legally you are a grown-ass woman, and I know you have money of your own."

"I do. A little from some inheritance." I wasn't sure where he was going with this.

"A little to you is probably enough for a family of four to live comfortably for a few decades." He snorted, not unkindly. "Then you have assets you can make liquid in a moment, right? Jewelry, designer purses and shoes, things like that?"

"Yeah."

"And you have your degree. I know you don't have any actual job experience, since you were trained your entire life to be a wife and manage a house. But you used to talk about teaching art to little kids. You have the degrees you need to do that, right?"

"Yeah, well, kind of. I would need to be certified to teach. What's your point?"

"So, if Mother Astrid"—he lifted his pinky and talked in a ridiculous accent that I thought was supposed to be cartoon-highbrow—"has decreed that you marry this Manwarring man, and you don't want to, what would happen if you just hopped on a train and moved and started your life over?"

The thought in full detail had never truly occurred to me. I had danced around it, thought about other women who had done it or who could. But I had never even allowed myself to dream of a situation where I could just up and leave. It seemed too cruel to think about.

"My mother would turn her attention onto Rose." I had taken the brunt of my sister's share of abuse, and if I left, there was no saving her.

"Isn't that going to happen anyway as soon as your bill of sale is signed in front of the priest?"

"What?"

"Bill of sale, marriage license. In your world, it's the same thing. But my point is once you are with your husband, isn't it Rose's turn?"

He was right. How had I not thought that far ahead?

What would happen if I just left? Could I do that?

No, I didn't know how to live on my own. I couldn't... I wasn't that brave.

Marco must have seen the wheels turning in my head and sensed the change in my mood. He cleared his throat to pull my attention back to him.

"But back to the matter at hand. We are trying to make lover boy jealous. I don't see how he could possibly be anything less than fuming when he finds out you are here."

"Really?"

"Darling, you are at a café that was recently rated as one of the most romantic brunch spots in New York. You're sitting drinking coffee under a scaffolding full of flowers. With a devilishly handsome man, who, okay, is more into men, but the lover boy doesn't know that. More than that, he bailed on you, and you found a better option seconds later. If he doesn't lose his damn mind, girl, I will buy you the ticket to run myself."

"Well, when you say it like that. I mean, I ditched him but..."

"Honey, that is just going to make him even angrier."

He cupped my cheek and brought my face close to his. From the outside, it must have looked like he was about to kiss me.

"You need to know your worth, and it has nothing to do with any bank account."

"I wish that were true. I can put on a brave face, but at my core, I'm just a weak, spoiled little rich girl who does as she is told."

"Bullshit. I don't know who fed you those lines, but you are a force, Amelia Astrid. Your mother refused to let you go to NYU, but you did it anyway. She forbade you from ever taking the subway, but I know you have a MetroCard and use it frequently. She'd dress you like a pretty doll in nothing but lifeless beige colors, and here you are in a vibrant sundress looking like sugar and spice. Your fiancé told you he'd take you home, and you told him to fuck off. You may pick and choose your battles, little girl, but you have a fire in you. Maybe you should let it burn a little more often."

Tears formed in the corners of my eyes, and I wished I was the woman he saw. "Marco—"

Whatever I was going to say was cut off by a scream and the screech of metal colliding with metal.

A black Bentley had run a red light, causing a car accident.

It drove up over the curb, scraping the paint on the bottom of the bumper and nearly running over several pedestrians, then stopped just before our table.

"What the fuck?" Marco said, standing up and pulling me behind him.

Luc Manwarring stepped out from the driver's side, his square jaw clenched and fury in his eyes. "Get in the car, Amelia."

"No!" I yelled back.

"Is that him?" Marco said over his shoulder.

"Yeah."

"Girl, damn, he is hot." Marco was drooling a little when Luc ripped off his suit jacket, threw it into the car, and rolled up his sleeves.

"I am aware, thank you." I pinched Marco on his side. "But that isn't the point."

"It wasn't, but it is now. Does he have a gay brother?"

"Amelia, in the car, now," my asshole fiancé barked again. "Don't think your little friend is going to protect you."

I moved to step around Marco, and he stopped me for a moment. "You going to be okay? Say the word, and I will figure out how to get you away from the sexiest man I have ever seen."

Marco's gaze went back to Luc for a moment, giving him another once-over, but then returned his attention to me. "Seriously, say the word."

His concern was touching. For a moment, I wished Marco

could help me, but having him intervene any more was just going to put him on Luc's bad side. I didn't know what he could do to Marco, but I really didn't want to find out.

"Yeah, I'll be okay," I lied.

Then gave him a weak smile. "And I guess I have my answer."

CHAPTER 23

AMELIA

I got into the car with Luc, knowing it may not be my wisest move, considering how angry he was.

But it was not like the man gave me much of a choice.

"Where are we going?" I somehow got the courage to ask.

"Home. Where you belong."

He squealed his tires around a corner, and I could see the white of his knuckles as he gripped the steering wheel. "I don't know why you feel the need to continue to test me."

Intense anger radiated from him as he drove recklessly through the streets toward his building.

I had never seen him this angry before, and I had to tread lightly if I wanted to make it out of this situation unscathed.

But fuck it, and fuck him. I was pissed, too.

I clenched my fists in my lap, my anger starting to boil over. "You don't own me. You may think you do, but you don't."

He didn't respond, but instead gave me a side-eye as his jaw tightened.

"You can't have me followed. I'm not a child."

"Then stop acting like one," he boomed. "And it's a good thing I do have you spied on. Clearly, by your actions today, I have to."

I shrugged, trying to put on false bravado, even though my heart beat heavily. "It's not like this will be a real marriage. Whoever I choose to associate with, and whoever I choose to fuck, shouldn't matter to you."

He shot out his hand, grabbed my wrist, and squeezed it painfully. "You belong to me, and don't you forget it."

He let go of me abruptly, turning the car in front of his building.

As soon as the car came to a stop, I was out of my seat belt. "You can't spy on me!"

"I can. I will," he shouted, grabbing me roughly by the hair and pulling me toward him. "You're going to be my wife, so get used to it."

My pulse raced as I realized what was happening.

I had to fight back, protect myself.

But as Luc's lips crashed onto mine, a strange sensation washed over me. It was a mixture of fear and excitement, and as much as I hated to admit it, I couldn't help feeling a sense of arousal.

Luc's hands roamed over my body and I knew I was in trouble, but I couldn't stop the sensations coursing through me. All I could do was give in to the darkness that consumed me, and hope that I came out of this with some dignity when it was all over.

"We're going to go upstairs to my place," he said after breaking the kiss. "You are going to behave, or I swear to God I will make a scene you won't like right in front of the doorman who is waiting to open your door right now."

I tried to swallow down the fear that had lodged itself in my throat, knowing that any wrong action could result in a violent outburst from Luc, and he would make good on his promise.

I regarded him, fear and anger mingling inside of me. "I will not be controlled by you. I will not stay with you just because you say so. And I will definitely not love you in this forced marriage."

He led me into the building, giving the doorman a quick nod before dragging me to the elevator.

I had never been so nervous in my life, but I was mostly nervous about how I was going to handle the situation. I didn't want Luc to hurt me, but I couldn't just roll over and give him what he wanted.

The elevator dinged, and we stepped in. Luc pressed the button for his floor, and the elevator door closed.

Luc's body made a cage around me, blocking me off from any kind of escape. His mouth came down on mine, cutting off another of my threats, his tongue forcing its way in. His erection pressed against me, the stiff material of his suit making it difficult to ignore how hard he was.

I struggled against him, pushing my hands against his chest as my anger flared.

The door opened, and Luc gripped my arm and dragged me from the elevator toward his place.

I stumbled, lost my balance, but Luc was there to hold me close.

I was so confused. His blatant disregard for my personal space made me feel small and helpless, yet the way he held me made me feel protected.

It was such a conflicting feeling, and one that I didn't know how to process.

He opened the door to his penthouse, the lust in his eyes evident as he glared at me. Once he'd kicked the door closed behind him, he led me to the living room, where he pushed me against the wall and pressed his lips to mine in another fiery kiss.

As much as I wanted to fight him, the battle was lost.

"You're mine. Say it," he demanded.

I bit my lip, annoyed that he would force me to say something I didn't feel. "I'm yours," I lied.

"No, don't lie to me." His eyes burned into me. "That will only bring you more trouble."

I didn't respond, but instead just looked to the side, avoiding his gaze.

"Not a good idea, sweetheart," he said, his voice gentle. "You know I will only punish you until you submit."

I struggled, trying to pull away from him, but Luc held me, the strength in his hands seemingly impossible to fight against.

He pinned me against the wall as he trailed his hands down to below my waist where he grabbed handfuls of my skirt and yanked it up. I thrilled at the thought of him taking me by force. It was not like I wanted him to, but I couldn't deny my excitement.

"You're lucky I didn't kill your friend," he whispered into my ear. "Is that what you wanted to see? Just how far I'd go to protect you?"

My breath caught, and my lips trembled as Luc held me, waiting for my answer.

"I need to be protected *from you*," I replied.

He chuckled as he kissed me again. "You don't know how right you are."

CHAPTER 24

LUC

A fine line existed between anger fucking...and hate fucking.

And I couldn't tell you which one I was about to cross over to.

Probably both.

But one thing was for certain, and that was that my dick was going to be buried so deep inside Amelia's pussy she'd never again doubt who she belonged to.

I detested games.

I hated bratty antics, and for that, there would be consequences.

I grabbed her firmly by the back of the neck and held her still for a kiss.

She was resistant at first, still struggling, but my demanding lips parted hers, forcefully exploring her mouth.

My cock strained against my pants, desperate to feel the tight clench of her body, but I wasn't going to make this quick and painless.

My little bride needed to pay her penance for acting out.

She moaned under the brutal press of my lips even as she pushed against my shoulders with her hands. I allowed her resistance... for now. I was quite enjoying tasting and taking.

Breaking her down.

Amelia whimpered, and my cock throbbed in response.

I was doing this all wrong.

Kissing her like this.

Touching her like this.

I should be dragging her to my room, ordering her to undress, and spanking that round, perfect ass of hers to teach her a lesson about defiance.

I pulled back to look at her.

Her face was flushed from being so close to me. Her eyes were glazed over and dazed. They reminded me of a doe's, vulnerable and weak.

"What if I don't want you to touch me?" she asked.

"Stop talking," I told her.

I pulled her by the hand toward my office, slammed the door behind her and threw her down on my desk.

She looked up at me as she scrambled to her knees, stunned and afraid, and damn if that didn't turn me the fuck on.

I had to control myself. I had to make her earn it.

She needed to be eye level with my cock. I climbed up and stood on the desk as I reached down and slowly unzipped my pants. My dick was so hard that I was sure it looked painful; hard and long, the purple head slick with precum.

Amelia stared at it, and for a moment, she didn't look afraid.

She looked interested.

Fisting her hair, I wrenched her forward. She slid on her knees over my desk's slick surface until her lips were only inches from my cock.

She gasped, trying to pull back, but my grip on her hair held her in place.

"Open your mouth," I growled.

She shook her head, but I refused to relent. "I don't do this. I'm not this type of girl."

Her breath was hot on my sensitive skin, and I couldn't fucking wait for her to open those pretty lips to let me in.

"Suck me off, Amelia," I ordered harshly.

She shook her head again, the tension in her jaw visible as she stiffened.

"Open your fucking mouth," I growled, "or I'll pry it open."

She watched me, gasping, wide-eyed and afraid.

Taking advantage, I pushed between her open lips. The head of my cock brushed against her tongue. Placing firm pressure against the back of her head, I pushed her mouth further down on my length, watching her lips stretch around my girth.

"Don't forget the balls," I told her.

She looked up at me with her big, doe eyes and, after a slight hesitation, slid her mouth off my shaft and opened her lips wider, taking in both of my balls. Slowly, she began to mouth them, rolling them over her tongue before returning to bob on my shaft.

I grunted and grabbed her head, guiding her as I closed my eyes, feeling the heat of her mouth around me. She was inexperienced but eager and learning quickly.

Her slow, tentative tongue drove me fucking crazy.

I needed to feel her... needed to feel her throat.

"Deeper."

She took my dick as far as she could, before gagging.

I let her recover then brought her up and down a little faster this time.

She got the idea, clearly warming up to it.

I shifted my hips back, sliding out, and she whimpered. Giving her what she secretly craved, I pressed my cock against her lips again and ordered her to open wider.

She let out a little sigh and parted her lips.

"Good girl," I praised.

I leaned back, allowing her to take me in as far as she could handle. Then I pushed her past her limits.

She resisted at first, but I pressed my cock all the way to the back of her throat.

She gagged and pulled back.

Tightening my fist in her hair, I slowly eased her back down along my length until her lips were pressed against my groin.

"That's it, babygirl. Take it all," I told her.

Amelia tried to shake her head and pull away, but my grip was too strong.

She pulled in a deep breath through her nose and obeyed me, sweeping her tongue at the sensitive part of my shaft where my balls were.

I groaned, and my cock throbbed in her mouth.

I was going to come.

Easing my cock out of her warm, tight mouth, I caressed her swollen lower lip with the pad of my thumb. She looked up at me with those sweet, still-innocent eyes and flushed cheeks. She was so fucking gorgeous. I reached down and pulled her dress over her head and threw it across the room. Her porcelain skin glowed, contrasting with the black lace panties and bra she still wore.

I reached forward and pulled down the straps of her bra so that her tits spilled free.

She averted her gaze as I took one of her hard nipples in my mouth. Whimpers escaped her as I sucked on it, and when I grazed my teeth over the sensitive skin around it, she gasped.

"Do you like that?" I asked her.

She nodded and closed her eyes.

I reached out to palm her ass, pressing her stomach against my hips.

I'd spank her later for her performance with that man, but for now, I wanted to taste her, to bury my tongue inside her dripping wet pussy to savor her juices and feel her come.

After laying her on her back on my desk, I kneeled between her open legs as I tore the delicate fabric of her expensive panties until they were nothing more than a shred of silk. She was glistening and wet, her pussy lips swollen, begging for my cock.

"You're perfect, Amelia," I told her.

"No, I'm not," she said.

"Yes, you are."

Ever so gently, I spread her pussy open with my fingers.

"Oh my God," she breathed.

I slipped two fingers inside of her, and she threw her head back and gasped.

I kissed up her thighs, my fingers still inside her.

She was panting sweetly now.

I bent down to bite her on the inside of her thigh, wanting to mark her fair skin.

Brand her as mine.

She moaned and thrust her hips toward me, begging for more.

I licked up her other thigh, stopping just short of her pussy, and she thrust her hips toward me again, trying to get me inside.

She whimpered when I looked at her and thrust my fingers inside again. She was so fucking tight, I needed to prepare her pussy for the pounding I was going to give her with my cock.

"Take a deep breath." I pulled my fingers out and slowly eased a third one in, opening her while pressing my thumb against her clit.

With my free hand, I slipped my arm under her lower back, arching her body toward mine as I positioned the head of my cock at her entrance.

"Moan for me, baby."

I knew she was lost in the moment when she obeyed without a protest or a fight.

The moment the sweet sound left her lips, I thrust inside, wanting to feel the vibrations of her submission along my shaft as her tight body clenched around me.

I thrust several times, easing the rising pressure in my balls… but it wasn't enough.

I needed more…violence, more…power, more…pain…more domination over her.

I pulled free and got to the floor. Kissing her inner thigh, I reached up, took her by the arm, and pulled her off the desk to her feet.

I kissed her, hard, before turning her around and bending her over my desk.

I spread her ass cheeks apart and slipped my cock into her tight pussy from behind.

She groaned as I reached around to grab her tits, my hard shaft pushing past her hole, claiming what was—and would forever be—mine.

I spanked her ass and let her feel my cock pulse inside her.

"Luc," she choked out, and I spanked her again.

I fucked her slowly, pounding deeper and deeper inside her with each thrust until I was balls deep.

Her flesh clenched around me, and it was fucking amazing.

But I wanted more. I needed to hear her scream in pleasure.

I grabbed her hips and pulled her back, slamming into her as hard as I could.

She gasped as her body shook.

I spanked her ass again, leaving a red handprint on her fair skin. She cried out as I grabbed a handful of her hair and pulled her head back, kissing her neck and sinking my teeth into her exposed shoulder. Her body slapped against the desk, and I no longer cared about being gentle.

I spanked her ass again, and her pussy clamped down on my cock.

"Fuck," I growled.

"More," she whispered.

"Beg me for it."

"Please," she begged, "spank me again. I want you to fuck me hard."

I fucked her harder, and she cried out, her moans mixing with the slapping of my balls hitting her pussy, my cock sliding in and out of her hole as she took all of me.

I pulled out of her, spun her around, and pushed her back against my desk. I lifted her, holding her up with my cock pressed against her entrance.

I spread her legs and pulled her to me, thrusting into her and kissing her. Her pussy tightened around my cock, sending a shiver of pleasure down my spine.

The visuals of my cock spreading her pussy and her juices leaking down her legs had my cock teetering on the edge of exploding inside her. Her pussy was so fucking hot.

"You're going to come," I told her.

"I'm going to come," she repeated.

She kept her legs spread, her pussy open and glistening around my thick cock. I thrust into her while her pussy milked my cock, the muscles contracting as she mewled my name.

My balls tightened, and I thrust into her again.

Her pussy convulsed around my cock as she came. She moaned, and her body shook as I roared out in pleasure, filling her with my seed.

But I wasn't done yet. I kept stroking my cock, wanting to cover her from the waist down in my come. I shot a few more streams of come onto her cunt, and then, as juice leaked out of her, her pussy pulsing from her orgasm, I stroked my cock one more time and shot the last of my come onto her lower stomach.

I wanted to mark her with every part of me.

Coat her in my possession.

Spreading her pussy lips, I drenched my fingers with my come then painted her breasts, her collarbone, and then her lips with my completion.

I swirled the sticky substance around her nipple. "Don't ever test me again," I warned. "Or I'll make you wear my come all day."

CHAPTER 25

AMELIA

This couldn't keep happening.

Three times now, we had been together. Three glorious times, never the way I wanted, but I couldn't pretend I didn't like it.

It was too obvious how much I loved it. How it made me feel wanted when he was taking me to prove a point.

How he claimed me in a way that felt deliciously primitive.

What was wrong with me? How could I get off on him being such a controlling asshole? How could I lose myself so completely? When he touched me, common sense flew out the window. I didn't think about where we were, what he was doing, what would happen if we were caught or any other repercussions.

I sat straight up in the bed when I realized we had never discussed any of the repercussions.

He never used a condom. I wasn't on birth control. What if I got pregnant? What would people say if I was showing or if I didn't drink at my wedding? It would reflect badly on him and me, which meant my mother would be furious. The scandal it would cause, and the rumors about paternity.

That could not happen.

I added "look up birth control options" to my mental to-do list for later. Maybe I could broach the subject with Luc, and have his assistant get me something to fix it if it had already happened, or to prevent it from happening. I was expected to bear his children quickly, but not conceive until after the wedding.

I lay on the bed for a few moments. The soft silk sheets felt wonderful against my still-heated skin as I looked around Luc's room.

It was very him. Tastefully decorated with dark wood and brass hardware, the room blended a minimalist style with impeccable quality and taste. I still hadn't asked about what our living situation would be, assuming he still wanted to go through with everything.

Somewhere, a clock chimed four times, and I remembered I was supposed to have tea with Mother today at five. I needed to get back to my home and get ready. My red sundress would not be appreciated by her highness, and to be fair, it wouldn't be the most appropriate attire for high tea at The Wharton.

The company may be less than ideal, but I still looked forward to tea. Even spending time with my mother was worth it to enjoy the softly playing live piano and the massive glass-domed ceiling with its stunning Art Nouveau details. The room was a work of art, and it made me feel like I was in a scene worthy of the greatest painters in the world.

Mother insisted on going to see and be seen. Rose went for the cucumber-and-cream-cheese sandwiches, mostly because it was the only place we wouldn't be scolded for eating cream cheese or bread. But I loved it for the ambiance. The room simply felt magical.

It was the fairy tale people thought I lived in, where even my harpy of a mother was sweet and loving. It was only because conversations could be easily overheard, but I'd take what I could get.

When I left his room, my dress back in place, Henry was waiting for me.

"Hello, miss. Mr. Manwarring insisted I give you a ride home. He was called into a meeting with his father."

I considered declining the ride, but that would be rude, and Henry, though he had made that file on me, was merely doing his job. There was no need to be rude to him. Besides, I wasn't sure if I could get from the Financial District to my home in time to change if I took the subway.

"Thank you, Henry. I appreciate the ride."

"Of course, miss." He led me downstairs to the black Bentley that had been run up on the curb not too long ago.

I climbed in the back and watched the city go by in the softer, warmer tones of the afternoon light.

Henry was an excellent driver, and I made it back to the mansion with about fifteen minutes to get ready. I ran full tilt to my room, boasting its new door after what my mother had told people was a failed burglary attempt.

She still didn't believe what happened. She'd been told that Luc and I had an altercation, but she'd refused to hear of it.

As I reached my door, my mother called me from a dressing room a few doors down. Cautiously, I moved to the other door, trying to smooth my hair and my dress so it wasn't obvious what I had spent the afternoon doing.

The door opened to probably the most horrifying scene I could ever have imagined.

My mother stood in the middle of the room looking through dozens of racks of poofy white monstrosities. Three assistants fluttered around her, refilling her glass, and displaying design books. And Rose was huddled in the corner watching the carnage.

"There you are, perfect. We need to pick your wedding dress."

"I thought we were going to the Wharton for tea," I stupidly said.

Her eyes were laser-focused on me the second she heard the whine I wasn't smart enough to suppress.

"Darling, you are going to have to fit into another wedding dress. The last thing you need is more carbs or sugar."

She looked me up and down. "We should probably get you on a fasting diet as soon as possible. Maybe take you to the doctor and get you on that medication for obese people. You could clearly use it. No one wants to see a whale waddle down the aisle. No doubt this groom will run away screaming as well."

Shame burned through my gut. Logically, I knew I was not overweight. For all our problems, Mr. Manwarring did not find me unattractive and would not be running from me at the altar. Her words were just thrown out there, intending to hurt me. No matter that I should be immune given how many times she tossed insults at me, they still cut deep.

"Of course, Mother."

"Now we have a lot of work to do to find something that can make you pass for a beautiful bride."

I bristled under her criticism, but I knew better than to say anything. Technically, there may have been other people in the room, but I knew, and my mother knew, they would never dare speak a single word against her. She was also not above moving from verbal to physical abuse, and Luc had already left me sore enough for one day.

"There are some undergarments sitting on your bed. Go shower and change into those, and I will pull the first few options for us to consider. I insisted on a full corset this time. If you won't lose the weight, we will just force you to a smaller size."

"Yes, ma'am."

I rushed back to my room, stripped off my sundress, put my hair into a high twist to keep it dry, and stepped into the shower.

The water was scalding as I tried to scrub off the memory of Luc's lips, his hands, and his cock. Or at least any outward sign of what we had been doing. I almost regretted it. As soon as his smell was washed away from my skin, replaced with my lemongrass body wash, I missed it.

My momentary regret was far less troublesome than whatever my mother was about to rain down.

My only goal for this upcoming interaction was to keep my mouth shut and not provoke her. The pours of champagne were no doubt heavy-handed, so she would already be in a mood.

Wrapped in the Egyptian cotton towel, I moved back to my room and saw a white box wrapped in a black ribbon sitting on my bed.

Lifting the lid, I found a white corset with white panties, a garter belt and silk thigh highs, and a white satin robe. I didn't need to wear it all just to try on the dresses, but if I went back into that room without every bit of this on, it would further fuel my mother's wrath.

So I did as I was told. Again. I tamped down my wants and my desires and did what she demanded of me. Marco was wrong. This was who I was, what I was.

As I wrapped the satin floor-length robe around me, I drew a deep breath and returned to the dressing room, hoping I could down a glass of champagne before the pain started.

Not for the first time, I wondered if I should hide a bottle of whisky in my room for these kinds of situations. But then I would end up being just as much of a drunk as she was.

"There you are." My mother's claws closed around my arm as

she pulled me into the center of the room and put me on the large, carpeted pedestal there, my image reflected back from all the surrounding mirrors. "Stand there, and you"—she snapped her fingers at one of the girls— "grab the robe."

I smiled at my sister, who hadn't moved out of the corner. It helped to know she was there, even if she couldn't do anything to help.

I slid off the robe and handed it to the poor assistant who'd been summoned, then reached for a glass of champagne, which my mother yanked out of my hands before I even got it halfway to my lips.

"Champagne is for brides who don't need to lose at least ten pounds before their wedding."

Losing ten pounds would make me medically underweight, but I didn't dare point that out. What was health, when fashion was on the line?

"Put her in this."

She tossed a dress to one of the other girls, who helped me into it. It was the ugliest thing I had ever seen, with ruffles and sequins all over the place. I couldn't even put my arms down without risking crushing something on this taffeta-and-tulle monstrosity.

"I don't know." She took a step back and eyed me, her champagne flute resting against her chin while she studied me. "She doesn't have the grace to pull this gown off."

Thank fuck.

My relief was short-lived because a moment later that dress was being stripped off of me and another just as terrible was being put on. Part of me wondered if that was her plan. If she was intentionally putting me in tacky dresses so that it was easier for her to upstage me. She would whisper to her friends about how she had tried to talk me out of the avant-garde dress into something more timeless, but her willful, artistic daughter just wouldn't listen.

She would shame me and make herself the victim in one sentence.

With each dress I tried on, the more I was sure that was the case, and that hurt more than all the digs about my body or my complexion. No one could carry off a white so bright it made my eyes hurt and every pimple, line, and pore I didn't even have stand out.

"None of these dresses are right. Maybe you just can't carry off a couture gown. What I ever did to get such a homely daughter, I will never understand," she slurred.

"Maybe if we look at a silhouette that is a bit more classical, a mermaid or trumpet perhaps?"

The assistant next to me started nodding and went to pull something from the rack.

"It doesn't matter anyway," Mother said, fire in her eyes. "You already lost a much better match. I doubt this Manwarring will care how you look at the altar. He just cares how you look on your knees."

"Mother..." I warned.

"No, you are a disappointment. Dubois would have done so much more for this family, but you have to be too much of a fat, slutty cow to secure a good match. You threw away the life I handed you, now look at you." She motioned to me with her champagne flute, sloshing champagne over me and the dress. "Now your sister will be forced to make an even better match to cover up that you're the shame this family endures."

The last one crossed the line.

"I am not the one who lost Mr. Dubois. He was at the altar about to say 'I do' when you stopped the wedding. Whatever Mr. Manwarring said to you had nothing to do with me. I am being used to pay for whatever sins are in your closet," I said, slipping out from the now stained dress. I grimaced at the girl who brought a hoop skirt for me to step into for the next one.

"You think you get to talk down to me like that?" She sauntered to me, stumbling a bit, her words slurring even more.

I'd assumed she was too drunk to do much damage, so I didn't see her hand fly through the air until it slammed into my face hard enough to throw me so off balance that I fell off the pedestal and landed hard on my hands and knees.

"You are nothing but a whore who can't keep her legs closed. I don't know what I did to be cursed with such a willful slut of a daughter. Your father is ashamed of you."

She hovered over me.

The boning in the corset was digging into my sides, and tears were spilling down my cheeks as she placed her stiletto on top of my hand. The sharp pain made me cry out and I gripped her ankle in my free hand, trying desperately to pull my trapped hand out from under her.

"Get off," I begged. The heel of the shoe was sharp, and she dug it between the knuckles of my middle and index fingers. "Please, you're hurting me."

"No, you will learn your place. It's here under my fucking shoe."

"Mother, please." Rose tried to interrupt, and she threw her champagne glass at her, shattering it on the wall above her head.

"Don't you dare start. You're just as ungrateful as your sister! Why did I have to be burdened with two ugly, ungrateful daughters? The rest of my life has to be spent making sure you two don't become even larger burdens to your father and I."

"I'm not yours anymore. In a few months I won't be an Astrid. I won't be your burden." I kept trying to pull my hand out or move her, but she leaned heavily on the shoe that was close to puncturing my hand.

"I don't give a fuck what your last name is, or how you let

that man debase you. Your loyalty is to this family first, your children second, and then your husband. You will always answer to me first." She pressed down harder, and I couldn't hold back the cry of pain.

The door flew open, and my father, soon-to-be husband, and father-in-law all came in holding papers before my mother could say something else.

"Get out!" she screamed, lifting off my hand, and I crawled back, cradling my hand to my chest. "You can't be in here. She isn't decent, and it's bad luck to see the dress—"

"What the fuck is going on here?" Luc demanded, staring daggers at me.

I tried to cover as much of myself as possible with my hands and duck my head so he couldn't see the tears or the burning handprint on my face.

One sideways glance at one of the many mirrors confirmed my state—the bright red marks on my face and hand, mascara running down my cheeks, my hair fallen from the clip.

In short, I was a mess.

"You need to leave!" my mother screeched.

She turned on my father. "What kind of man are you, bringing these men into this room when your daughter is practically naked?"

"We need you to sign for this deal with—" My father didn't even get to finish his sentence before she was screeching again.

Crouching down further and trying to hide my body with my arms, I kept my eyes on the floor, not wanting anyone to see me. I prayed I could just disappear into one of the mountains of tulle, that one of these hideous dresses would just come to life and consume me.

I remembered what happened the last time Luc saw a mark on me. I wouldn't give my mother the satisfaction of knowing that he had found me lacking every time she marred me.

The way she was screaming, I expected the men to retreat. Instead, a pair of polished black loafers stepped on the carpet in front of me.

A moment later, a warm jacket was draped over my shoulders, and I was surrounded by his scent again.

Luc knelt then cupped my chin gently, bringing my gaze up to meet his.

He looked into my eyes, then at my cheek and my hand. His jaw clenched, and he ground his teeth as he stood back up and demanded everyone leave the room.

"This is my home. You can't just walk in here and—" my mother tried.

"I think you know damn well what will happen if you don't get the fuck out of this room now," he seethed, and I heard some shuffling and the door slam.

"They are gone now." His voice was softer, gentler.

I didn't trust it.

"Amelia, look at me.

CHAPTER 26

AMELIA

"*A*melia, babygirl, please stand up," he said softly.

I did as he said and stood back on the pedestal.

Parts of my hair hung in front of my face, but the mirrors surrounding me still showed the handprint—bright red and clear as day, there was no way to possibly hide it.

"Tell me what happened."

He stood in front of me. His strong hand was still on my waist, supporting me, yet I felt exposed and vulnerable.

"Nothing."

"Amelia. Tell me what just happened in here." His voice took on a harsh edge.

Somehow, he sounded angrier than he had earlier.

The tears flowed down my face more freely, a lump forming in my throat. I couldn't answer him. So much worse would happen if I told him what happened in this house. Or if he found out this wasn't the worst she had done to me.

She rarely left marks. She was always careful about that, but many ways existed to inflict pain without leaving physical marks.

"We were trying on wedding dresses," I answered with my head down, my voice little more than a whisper.

I was like a broken doll standing on a pedestal, in underwear and a suit jacket that dwarfed me. The sleeves even went well past my fingertips. It made me feel small and weak.

I guessed that was appropriate.

"And why are you crying?"

I looked back at the door my mother had gone through. She was probably right on the other side, listening for something else to berate me about. She always looked for more ways I'd failed her as a daughter. Still, better me than Rose. Though now I was terrified that she was Mother's next target.

He gave my waist a small squeeze. "Amelia, answer me."

I shook my head. I couldn't do it.

"Look at me." His voice came out hard, an order.

I swallowed the lump in my throat as I met his gaze.

His jaw was clenched tight, fury lighting up his blue eyes.

"Tell me what happened." The *or else* hung between us, unspoken.

"Do what you want to me. Your punishments aren't worse than hers."

His eyes widened, and he pulled me into his arms.

I tried to resist.

It was probably a trap, but the second his arms were secure around me, I melted against the soft cotton of his shirt, warmed by his skin.

"I'm not going to punish you. I want to protect you, but I need to know what I'm protecting you from."

Gentle words. They were a trap, they had to be, but the safety of his arms made me want to trust him.

"Amelia, I have made mistakes with you. I was trying to make up for them at the museum."

He drew a deep breath, moved a lock of my hair out of my face, and tilted my chin so I could look him in the eye.

"I can't promise I won't punish you again, but when I do, I want it to give you pleasure, not just pain. Every strike I give you on that perfect ass should sting but also arouse you. I will never lay a hand on you out of malice."

I stared into his eyes for a long moment, searching for the truth in his words. He at least believed what he was saying, but did I?

What other choice did I have?

"My mother said I was too fat for the dresses, and I was going to have to diet until the wedding." Not a lie, but not why I was crying.

"Don't you dare!" The venom in his words made me jump and pull away from him. "Your body is the sexiest thing I have ever seen. You have curves so perfect that altering you in any way should be a crime against God."

I didn't know how to respond to that, so I put my head back down on his shoulder, hoping to hide the blush that was now rising in my cheeks. He already saw me so well. I didn't want him to see the effect his words had on me.

"Your mother is a jealous, petty woman. She would have been making comments like that the second you started to outshine her. I'd bet that happened a long time ago. By now you would've built up a thick skin to that bullshit. You're too strong not to have. Tell me the truth so I can protect you."

He really saw right through me. He had been paying attention. There was no way Henry would have been able to tell him when my mother started insulting me.

I stayed silent but my tears stopped flowing.

He cupped my jaw, wiping away the remaining tears with his thumb. "Let's try this again. What happened?"

I looked back at the door.

"Don't worry about her, worry about me. Tell me what happened. I won't let her touch you again. You have my word."

"Is your word any good?" The words slipped out of my lips before I even thought about it.

"Excuse me? Do you want to repeat that, princess?"

"I just mean... I don't... I don't..."

He leaned closer to me. "Say it," he whispered in my ear. "Tonight, I want to show you what kind of husband I will be. I need you to be honest, and I will do the same."

"If a man resorts to blackmail or extortion to obtain a bride, whatever the reasons, can his word be trusted? I don't know. I heard you say to Mr. Dubois that it's just business, and I don't know what that means for your character."

"Have I ever lied to you?"

I thought about that for a moment.

He hadn't lied. He had spanked me, pushed me well past my limits, and taken what wasn't rightfully his until after the ceremony, but I had ended up reveling in his depravity.

I liked the way he took me, and he made sure that I found my pleasure in his touch, a trait not common among powerful men, if the maids were to be believed.

He was right. Every time he gave me pain, it added to the pleasure. Even when he was angry, that anger never fueled his strikes. He left me with a sore ass, but never really hurt me.

He had also let me think he cared, when all he had done was have his assistant spy on me.

But wasn't that caring? His assistant must've had more important things to attend to, and even if his assistant had set up everything, he had made the time to do something he knew I would enjoy.

I was so confused.

This man was a tycoon in his own right. He had an empire he was preparing to run. He wasn't a prince sent to save me from an evil queen, but maybe he was the king who would protect me from everyone but himself.

There was no way of escaping him, not really, so maybe the smart move was to embrace him, let him protect me, and then learn to live within his rules. I'd end up there, anyway. Why not make it easier on everyone?

"No, you have never lied to me, but you scare me," I admitted.

"I will never break a promise to you, Amelia. This may not be a love match. This union may have started in order to stop a business deal from happening, but the result is still that you are going to be my wife. I will never break my word to you, and I will always protect what is mine. Now tell me what happened in this room before I got here."

"Mother was forcing me to try on awful dresses. She was degrading me, but you're right. I barely feel it anymore..." I swallowed, not sure how much I should tell him.

"Keep going." It was more of a command than a request.

"She was drinking. She said that I was a disappointment, and my father is ashamed of me. She called me a whore and said that I ruined a more lucrative match."

"This is because you're going to marry me and not Dubois."

I pulled his jacket around me tighter, wincing as my sore hand twinged, and nodded.

"She struck you because she thinks you are the one that let that happen," he repeated like he didn't quite believe me.

"I may have..." I did not want to anger him further.

"You what?" he pressed.

"I said she was the one that ruined the match by having whatever secret you are holding over her head."

He raised one eyebrow as his mouth lifted in a grin. "You fought back?"

I nodded.

"Then what happened?"

"She hit me. I was stupid. I wasn't watching out for it. She had drunk almost a full bottle of champagne. I thought she was too drunk to—"

"Did you pick out a dress?"

"No."

"Which of these do you like?" He turned abruptly to rifle through the racks.

"None of them."

"Did you just not want to... what is it the kids are saying now? 'Say yes to the dress?'"

I gave him a soft smile.

"I guess just nothing that was ugly enough."

"Ugly enough?" He turned to look at me again.

"Even at my own wedding, my mother is trying to outshine me. These dresses are the most avant-garde dresses from the top couture designers. They are all either hideous, more concept art than wearable gowns, or made for a different body type and skin tone," I explained.

"So you don't like any of them?" He looked at me another moment then back to the dresses. "None of them really looks like you. They are all so stark white, still and lifeless."

"That's because they aren't for me." I shrugged, then was hit with an overwhelming sadness.

She would never love me, never want me to really succeed. Why couldn't I have been born into a family like Marco's? Where people were cherished and supported.

"Shh, it's okay, I have you now." He reached out and grabbed my hand.

He pressed where her heel had dug into my hand.

The pain was instant. I jerked back my hand and let out a cry of pain.

Cradling my hand to my chest, I looked up at Luc, and his jaw was clenched again.

"Give me your hand, Amelia." He held out his hand for mine.

"Please." I pressed it harder against my chest.

I didn't know if he wanted to see why I yanked my hand away or if he was going to dig his thumb into the forming bruise from my mother to punish me for pulling away.

I knew what he'd said earlier, but I didn't want to risk it. I couldn't take any more pain tonight.

This day had already been one of the longest of my life, filled with emotional highs and lows. One thing right after the other.

I was exhausted, and my nerves were frayed. It was too much.

"Give me your hand, Amelia. I'm mad, but not at you. Let me see how bad it is, babygirl." His tone was so much softer.

I still didn't trust him, but I didn't have any other options. Slowly, I offered my hand to him, palm up.

Gently as he could, he grasped the ends of my fingers to flip my hand to the ugly red welt that was forming on the top my hand.

"What made this mark?"

"It doesn't matter."

"It matters to me. Who did this to you and with what?" Then, more to himself, he said, "We should get this looked at by a doctor."

"It's nothing," I tried to argue again.

"Amelia, I have vowed to never break a promise to you." His blue eyes stared into mine. "Can you please promise me that you won't lie to me again, especially not when it comes to your safety?"

The sincerity in his gaze made me pause again. I was seeing such a different side of this man. I didn't know what to believe.

He meant what he was saying. Or did I just believe what he was saying because I wanted to? I was going to marry him. He would be my husband soon. I wanted...if not love, at least kindness.

A thud at the door drew my attention away from him. She was listening. She had to be. I was already going to pay for telling him what she said about my weight and the comments he made about her.

"Did your mother do this, too?" he said, lowering his voice.

I nodded.

"With what?"

"Her stiletto."

I looked down. I couldn't stand even the idea of having him pity me.

"Okay."

"Okay?" I looked back up at him. I expected pity or anger. Instead, I saw resolve.

He buttoned his jacket over me, covering me from shoulders to mid-thigh. Then he scooped me up in his arms. I immediately grabbed his shoulder with my good hand, and he carried me out of the room.

CHAPTER 27

AMELIA

*M*y mother was waiting on the other side of the door. He went right past her without even sparing her a look and only stopped in front of our fathers.

"Amelia isn't safe in this house. She's moving in with me, effective immediately."

"No, that isn't proper. You can't! I won't allow it," Mother sputtered.

"I wasn't asking. I was informing. Amelia needs to see a doctor about the wound on her hand. Then she will move into my penthouse. All wedding arrangements will be made by her from there."

"I will not allow my daughter to live in sin!" Mother shrieked, and I ducked my head, burying it in Luc's neck.

His arms tightened around me, and he made me feel safe.

"Then I'll call a judge now, and we can be married tonight. Either way, she is not staying in this house with that drunk, abusive bitch another night. She is mine, and no one"—he turned to glare at my mother— "and I mean no one, touches what's mine."

"The wedding will go on as planned," his father said. "If the young couple wants to cohabitate before the wedding, I think it's a fine idea. This isn't the 1800s. Let the kids play house for a while."

"No!" my mother shrieked. "Why would he buy the cow if he is getting the milk for free?"

"Madam, the only cow in this house is you. I said I was going to marry her, and I will, either in the church in a few months, or tonight with a judge. I really don't care which. All things considered, I don't think you are the best person to opine on who does, or doesn't, pay for milk."

I had no idea what that meant, but it shut my mother up. She just glared, her face turning crimson as she glowered.

"Amelia, do you want to leave with Mr. Manwarring?" my father asked.

"Of course she doesn't," Mother started.

"Yes," I answered my father, keeping my voice low but loud enough I know he heard.

"Okay, then. The wedding will proceed as scheduled. So, please try to keep this out of the papers, and I'll have the staff get your things packed and delivered."

I nodded as my fiancé carried me out of my childhood home.

The second the front door closed, I could hear Mother screaming again, but it was no longer my problem.

I looked up to see Rose in her window, gazing down at us. She raised her hand to wave, and I did the same, relieved she was safe in her studio.

"Where are we going?" I asked as we got into the car.

"First, I am taking you to my private doctor. I would have him just meet me at home, but I think your hand will need X-rays."

I nodded and watched the place I used to call home disappear as we turned a corner.

Luc made a call to the doctor.

"Did you mean it?" I asked when he hung up the phone.

"Mean what?" He held my uninjured hand.

"When you said that I was moving in with you."

"I did. In the Financial District. We will start by living there. If you like it, we can stay. It is convenient for work. If you don't like it, we will start house shopping whenever you like."

"What about the wedding?" I asked.

"What about it?"

"Did you just want to go to the courthouse and get it over with?"

"No. I would have if I needed to in order to keep you safe and get you away from your mother. But a large wedding is expected, and I am kind of looking forward to it. Standing in front of God and the entire world and telling them you are mine."

He wrapped his arm around me and pulled me in to his side.

"If you want help planning, I'm sure we can get Rose to come over, and my sisters would love to help as well. I was waiting for your name to change to add you to what will be the joint accounts, but I'll have Henry acquire a card for you to do that planning."

I nodded, not sure what to say. He was giving me total control and offering the resources I'd need. That had to mean something, right?

The doctor was waiting for us when we arrived at a brownstone. He led us to the basement level, where he had his office and some basic equipment. If he thought the state I was in was unusual, he didn't say anything about it. Just looked at my hand and took a few X-rays. There was some serious bruising, but no permanent damage.

The doctor even brought Luc out of the room while his nurse, a woman I was pretty sure was the doctor's wife, wrapped my hand.

When the men were out of earshot, she looked at me with a comforting hand on my shoulder.

"Honey, are you okay? Do we need to call the police?"

"Why would you need to do that?" I asked, confused.

"Your hand, sweetheart. Are you safe? If not, you can tell me. We will help you."

I was touched by this woman's generosity, but I assured her I was fine.

"I'm safe now. He took me out of a bad situation. He saved me tonight."

"Good." She nodded. "My husband has several clients like Mr. Manwarring. He has been that boy's personal doctor since he was a child. He is one of the good ones."

"He really is." I smiled at the older woman. "Why don't I get you some clothes?" She disappeared before I could tell her it wasn't really necessary. She came back a few moments later with a simple, emerald-green sundress.

"Here. It isn't much. Our daughter left it when she went off to college. It should fit you."

"Thank you." I got changed, putting Luc's jacket over my arm as I met him out in the main room where he and the doctor were discussing something.

"Ready?" I asked, interrupting them.

Both men looked at me, and the way Luc's eyes heated when he took me in wearing that green dress, I knew he was thinking of the night of the opera and a very different green dress.

"Let's go." He offered me his arm. I took it, and he led me outside, sweeping me off my feet when we got to the pavement since I wasn't wearing shoes.

"Where are we going now?" I asked as he settled into the car next to me.

"Home."

CHAPTER 28

LUC

*A*melia stood in front of the fireplace in my bedroom, rubbing her hands up and down her arms, no doubt attempting to pull her mother's chill out of her bones.

"No one will ever leave bruises on you again," I vowed, still biting back the anger and rage bubbling inside of me. "If your mother were a man and not related to you, she'd be dead."

Amelia didn't turn to face me but instead stared into the flames. "I'm surprised you actually have a real fire in your room. We were never allowed to use the fireplaces in my home. They were purely for decoration. Mother always said they'd leave soot on our expensive furnishings."

"I don't like to be cold," I confessed. "I spent a large part of my life in frigid and drafty boarding schools. I promised myself that once I was a grown man, I'd never crawl into a cold bed again, shivering as I waited for my body heat to warm the blankets."

"I'm embarrassed." Her soft voice stating those words nearly took me out at the knees.

"Never be embarrassed, Amelia," I said as I closed the distance between us and stood next to her in front of the fire.

When she didn't look at me, I took hold of her chin to force her to lock eyes with mine. "I will make sure you never feel the way that woman made you feel ever again."

For a moment, silence stretched out between us, broken only by the crackling of the flames. Then, without warning, Amelia turned and stepped closer, wrapping her arms around me and burying her face in my chest. I hesitated for a moment, then wrapped my own arms around her, pulling her tight.

"Thank you," she whispered. "No one has ever... fought for me before."

Without thinking, I leaned in to press my lips to hers. The kiss was gentle at first, but then it deepened as Amelia responded, her hands coming up to tangle in my hair. I broke away and rested my forehead against hers.

Unfamiliar feelings were rushing through me. It wasn't just the need to possess this woman, to control her, and to dominate.

No... I felt this almost animalistic sensation to protect her at all costs.

I wanted to keep her wrapped up in my arms and never let her go for fear that something bad could happen. I wanted to—

I kissed her again, deeper this time, pouring all my pent-up emotion into the kiss. Amelia explored my body with her hands, pulling me closer to her. She shivered against me, and just as I was about to lift her and carry her to the bed, a knock sounded at the door.

Remembering what I had planned to help lighten the mood and help Amelia relax, I went to the door to retrieve what I had asked for.

When I turned to face Amelia with a silver tray full of everything needed to make s'mores, I said, "We can use that fireplace for more than just warmth."

Amelia's eyes lit up as she took in the tray filled with marshmallows, graham crackers, and chocolate bars. "S'mores?" A smile spread across her face. "I've never had those. My mother always said they were too messy and unrefined."

I chuckled. "Well, I'd say she was missing out. There's something about the combination of chocolate, marshmallows, and graham crackers that's just...perfect."

Amelia watched as I skewered a marshmallow on a long metal rod and held it over the flames. The marshmallow began to puff and turn golden brown, and I carefully slid it off the rod onto a square of graham cracker. I added a piece of chocolate and then topped it with another graham cracker, pressing down gently to let the marshmallow and chocolate melt together.

"Here, try it," I said, holding the s'more out to Amelia.

She took a tentative bite, the marshmallow oozing out the sides of the crackers, and I watched as her eyes widened in surprise and delight. "This is amazing," she said, grinning at me. "But my mother is right about one thing. I do have to fit into a wedding dress." She eyed the dessert longingly. "A taste is all I need."

"That's ridiculous. Your body is absolutely perfect, and don't let anyone, especially your shrew of a mother, tell you otherwise."

Amelia blushed at my words, but they clearly pleased her. She took another bite of the s'more and savored the sweetness as it melted in her mouth.

"You know," she said, looking up at me with a mischievous glint in her eye. "I think this is the first time in my life that I've ever done something... young and carefree."

I felt a surge of satisfaction at her words, and a warmth spread through my chest. It was a feeling that was foreign to me, but I liked it. I wanted to do everything in my power to make sure that Amelia was happy and safe, and that she never had to suffer again.

"Well, we'll have to change that," I said, grinning at her. "I've got plans for us, and they involve a lot more than just s'mores."

Amelia raised an eyebrow. "Oh really? Do tell."

I leaned in, speaking softly so that she couldn't miss my sincerity. "I'm going to show you the world, Amelia. And I'm going to make sure that you experience everything it has to offer. The good, the bad, and the beautiful. And I promise you, when we're done, you'll never be the same again."

Amelia's eyes widened at my words, excitement growing in them. She took another bite of the s'more and grinned. "What would society say if they knew we were roasting marshmallows in your bedroom? I shouldn't even be alone in here with you prior to marriage. We're breaking all the rules."

"Good. The only rules I follow, and the only ones I want you to follow, are mine."

I leaned in to brush a kiss to the tip of her nose, and then kissed her lips gently, licking off the sweetness there .

"And right now all I want to do is continue breaking all the rules."

I hadn't planned to fuck Amelia tonight—not after everything she had just gone through—but having her sitting next to me, so close, so vulnerable, I couldn't deny the inner beast still rattling the cages inside me.

I wanted her. And I wanted her now.

I tore my lips away from hers then started kissing down her neck. When I reached the soft, creamy skin just below her jaw, I sucked hard, leaving a dark red mark in my wake. Out of the corner of my eye I could see how Amelia's breath was coming in short, sharp gasps.

"You taste better than the s'mores," I whispered, placing open-mouthed kisses on the mark I had just left.

"You're leaving a mark. What will people say if they see it?" she said breathlessly.

I gave her a long, hard look before I picked her up and carried her to the bed.

"You are mine, Amelia. It's about time the world knows it. And like I said, I don't follow anyone else's rules," I said. "And I will do whatever I want to you."

Her pupils dilated at the sound of my harsh voice, and her eyes were filled with the same want that I felt.

I stood up and pulled my shirt over my head, quickly followed by my pants and boxers. Her eyes followed my every move, widening slightly when she saw my cock spring to attention.

I returned my focus to her and spread apart her legs. I settled my hands on her knees and ran them up the smooth, soft skin of her thighs. After slowly removing her panties, I paused to look up at her.

"Maybe you've never been told this, or maybe not enough, but you truly are a stunning woman. Beautiful."

Amelia shifted under me, her hips rising to meet my face.

A small smile of satisfaction spread across my face when one of her hands moved to the back of my head.

She didn't want to admit it, but she wanted more.

And I was going to give it to her.

I kissed the insides of her thighs, moving slowly inward.

Her taste was sweet, just like I remembered it from the last time I devoured her cunt. I opened my mouth and began to lap at her, torturing her with my tongue.

Her hands tugged at my hair, pulling me even closer to her.

She made little mewling sounds while I continued my assault. My name fell from her lips in a soft whisper. Enough for me to feel her orgasm come on. When she began to spasm under me, I spread her legs even further and moved my face up to her perfect pussy.

"I'm not going to stop," I said, looking up at her. "I'm going to make you come until you can't think of anything else but me. And then I'll do it all over again. And again. And again."

My words seemed to only increase her pleasure, and I continued to lick her until she was covered in sweat, her gasps coming more slowly and in longer intervals.

Bracing my head on my elbow, I studied her face as I brushed her soft curls away from her cheek.

It had been a brutal, stressful day, and now I had worn her out. There was something strangely comforting about watching this beautiful creature succumb to sleep as her eyelids slowly drifted closed and her head shifted to the side.

It took trust to fall asleep in another's arms.

Her chest rose and fell with her breaths.

I gently removed the rest of her clothing and pulled the covers up over her naked shoulders. She was still so warm and pliant and open to me, and I liked it. I loved being able to have this effect on her and bring her right to the edge of oblivion.

"Sleep now, Amelia. I'll be right here when you wake up."

I climbed into bed next to her and pulled her into my arms— flesh against flesh.

Warmth against warmth.

She was still breathing heavily, and I could tell she was on the edge of sleep, but I was surprised when she turned and nuzzled her face into my chest. She brought her hand to my cock and began stroking it.

"I want you," she said softly. "I want you inside me."

I groaned inwardly as she began to move her hand faster, and I could feel myself growing closer and closer to the edge.

Desire and lust were winning over my good intentions, and I wanted nothing more than to shove my cock deep inside of her.

She didn't stop stroking me, and I began to push her hand away, but she only gripped me harder. I closed my eyes, wanting nothing more than to sink into her tight wet pussy.

"Please, fuck me."

I rolled over with Amelia, so that she was on top of me. She spread her legs around me and I lifted her, moving my face to her pussy. She let out a soft moan at the feeling of my breath on her, and I gently tongued her clit.

"Oh, God," she sighed.

I flicked my tongue against her clit, causing her hips to gyrate on top of me. I loved feeling her naked body over me, and I wanted to feel more of it. I sat up, taking her with me, and held her steady while I stroked her breasts. Her body quivered under my hands.

"Please, Luc. I need you now. I want you inside me. I need to forget about everything else."

Her words were all the encouragement I needed to lose control. I flipped her over and spread her legs apart. I moved up on top of her and pinned her arms above her head.

I could see the longing in her eyes, and I wanted to give her what she wanted. I also saw the sincerity there, shining back at me. She wanted this. She wanted me.

I pressed my cock against the entrance of her pussy, and she threw her head back and moaned. I teased her opening with the head, and she began to squirm under me, trying to get me to penetrate her.

"Luc, please," she begged.

"Say you want me," I whispered into her ear.

"I need you, Luc. I want you. Please, say you want me."

I smiled and leaned down to kiss her, my cock pressed against her pussy.

"I want you, Amelia. I want you so much."

I pushed my hips forward, plunging myself deep into her. I let out a long, loud groan.

She was so tight and wet for me it was almost too much to bear.

"Are you okay? I asked.

She nodded, breathing harder. "Please. Move. I want you."

I pulled out of her slowly and then pushed back in, deeper and harder. Her breathing sped up, and it turned me on even more. I slammed into her again and again, and her pussy began quivering around my cock.

Her noises were growing louder, and her nails were digging into my back. She was close, and I wanted to give her exactly what she wanted. I released her arms and pushed her legs up so that they were on either side of my head. I began driving into her harder, and she began to scream in pleasure.

"Oh God, Luc. Oh, my God. I'm going to—"

She threw her head back, and her pussy walls tightened around my cock. I moved my face to her neck and breathed in deeply as she orgasmed, her body bucking wildly underneath me.

I made small circles with my hips, prolonging her orgasm and enjoying the feeling of her pussy gripping my cock in a vice-like grip.

I could feel her coming undone under me. When she finally tensed and shuddered, I couldn't hold it back any longer. I let go, and my orgasm swept over both of us. I bucked against her, allowing myself to be lost in the moment.

When I finally came to my senses, I collapsed on top of her. I pulled my body off hers and rolled her to my side. I wanted her to be next to me, in my arms, where she would be safe.

"Amelia?"

"Mmm hmm," she murmured, her eyes still closed.

"I want you to stay with me. I didn't ask you when I took you away from your home. I didn't give you a choice, but I'm telling you right now that this is what I want."

"I'll stay," she whispered.

I didn't say anything more, but I pulled her close to me. She fit perfectly into my body, and her soft breath was warm on my chest.

This was something money couldn't buy.

This was something power couldn't give.

I kissed Amelia's head as I took in just how warm I was. I had come a long way from the cold boarding school boy, although I still wasn't sure if that was a good thing.

CHAPTER 29

LUC

"*S*ir." Henry's voice came from my bedroom door. "I'm terribly sorry to disturb you, but your father is here. He is in your office and is quite insistently demanding an audience."

The room was still dark thanks to my blackout curtains covering the floor-to-ceiling windows. A thin but bright line of light streamed in at the very top, just allowing me to see around my room, and the naked woman still sound asleep on my chest.

"Thank you, Henry," I said as gently as possible so as not to wake Amelia. "I'll be out in a moment to deal with him."

I had been awake for a while now, watching Amelia sleep.

She looked so peaceful it made my chest ache.

Seeing her last night in so much pain, letting me take care of her, then sitting in front of the fire and just talking— it all shifted something inside me. I don't think I had ever opened up like that to anyone. Not even my therapist.

"Coffee has been made and is waiting for you," Henry added before gently closing the door.

I hated my father for interrupting the time I had with Amelia.

She was sound asleep in my arms, lying on my chest, her delicate little fingers twirling my chest hair while she dreamt.

The silk sheet she was wrapped in clung to the perfect shape of her round ass, and her breasts were exposed. My mouth watered as I thought about leaning down to pop one of those perfect pink nipples into my mouth and sucking until she woke with a moan of pleasure.

This was the most satisfied and content I'd ever felt.

Usually, on Saturday mornings, I would have already been working in my home office. Instead, I was in bed with a beautiful naked woman making a mental list of all the things I wanted to do with her that day.

Maybe take her back to the Met and tell Henry I was not to be disturbed. Or if Amelia didn't want to live in my bachelor pad condo, we could start looking at houses, or even scout out venues for the wedding.

Better yet, we could've spent the entire day in bed hiding from the world and talking, learning even more about each other, and making love.

That last option was my first choice.

I didn't think I had ever made love to a woman before.

In fact, I was sure that was a first.

Every woman I had ever been with I'd fucked hard and fast.

Sometimes, my partners and I indulged in more violent delights, and with others it was all passion, heat, and chemistry. I had ripped women's clothes from their bodies, desperate to get to their bare flesh. I had chained women to crosses and whipped them to orgasm.

The quick fucks in the more private spots in the club had been erotic but impersonal. I had possessed every woman I had ever enjoyed.

Even with Amelia, the first few times I'd played with her, I'd owned her.

Last night had been different.

Last night I had taken her to show affection.

I had been gentle as I'd explored her body and coaxed her into pleasure before giving in to my own. I hadn't taken or demanded. It had been profoundly different.

Something told me Amelia was the woman who was meant for me, that no matter who I had been with before, she was the only one who could have given me what we had last night. It was the kind of thing that made a man want to love his wife.

For the first time in my life, my mind was still.

It wasn't buzzing about the next person who was coming after me.

I wasn't strategizing how to destroy someone for having the audacity to inconvenience me. I hadn't even thought of ways to have my father removed as head of the family all morning.

It was just me and my wife-to-be cuddled in bed.

She was safe and happy, and I was content.

Now I had been notified that my father was here and wanted to speak to me, and he knew I was home, so there was no way to make him fuck off. He was still head of the family, for now, and it was simpler to let him think he was still in charge. Besides, if Henry had entered this room, it was clear he had tried to make my father leave and it hadn't worked.

As carefully as I could, I slipped out of bed, trying not to disturb Amelia.

She immediately reached for me, and the cutest little line appeared between her brows when she couldn't find me. A strange ache bloomed in my chest, and I wanted to crawl back into bed. Instead, I took my pillow, still warm from my body and still smelling like me, and slid it over to her.

She immediately pulled it in close and fell back into a deep slumber.

I'd be back in this bed as quickly as possible, so I slid on black silk pajama bottoms and a robe. With any luck, the casual appearance would help my father realize it wasn't a good time to visit.

"He is waiting in the study, sir," Henry said. "And I finished that report you asked for."

"Thank you, Henry. Go home and spend some time with your family."

"Sir? It's nine a.m. on a Saturday."

"Exactly, go home. Take a day off. That's an order."

"Yes, sir. I'll see you tomorrow." He turned to leave, and I called out to stop him.

"Make that Monday, Henry. I'm taking the weekend off. You should do the same."

"The entire weekend, sir?" He stared at me, blinking like he had misheard me.

"Keep your phone handy in case I have a question, but don't count on me calling you," I said. He looked at me like I had lost my mind and opened his mouth like he was going to say something, then thought better of it.

"Have a good weekend, Mr. Manwarring."

He headed toward the front door while I went to my private study. It was one of the few places my father knew I didn't like him in, which of course was why he was there. I wasn't even surprised to see him sitting in my desk chair. He held a cup, so he was drinking my coffee, his filthy polished Italian leather loafers on my desk right above my keyboard.

The old man was pushing me too far.

"Luc, there you are. You took your time. It's already nine a.m. You should have been up hours ago."

"I was otherwise occupied."

"Yes. That was quite a show. I don't think I have ever seen that old bat's face turn so many colors." He smacked the top of my desk as he laughed. "It was about time someone took a firm hand with her."

"Yes, well. I needed to ensure she knows that Amelia is mine now, and she won't be used as a spy in my home."

Amelia telling her mother my secrets had never even crossed my mind, but my father wouldn't understand that I wanted to protect her because I felt something deeper for her. The most Lucian Manwarring had ever felt for a woman was an erection.

Until Amelia, I had thought I was the same, but she had stoked something more inside me. I didn't know if I would call it anything as innocent as love. We had made love last night, but that wasn't the right word for how I felt.

What I felt for her was darker, primal, and possessive.

Maybe it was the only way I knew how to love, to covet her with the same ferocity I coveted power.

Still, my father wouldn't understand that, and trying to explain it was an exercise in futility I didn't have the time for. The longer I stayed and talked to him, the longer I was away from her.

She was my priority right now, just getting back to her.

I took the steel decanter of coffee Henry prepared every morning from my father and poured my first cup of the day. Henry always prepared the finest French roast coffee. I took my first sip as I settled into one of the other leather chairs in my office, as if it was business as usual. "Did she sign the contract?"

"Yes. The bitch ranted and raved for about another twenty minutes. Astrid finally calmed her down by asking what you meant about cows." He let out a boisterous laugh.

I hoped it wasn't loud enough to wake Amelia, though maybe if he woke her, I could taste her sweet pussy again before we figured out what to do for the rest of the day. I thought she was going to be my new favorite breakfast each morning.

"I want to move up the wedding." The words just flew from

my mouth before I had even thought them through, but the second I said it, I knew I meant it.

"Why on earth would we do that? It's clear you have had that girl in your bed. She's ruined now. We can string them along forever. Just holding the threat of dumping the little bitch will be enough to make her father agree to anything."

"No, I want to get this done. I don't want to give them a chance to figure out a way to wiggle out of this deal."

"No one is wiggling anywhere." My father scoffed. "We have them right where we need them. Astrid can't strike while you can still replace his daughter and make her the laughingstock of society. He knows that with a few well-placed rumors, she will have to move to another country to find a husband. She will be damaged goods. Her life was ruined the second she climbed into your bed. We should hold that advantage."

Strategically, he was right. This would make them our bitch, and the advantage it gave us was unmistakable. I still couldn't stomach it. She was mine. I needed to make that fact known. Not she could be mine, or might be mine, or even would be mine, eventually. She was mine now.

"I don't want to wait that long," I said.

My father laughed. "What's the rush? You already have her freshly fucked in your bed. There is no advantage to pushing this faster, and every advantage in stretching it out."

My jaw tightened, and I clenched my fists. My heart pounded and demanded retribution for what he said. She was mine. No one spoke about her like that.

"She isn't a whore. She will be my wife and the mother of my children." I kept my tone as even as possible, but my patience was running thin.

"Are you sure about that?" My father finished his coffee and poured himself another.

"What do you mean?"

"The only reason she is in this mess, in your bed, is because her whore mother couldn't keep her legs shut. If the boy, Harrison, wasn't a bastard, then Amelia would be Mrs. Dubois and spend her nights bouncing on Marksen's dick, not yours. You bought and paid for her, which makes her a whore."

With a deep breath through my nose, I held on tight to control my rage and stop myself from making a mistake and showing my father how important she was to me. Lucian Manwarring was a vicious man, and soon I would usurp his kingdom. The last thing I wanted or needed was for him to have leverage to use against me.

"Don't tell me you are falling in love with the girl." He set down his coffee mug next to the coaster and sat up.

"Don't be ridiculous," I said. "I don't love her. She is nothing more than a means to an end. Well, several ends. A woman like that is a tool used only to combine and grow empires."

"Then why the rush?" He leaned forward and narrowed his eyes, searching me for any weakness. I refused to let him see the truth, so I explained it in a way I knew he could understand, even if it was complete bullshit.

"Because Harrison is smart, and I want to make sure this is a done deal before he catches on to what we are actually doing. He is preoccupied right now, preparing for elections. But eventually, he will check in on his family, and I don't want there to be any possible avenues for him to step in and stop any of this."

"You worry too much. I doubt he would care about one of the women in his family. Besides, we can just threaten to expose his true parentage, and he will fall in line just like his slut mother."

"That isn't—" A thud sounded in the hallway, and I turned to look. It was empty, but I could have sworn I heard something.

"Don't be such a little bitch. The contract is signed, the girl is ruined, the boy is still a bastard, and the Astrids will do whatever we say. Tonight, you will join me. We'll go to the club for a proper celebration. But until then, we need to discuss what our plans are for the new distilleries."

My father kept talking, but I was still looking into the hallway, sure I heard something.

"I still want to move up the wedding."

"Give me one good reason." My father rolled his eyes.

"My sisters. Olivia. She will need to be settled soon. She shouldn't marry until I do. Charlotte is also of age. We need to prepare them for their own matches."

I kicked myself for not bringing them up first. All I ever had to do was show why something would be good for him and he would go along.

My father stroked his chin as he thought that over. "That is a valid point. Okay. We will move it up to this fall or winter."

"Fall. Let's just get it over with so we can move on. I will have Henry make a list of wedding planners for Amelia to call and get everything started."

There was another sound further down the hall.

It was probably a cleaning lady, letting herself in.

Amelia was safe in bed, still asleep. Right now, I just needed to get rid of my father, then go back to bed and spend some more quality time with her, getting to know every single inch of her body.

Later, we'd discuss moving up the ceremony and what she needed me to do to help her plan the wedding of her dreams. I suddenly didn't want to leave all the plans for her and my sisters. I wanted to be involved.

My sisters were another concern. I had to find matches for them that were advantageous enough for my father to agree but to men who would actually treat them right. I didn't want them to end up with men who would treat them like I had first treated Amelia, or worse. They deserved better. I wanted them with honorable men, and those were few in my world.

Amelia Mae Astrid was more than I could have ever dreamed. I had nearly ruined any chance of happiness with her, but after last night, I believed she was giving me a second chance and I wanted to prove to her I deserved it.

When I heard the front door close, I got a sick feeling in my stomach.

The cleaning lady was probably just letting herself out.

She usually came in the mornings to check the fridge, then went shopping.

That had to be it.

CHAPTER 30

AMELIA

*H*ot tears flowed down my face as I crept back through the condo to Luc's bedroom.

I was so stupid.

I had believed his honeyed lies.

He had told me he wanted to be with me.

I thought we'd bonded over s'mores and sex. The sex had been different from all those other times. It had felt intimate, affectionate, and just so much more than it had been before. He had been sweet, gentle, and it was deeper, more personal. It felt like an expression of affection and intimacy, instead of the previous carnal shows of possession.

It had all been an act.

Now I just needed to figure out what to do with all this new information.

After hearing what Mr. Manwarring said to Luc, and how he didn't deny it, I felt ill. He'd laughed. He'd thought I was still asleep in his bed, and he was sitting in his office with his father, laughing about how I was a stupid, ruined little girl.

He was only trying to make me happy to placate me into

marrying him faster, so my brother didn't stop the wedding. No, they weren't worried about him stopping the wedding. They were worried about my brother insisting on more favorable terms. That's what I was, a bargaining chip, just another line on a contract. They wanted this contract done so they could move on and arrange his sisters' marriages next.

Just the thought of more young women having to go through all of this made my stomach roll. Listening to them talk about his sisters made me realize once this was done, my family would likewise move on to the next Astrid daughter.

I had been sold to a monster to keep a secret.

What was Rose going to have to endure at the hands of whomever my mother deemed appropriate?

And hearing that Harrison and I didn't have the same father.

My stoic, protective older brother, who always cared for me and Rose. He'd even shielded us from Mother when we were younger. And he was a bastard.

My heart broke for him.

Scandals like that could destroy him, not to mention make my father the laughingstock of the city.

Marco's words from yesterday echoed in my head.

What if I just left and decided to live my own life? What if I took my life into my own hands and designed the life I wanted to live?

Could I escape the gilded decadence that defined my life? That defined my everything.

It was not like I was doing any good here.

With a determination I was pretty sure would fade the moment I left, I got dressed, stealing sweatpants and an undershirt from Luc's drawers. I grabbed his cell phone, since mine was still at the house.

As quietly as possible, I snuck toward the front door.

When I reached the office again and had to pass the open

door, Luc and his father were heavily debating someone's involvement in a new distillery.

I glimpsed inside.

His father was still sitting at his desk, leaning back in the chair and staring at the ceiling, looking like he didn't want to have that conversation again.

Luc was talking with a determination I hadn't seen before. My heart raced, and I hated how even seeing the back of his head and hearing his voice was enough to make me ache for him.

It didn't matter; he was distracted.

It was now or never.

As I was about to take a step to pass the door, he stood up, and I froze. He leaned over the desk, planting his fists on the wooden surface. His tone was lowered to a whisper, but I could hear the anger in his words. It didn't matter what he was saying. His back was to me, and his body would block his father's view of the door. I was able to slide by undetected.

Once I made it to the front door, the rest was easy.

It took less than forty-five minutes for me to be standing outside the Astrid mansion gate, waiting for Rose.

I was leaning against the wrought iron bars, sticking close to make sure I couldn't be seen from the estate's windows.

My mother's rooms were on the other end of the mansion. Logically, I knew she wouldn't be looking out the windows, anyway. This early on a Saturday, she would be sleeping off the hangover.

Finally, I saw Rose as she ran down the lawn in a pink dress and bare feet with two duffle bags hanging from her arms.

"Okay, this one has your phone, and like a week's worth of clothes." She passed the bag through the iron bars. "This one has a few high-end handbags and pieces of jewelry that you should be able to pawn for immediate cash."

"Thank you."

"Don't thank me for this. All of this is yours and the maids already had it packed and ready. Thank me for calling Harrison." She shrugged.

"You what?" I had told her not to tell anyone. I needed to be gone before anyone knew to look for me. "Is he going to tell Mother?"

Fuck, I didn't even want to think about what would happen if she caught me. "Or is he calling Luc?"

"Oh, it's Luc now?" She raised a brow at me.

"What is Harrison going to do?" I didn't have time for her to grill me about the familiar name I used for the man I was running away from.

"Harrison thinks this is a good idea. He doesn't like what Mother is forcing you to do. He says it's barbaric and outdated. I asked him to transfer some money into your accounts, and he said that Mother's name is still on them, so she can track them. He says he is going to get her name off those accounts and once he does, he will contact you and send you some money to help get you settled."

I reached through the bars and hugged my sister, happy tears stinging my eyes. "Thank you."

"He is the one that suggested selling the purses and jewelry for cash. Our brother can be surprisingly useful."

"Yes, he can," I said.

Words couldn't express how grateful I was, just knowing I had one male sibling who saw me as a person and not a bargaining chip.

"Do you know where you are going?" she asked, worrying her bottom lip.

"Not yet, and you know what? For the first time, I think that is exciting." I smiled like I believed what I was saying.

Truth was, despite the summer heat, I had a cold, creeping feeling of dread.

I was terrified.

I had traveled before, of course, but always with my mother, sister, or a group of friends.

Never on my own; never like this.

Anxiety was bubbling away in my stomach, and I wanted to throw up, then hide under a blanket like a child, but that was not an option.

She gave me a bright smile. "That is awesome, but go before they figure out you are gone, and have a room ready for me in case Mother pulls this stunt with me, too."

"You got it. Here, take this." I handed her Luc's phone. "Give it to him when he comes looking for me."

"I'll give it to Harrison and let him decide what to do with it."

"Even better." I hugged my sister through the wrought iron bars one more time.

"I'm going to miss you," she whispered, holding me tighter.

"I already miss you," I said back before pulling out of her tight embrace and turning toward the nearest subway station.

The pawn shop was easier than I expected. Several were located not too far from where I was, just a few quick subway stops down.

I entered the first one, which had an Alexander McQueen bag in the window.

The attendant, an older woman with deep lines, bottle-blonde hair, and massive hoop earrings, was sitting behind the counter. She was nice enough to let me use her bathroom to change into my own clothes, popping her gum and pointing the way with a long, bright-pink stiletto fingernail.

I got changed into another summer dress I remembered buying at Saks last summer. Mother had curled her lip at the red paisley flutter dress by Tommy Hilfiger, but I loved it. It felt young, free, and the hem was just short enough for me to be a little daring.

The maids could have packed this, but I liked to think there was a reason it was in the bag Rose grabbed for me. It was a sign. I needed to be free and daring.

I slipped on the dress and a pair of comfortable wedges. Holding the clothes I stole from Luc, I considered throwing them in the trash can, but they still smelled like him. In a moment of weakness, I stuffed them into my bag and went back out to the front desk.

When I approached the counter, she was flipping through a Vogue magazine, looking uninterested until I started pulling designer bags from the duffle.

I set a few Saint Laurent bags, a Gucci from this season, and three Hermès Birkin bags all on the glass counter.

She immediately wrapped her hands around the Birkin made from ostrich leather dyed to a creamy color called Parchemin. I didn't think I had ever even carried that bag. I had asked for the one in a rich sky blue called Bleu France, but Mother had decided the ostrich was more ladylike.

"You steal these?" The attendant examined the bags and jewelry as I laid them out on the dingy, scratched glass counter.

"No, I'm Amelia Mae Astrid. You can call the designers and give them the serial numbers on the inside lip of the bags. They will confirm I'm the owner." I handed her my ID. "Just please don't tell anyone I'm here."

"One minute. I have the database. You aren't the first wealthy woman that needed to buy herself a new life." She tapped away on her computer as I looked around the small, dusty shop. It was full of lost treasures, and I wondered what had happened to make people give up pieces of their lives.

I considered what she had just said—not the first woman who needed to buy a new life. What did that say about my world if this had happened before, and from the sounds of it, fairly often? I didn't have time to think about those women. Right now, I needed to worry about myself.

A pendant in the corner caught my eye. It was bright red, almost orange, and the way it caught the light was stunning. It was large and clunky, and my mother would call it garish.

"How much for this?" I asked. The attendant looked over the rim of her glasses.

"You don't want that, it's not really your style." She motioned to the things I was selling, all high-priced, dainty, and chic.

"Maybe I am looking for a new style."

She regarded me for a second and nodded before unlocking the case and pulling the necklace out. "It's a Mexican fire opal. This one is large but flawed. I can give it to you for two hundred and fifty dollars."

"Sold." I shouldn't be buying anything. I needed to save my money, at least until Harrison was able to get my bank accounts freed from my parents.

"Okay. I checked out the bags. You are good to go. I can buy all of them today except for this Birkin. There isn't enough in the till." She reluctantly handed me back the bag that I had thought was just dull.

"Tell you what, could you trade it for that red Alexander McQueen bag in the window?"

"The large bucket?" she asked, curling her lip.

"That is the one."

"That's nowhere near the same cost."

"Then call it a bargain. Or put the money for the McQueen bag in yourself and take home the Birkin." I shrugged. "Your choice."

Her eyes lit up. For so many women, owning a Birkin bag was something that they could only dream of. Even if they could get the money together, it was still almost impossible to get their hands on one.

"Are you sure?" Her eyes were still huge.

"Yes, but I need you to do me a favor."

"Anything."

* * *

I TOOK my cash and my new imperfect fire opal necklace and red purse and caught a cab to Penn Station.

Twenty minutes later, I was standing waiting for my train, holding a ticket with another woman's name on it.

I looked up at the beautiful skylights and watched the darker clouds move in when a streak of lightning struck across the sky.

Thirty seconds later, thunder rattled the glass panes, and a light summer rain started. In minutes, it was pouring, and the rain beat down on the glass ceiling.

It seemed appropriate. I'd hated the rain in the summer when I was younger, the way the air seemed to hang heavy right before the sky opened up. It would be hot and humid, then the rain would force us inside. It made everything wet, and the bright blue sky was replaced with a depressing gray.

It took me a while to understand that rain could be wonderful.

Just before it rained and while it stormed, I was miserable, stuck inside but after... After the rain, that was what was important.

The sky came back, seeming stronger, more brilliant than before.

The sun dried the dampness, and everything was brighter, cleaner, and fresher. It was like looking at the world through a window that had just been cleaned, even though you hadn't realized how dirty it was.

It was a fresh start.

Was this my summer storm?

Would everything be hard and depressing for a bit, but brighter when I reached the other side? Could this be what I needed to reset my life?

The loudspeaker came on, announcing my train's arrival. A few moments later, it pulled into the station and people disembarked. I gathered my stuff, ready to find my seat, when a text from Rose pinged on my phone telling me that Luc was at the house looking for me and raging.

Harrison had arrived just before he did and was handling him.

Little dots appeared on the screen. She was ready to fill me in on all the drama. I closed the message and turned off my phone as I boarded the first train west, not sure when or where I would get off.

I sat in my economy seat and leaned against the window, just staring out at the station, then the city I called home. I daydreamed about Chicago, or Los Angeles, or maybe some little, tiny town in Arizona or Colorado, where no one knew or cared who the Astrids or Manwarrings were.

The day's adrenaline had finally worn off as the train pulled from the station, and I realized I had no idea what I was doing.

I didn't know how to do anything myself. I had no actual skills, no trade, no friends or family I could turn to, and I had a limited amount of money.

Suddenly, despite the midday rain already slowing and the sun peeking from the clouds again, I felt cold, alone, and scared. I watched the city I loved disappear behind me and wondered if I had just made a huge mistake.

CHAPTER 31

LUC

*I*t took forever to get my father out of my goddamned condo.

He wanted to go over everything in excruciating detail.

It had to be intentional. He wanted to rehash the finer points of the contracts we made with Astrid over and over like it wasn't already a signed and done deal. This man wasn't planning. He was gloating, and it was tedious. Then he wanted to relive the moment I put Mrs. Astrid in her place.

He found this particularly amusing. If I hadn't been in such a rush to get back to my warm bed with my beautiful bride, I would've told him what happened when Mrs. Astrid had shown up unannounced here. But I didn't want to risk him asking so many questions that the story took longer to tell than it did to happen.

After that, he insisted on talking about other business, mostly having to do with the men I wanted out of our business. They were too much of a legal risk, even if the DA was family. If I was being frank, I also didn't want them anywhere near my wife.

Finally, after he drank most of my coffee, I convinced him to get out, and I was ready to crawl back into bed and wake Amelia for another round. I even toyed with the idea of rousing her by licking her perfect little pussy and making her come on my tongue. Maybe that would be a new part of my morning ritual.

After all, my good girl deserved a treat. My cock hardened as I thought about her, still in my bed, wrapped in nothing but my sheets. I couldn't help my smile as I headed from my front door back to my bedroom, my cock tenting my silk sleep pants.

When I got back to the bedroom, I knew something was wrong even before I opened the door. It felt wrong, lifeless. Hollow. I pushed open the door and my heart stopped. The bed was empty. My heart started hammering as I checked the closet and the bathroom. They were both empty.

She was gone.

No, no, no, no.

I searched every inch of the condo. There was no sign of her. The bed was cold, and I had no idea how long she had been gone. My phone was gone, too.

Fuck!

My heart was beating out of my chest, and it felt like I couldn't get enough air. Spots danced in front of my vision as I picked up the landline and called my head of security.

"Did you see her leave?" I demanded the second he picked up.

"Yes, a little over an hour ago. I pinged you when she left. She got in a rideshare and went back to the Astrid manor."

I slammed down the phone and got dressed. I had no idea why she'd left—if someone got to her, if something happened. Had she heard my father? Had something happened at her parents' house? Had she just realized I didn't deserve a second chance? Or worse, had she seen who I really was last night and decided she couldn't be with me?

* * *

THE MORE I was at this awful house, the more I hated it, with the antiquated details of its old-world décor and the figures above the arch that seemed to mock me as I marched up to the front door. I banged on the door with the side of my closed fist until someone finally opened it.

I expected a maid, or maybe even Mr. or Mrs. Astrid. What I got was a very annoyed Harrison Astrid, still in a three-piece suit straight from the office despite it being early afternoon on a Saturday. He stepped up to me, forcing me to back away and down a few steps, making him several inches taller. He always did like to hover over people. It was as if he knew the best ways to increase the intimidation and power he held with minimal effort.

"What do you think you are doing?" He towered over me, and I knew it was an intimidation tactic that I would normally not let go unanswered, but I had more important things to worry about.

He had to terrify criminals and people who got in his way. He had to present as a stern-faced, meticulously put-together lawyer who could rain down hellfire while he stared into their soul. I wasn't a criminal. Well, at least not that he knew of. I had no soul for him to stare into, and I had no intentions of backing away from his sister.

"Where is she?" I demanded.

"She isn't here," he said. "You know, I thought better of you, Luc. I knew you were a ruthless businessman. It's not a secret that your family interprets the law as they see fit, loving to bend it in all kinds of directions but never quite seeming to break it. I knew you were going after my sister to fuck with Dubois."

"What is your point?" I didn't have time for this.

"I let it stand because, frankly, I dislike that oily little weasel a fair bit more than I dislike you. But I didn't think you would be so vindictive when it came to your personal life."

"I don't have time for this, Harrison. Where is Amelia? She is mine. She belongs with me."

"No, she doesn't. You had your chance to do right by her. You squandered it."

"Harrison, I swear to God, if you don't give her back to me, I'll—"

"You'll what? What will you do, Luc? Tell the world I'm a bastard? The product of my mother having an affair?" He leaned in, forcing me to take another step back.

"You knew?"

"Of course I knew. I have known for years. I found out in high school when we tested our blood types."

He was so calm, so direct, he may as well have been saying the sky was blue. Though right now, clouds seemed to gather above us. "Had I known this was what you used to entrap my family, I would have let you know weeks ago. I intend on making the information public so no one else can use it against me."

"You can't. It will destroy—"

"It will destroy nothing but your hold on my family, and maybe my mother's reputation, but so be it." He shrugged.

"What?"

"My father didn't put me in office, the people of New York County did, and let me tell you a little secret. The people of Manhattan are not all over-privileged elitists that look down on others because of an accident of birth. It will do nothing to me or my career, except maybe make me a little more relatable to the average voter."

"Look, Harrison, this is fascinating, but it changes nothing."

"Aren't you listening? It changes everything. You have no claim to my sister."

"Please, just let me talk to her."

A lump formed in my throat, and I could see the future I had envisioned with her and our children slip through my fingers. "I need to at least talk to her. Things may have started the way you said, but they've changed."

"I'm not letting you near her again." Harrison took a step back so he was under the awning as the skies opened up and rain poured from the heavens. "Besides, she left. You don't get to know where she is, but she did leave something for you."

He reached into his breast pocket, pulled out my phone, and handed it to me before turning toward the door.

"What if I told you I think I love her?"

He turned toward me and raised a brow. "Then I *think* I can't help you."

"Stop." I reached out and put my hand on the door before he could slam it in my face. "Not think. I *do* love her."

"You love her?"

"Yes, I really do. She is infuriatingly stubborn, and kind to a fault, and I love her. Tell me what it will take. I'll do anything. You don't like the deal we made last night. Fine. I'll shred that contract with your father's signature if that's what you want. You can make that other deal."

"What other deal?"

"The one with Dubois. It's fine, I won't stand in the way of you making a deal with him if that is what it takes to prove to you I love your sister. I don't give a fuck that you are the DA and her brother. She is more important. I don't give a rat's ass that your empire can bolster mine. I want my bride back."

My chest ached, my heart was beating so fast, and my lungs burned as I held my breath, waiting for him to say something, do something.

"If she wants you, no one here will stand in her way. But if you pursue her after she tells you no, I will personally bring you and your father down on every single charge I can come up with, regardless of whether or not they have merit. I will tie your family and your businesses up in litigation so long your lawyers are going to bleed you dry."

"How do I find her?"

"If you knew her as well as you think you do, you would already know where she is. Or you can call her, see if she picks up."

Harrison glared at my hand, still on the door, and I took a step back. Before slamming it in my face, he turned to face me. "Regardless of what happens next, I won't be doing business with Dubois, like I won't be doing you any favors. The contract you signed with my father was fair. It can stand."

"Okay." I started scrolling through my phone, looking for her number.

"I'm serious, Luc. I don't care who you are married to. It will not protect you or your father from the law. Not now, not ever."

"Understood," I called over my shoulder as I ran back to my car. The driver was already waiting for his next order.

Amelia's phone rang twice and went to voicemail. I tried again. Same thing.

Harrison would want me to leave it at that. Maybe try again in a few hours once she had calmed down. He said that if I knew her as well as I should that I would know where she was.

I called my security team and had them send men to the Met to look for her. Others went to the cafés along Central Park, and to cover my bases, I sent a few to Saks. My gut told me she wasn't there, but I wanted to be sure.

Then I remembered her friend. Marco, the one she had cozied up with to make me jealous. Like I didn't already know he was gay.

The dossier Henry had made for me was still in my home office. He had expanded it to include the names and numbers of all known associates. With any luck, Marco's number would be there. Maybe he'd help me.

Two phone calls and many threats, begging, and bartering later, I was still nowhere. Worse, Marco hadn't narrowed my search, he'd broadened it.

Olivia took pity on me and called Rose. She didn't know where her sister was, only that she had given Amelia enough jewelry and purses to fund a trip anywhere in the world, and she had left on foot.

Within minutes, I had travel alerts set for her across the country, using pings from her cellphone, and my men were tracking her movements on CCTV.

Even I had to admit it was creepy and underhanded, when I saw her on a grainy black-and-white screen boarding a train. Had I taken things too far?

Then I realized when it came to her, there was no distance I wouldn't go.

My beautiful bride was boarding a train heading to Los Angeles. The newer trains also had cameras, and I watched as she sat down in a row by herself and looked out the window.

Standing alone in my home office, I watched her stare out the window as she left her home, tears running down her face.

I had done this to her.

She was running from everything she knew and loved because of me.

The entire time we had been betrothed, I had been focused on what the marriage meant for me, for my business, and how she would fit into my goals.

I'd never even thought about what she wanted. What would her days look like being my wife? I had simply assumed they would be spent going to charity events, representing me at different luncheons and galas. Eventually raising my children and managing my house.

Did she actually want any of that? I sat and watched her for a little over an hour, the entire time trying to decide what the right move was.

Did I show her I loved her by letting her go?

Or did I run after her and drag her back here, force her to listen to me? To tell me what she wanted, and I would give it to her. Anything at all, anything as long as it wasn't freedom from me.

That wasn't fair. She deserved more. I picked up my phone and called my head of security to have one of my guards figure out how to get to the next train station and board so he could follow her. The very least I could do was know where she ended up and see to her safety.

She lifted her head and for a moment, I thought she was looking at me. Then I saw she was looking at the monitor under the camera. She gathered her things and stood like she was getting ready to get off at the next stop.

She couldn't be too far from New York. Why would she take a cross-country train just to get off after an hour?

"She just got off the train. Do you know where she is?"

"Yes, sir. She is in New Jersey. I have a few friends out that way. I will follow her on CCTV and keep eyes on her until I have a man there. Do you wish for us to detain her?"

"No, follow her, but stay back. I don't want her to know I have her."

"Yes, sir." The line disconnected, and I ran down to the car.

If she left, really left, I would leave her alone, but she didn't. No one ran away from home to go to Jersey.

They said if you loved something, let it go. It would always come back. That was for people who believed in destiny.

Fuck that. I was going to find her now. She was mine, and she was coming home.

I made my own destiny.

CHAPTER 32

AMELIA

I thought I'd make it at least to Chicago before I got off the train, but I only stayed on it for about an hour when I saw an ad for the Grounds for Sculpture in New Jersey.

My father had taken me there a few times as a child, and I wasn't sure if I could say that was the place where I fell in love with art, but it was definitely one of them.

The ad flicked through a few pictures of their exhibits. When I saw the sculpture of Manet's *Dejeuner Sur L'Herbe*, the luncheon in the park, I knew it was a sign. I didn't know if it was from the universe or from God, and I didn't care. I needed to see that painting rendered life-sized, in person.

It felt a little dumb to get on a west-bound train to run away from home as an adult and still only make it as far as New Jersey, but I'd walk around for a bit, gather my thoughts, and make a plan.

The rain that was pelting New York when I left hadn't touched the park. It was midafternoon, the sun was out, and the grass a brilliant green. The air was sweetly perfumed by the wisteria tunnel, and its thick bunches of purple flowers hanging down attracted honeybees, as well as butterflies with their gem-toned wings.

This place truly was paradise, and it was exactly the distraction I needed.

With the paper map clenched in my hand, I followed the paths, looking at the art, trying to find the one sculpture I needed to see. Everything was so beautiful, and under any other circumstances, I would've taken the time these sculptures deserved to appreciate each one. Not now.

Now I needed to see that woman, freed from the confines of society and expectations up close. Something told me that if I could find her, see a version of that woman nude in the grass, freed from all expectations of decency, it would help me figure out what I needed to do next. She would somehow have the answers I was looking for.

It was silly, really.

When I found the sculpture, I kicked off my shoes and sat in the grass and just thought through what I wanted. The sun felt warm on my skin. The grass was cool under me, a little damp even, but it didn't matter.

I just sat with the sculpture, first studying her, wondering what her life was, what it could have been. Was she just a prostitute, like many art historians theorized, or was she more? Did she represent more?

That was the beautiful thing about art, and many people disagreed with me, but I always felt that the meaning of a piece could differ. Each person interpreted the piece in their own way, shedding the artist's intentions and deciding what it said. Of course, artists had different techniques to bring out specific qualities, but ultimately it was up to the viewer to see what they wanted and feel what they felt. Each person could have a different interpretation. Or maybe it was the same interpretation but through a different lens.

Each time I did something for me, something that I wanted, my mother insinuated I was a willful girl and a whore.

Was a woman who lived on her own terms, selling her body? Was saying it was so, a way to keep those women down and discredit them? Was I willing to let that happen to me? Did I care what society said?

No, I didn't. The only way I would be in good standing in society was if I married Luc, chained myself to a man who used me for a business deal, and just accepted that was all my life was ever going to be.

The more I thought about it, the less I found that acceptable. It was time for me to take control of my own life and live for me, not for society.

I thought it was the first time I considered wanting something that did not exist within the confines of my mother's expectations. The opportunities were limitless for a young woman of means. I just had to decide what I wanted to do with my life.

Sitting there for an hour, staring at the woman who might have been a prostitute, I could only come up with a single answer. I had no idea what it would look like, but I wanted to live my life.

Live, not exist to serve the needs of others. Not to be solely a wife or a mother, but to experience everything life had to offer: challenges, struggles, victories, and defeat. I didn't want to live in some bubble anymore, surrounded, both figuratively and literally, with endless shades of beige. My life needed color, and I intended to give it just that.

First thing I had to do was return.

Nowhere else in the world compared to New York, and I didn't want to give up the Met, and the smaller galleries in Soho and Brooklyn.

Why should I have to? New York was massive. And how hard

would it be to hide from Luc and my mother? The sad fact was that I didn't want to leave New York. I would always be a true New Yorker. It was in my blood. All I wanted was out from under my mother's thumb, and I didn't want to replace her control with Luc's.

New York was the most populated city in the country, and my mother stayed in a tiny block of the Upper East Side. Luc probably never left the Financial District. That gave me every-where else.

I could find a place in the city and hide in plain sight. The closest I had ever come to freedom had been college, and even then, I'd had a dorm room but had rarely been allowed to stay there. Mother wanted me home every night, which was fine. I'd told myself it was a reasonable compromise, but now...

I needed that time. For most people, college was their first taste of freedom and how they became who they were meant to be. I needed to figure out who I was, what I wanted, and what I was capable of. I needed the chance to fail.

Thinking about what I was going to do next, I stood up, brushed the dirt from my dress, and wandered aimlessly through the gardens, looking to the statues for some inspiration.

Even if I did return to the city and made it on my own, it left one large gaping hole in my life.

Luc Manwarring.

Even after hearing everything he'd said in his office, I wanted him. I hated myself for it, but it was true. I missed him in a way I didn't know was possible, that went bone deep.

A particular bronze statue caught my eye, and I headed toward it.

It was called *First Love*, and it was beautiful. Two figures sat next to each other, the more feminine one leaning on the chest of the more masculine one.

They were intertwined in an embrace, apparently completely

absorbed in that intimate moment, like nothing happening outside of their own little world was relevant. As long as they had each other, nothing could touch them.

That was what I wanted, a man who saw me as an equal, who was as enraptured with me as I was with him.

Was that kind of love too much to ask for?

If I had been asked yesterday if Luc was capable of that connection, I would have laughed.

That was before he'd played the part of my dark prince and pulled me out of my mother's clutches. The way we'd talked, the way he'd touched me, aiming to give pleasure instead of taking it… I just didn't know.

Then I'd heard him with his father, and I no longer knew which Luc was the real one. Was he the sweet man who'd fed me chocolate and marshmallows, the lonely boy who'd grown up in a drafty boarding school, or the ruthless man who'd laughed about blackmailing my mother to win my hand and my father's business deals?

Were any of them the real Luc? Were all of them? How was I supposed to determine which were real and which were acts?

My gut told me the lonely boy was the real Luc, but how was I supposed to know for sure? How could I trust that my gut wasn't lying to me because I missed his touch? Love had to be the enemy of logic.

This statue made me think of him, and I hated it for that.

It made me think of the way Luc held me the night before in front of the fire. It made me remember how it felt to be next to him, laughing and eating s'mores like a regular couple wanting to know more about each other. Wanting to know secret things, intimate things, things only the other knew.

I wanted the kind of intimacy those words promised me, the kind of intimacy given for its own sake, not to feign attachment with lies for power and money.

"Amelia." He called my name, and I wasn't even surprised he'd found me.

I thought I always knew it didn't matter where I went, he would find me. "Amelia."

He was dressed in his usual designer pants and black polo shirt, a style that made him appear both relaxed and somewhat sinister. My heart raced at just seeing him. I wanted to run into his arms and make him promise to never let me go.

I didn't.

He ran toward me, and I considered fleeing, but it was no use.

I stood my ground.

I turned and looked up at the statue again, perched up high on a stucco wall, and I wondered if that was the key to this piece. It looked so close; it looked achievable until you neared it, and you realized the figures were perched so far above you. That relationship, that kind of security, would always be just beyond my reach.

"Amelia." Luc finally reached me, panting. Upon closer inspection, he was a mess. His hair was disheveled, his clothing wrinkled, and small bags had formed under his eyes.

I didn't say anything and waited for him to share whatever he had come here to say. Maybe if he said the right thing, looking at him wouldn't hurt so much. Maybe he would say the words that would make me realize he could be the man I wanted him to be.

"Amelia, come home." He reached for my hand, and I took a step back.

That wasn't it.

"Amelia, let's go home. We will take the weekend to talk everything over and make a plan for the wedding. Just come home."

"No. I can't."

"You can. Every night can be like last night. We can get

married, and everything will settle down. Just come home with me."

Everything else would settle. That was what he chose to say. Everything else would settle. What he meant was I would be trapped. The business deal would be done, and I would be trapped in a gilded cage for the rest of my life.

That wasn't living. "Leave me alone."

CHAPTER 33

LUC

"*D*on't let her know you are there unless she tries to leave. I'm on my way," I yelled into the phone before throwing it in the passenger seat.

The agent had found her and followed her to a sculpture park. I had broken every traffic law on the way there. It didn't matter.

It took far too long to reach her.

The traffic was terrible.

It should have only taken me a little over an hour to get there, or maybe a little under an hour, since I was more than prepared to ignore the speed limit. Instead, it was two hours of pure panic trying to get to Amelia before she left and was gone forever. Somehow, I knew that if she was gone before I got to that park, that was it. This was going to be my last chance to convince her I was worth her time and attention.

Those two hours driving on I-95 gave me time to reflect, not only on every time I'd scared or intimidated her, but also on the filthy things I'd said to her.

Yes, at first I'd assumed she was more experienced than she

was, but that didn't matter. Whether I'd been the first man to touch her or not, I should have treated her with more respect.

Even if that could be excused, what the fuck was my excuse after I took her virginity the night of the opera? After that, I had known how innocent she was. Still, I'd pushed, and I'd punished her for her mother's indiscretions and for my mistakes.

The filthy things I'd whispered in her ear, how I'd touched her, how I'd made her touch me.

My stomach tightened with shame.

I should have been gentle. I should have guided her, taught her the art of making love, or at least helped her discover what she liked.

Instead, I had taken her, bent her body to my will, and used her.

The fact that I'd made her come for me over and over didn't help. I hadn't done that to give her pleasure. I'd done it to make her cunt grip my cock tighter and to make sure she knew I was the only one who could make her feel that way. It was just another way to exert my power and control over her.

Fuck, no wonder she'd run. I hadn't given her any other options.

I had thought I'd started to make up for that with the way we'd been in front of the fire. That had been a classic romantic moment not fueled by anger, rage, or even lust. That had been the only time we'd been together that was about more than my control.

It wasn't enough. It didn't matter that she'd matched me touch for touch. She'd still been following my lead, been the perfect little submissive girl. She deserved better.

My fists trembled as I tightened my grip on the steering wheel, heat flushing my face. More than once, I considered pulling over as my stomach rolled in disgust at my own actions.

There wasn't time. I needed to reach her. I needed to make

this right. Even the idea of having to live my life without her made a cold sweat break out over my skin as I screamed at the car in front of me for being stuck behind the same traffic accident.

"Fucking move!" I screamed again as we inched up another few feet and stopped. The driver in the car I yelled at flipped me off and the people in the car next to mine were staring.

"What the fuck are you looking at?" I snarled at them. It wasn't their fault I was behaving like a monster. It wasn't even the fault of the person in front of me. He was stuck in the same never-ending traffic jam I was.

This was my fault. All of it. Amelia leaving, my father still in control of my business and my empire. Everything was on me, and I was losing my fucking mind, banging on the steering wheel, yelling obscenities that would make even the vilest of sailors stand up and slow clap.

Self-control was something I thought I had, but apparently not when it came to her. Amelia Mae Astrid was my new favorite vice, the one thing that would make me lose my composure and my goddamned mind. Years spent perfecting the art of never letting my emotions show, never exposing my weakness to anyone, and here I was heading to New fucking Jersey in a panic. I was raging like a lunatic because I'd fucked up with the one person who didn't deserve my wrath.

By the time I was speeding through East Brunswick, I realized it didn't matter if I wanted her, not really, because I wasn't good enough. I didn't deserve her, and she certainly didn't deserve to be shackled to me. She deserved someone who always treated her with love and respect.

When I went through Cranbury, I prayed it wasn't too late, and by the time I merged onto the 195, I realized that if she would let me, I would spend the rest of my life making up for the mistakes I had made. All she had to do was give me a chance. I would prove that I could be a man worthy of her love.

I wanted to be a better man for her.

When I finally arrived, I alerted my security team and ran into the park.

"Where is she?" I asked when a man in dark glasses and a black suit approached me at the entrance. Inconspicuous he was not. Fuck it, it didn't matter.

"I left her sitting by the lake. Looking at a sculpture of some people in the park. She has been there for the last hour, not speaking to anyone or doing anything, just sitting."

He handed me the map, and when he pointed out the area she was in, I immediately knew which sculpture she had been sitting with. The way she had talked about that Manet painting at the Met, the different things seeing that naked woman in the park made her feel, there was no other choice. She had to be there.

She loved that painting, and if she was leaving me, leaving the life she was born into, it made sense that was the painting she would want to think on.

I sprinted all the way across the park in the blistering heat and suffocating humidity, dodging hanging purple flowers, insects, and aimlessly wandering tourists. This place was hellish, but if she liked it, then it was my new favorite place. I would bring her here every fucking weekend.

When I found the sculpture, she was gone. The only sign she had ever been there was a small dent in the grass where she must have sat.

"Amelia!" I called out.

A few random people milling about looked at me, but none were her.

I removed the map from my pocket and searched for other sculptures she might head toward. The muses on the lake seemed like something an artist would want to see, so I went in that direction.

With every step, I scanned the groups of sweaty tourists in their cheap shirts and denim shorts until I spotted my goddess standing in the middle of the field. She looked amazing in her red dress, as she just stopped and stared at a sculpture. She was so absorbed in her thoughts, she hadn't even noticed the group of men gawking at her.

One of them took a few steps toward her, like he was going to start up a conversation. I signaled for the security team, who stepped in and handled it before she even had any idea that they were there.

Her lack of awareness of her surroundings was somewhat concerning, but that was a problem for later. What was important now was that I had found her.

She was staring up at a massive bronze statue of two people sitting next to each other, embracing.

My heart stopped as I observed her, taking in the way she studied the art with pain in her eyes—pain I'd put there, pain I would spend the rest of my life trying to erase.

I called out to her, and she looked up at me, the expressionless mask sliding over her features. I hated that mask. The few times I had seen her without it had been the most real. With it, I couldn't tell what she was thinking or how she was feeling.

"Amelia, come home."

I reached for her hand, and she took a step back.

"Amelia, let's go home. We will take the weekend to talk everything over and make a plan for the wedding. Just come home."

"No. I can't."

"You can. Every night can be like last night. We can get married, and everything will settle down. Just come home with me."

That wasn't living. "Leave me alone."

"Amelia, you have to listen to me," I pleaded as I grabbed her hands in both of mine. I had never begged anyone for anything, but for her, I would fall to my knees.

"I really don't, Luc. I heard everything." She tried to pull her hands from mine. I tightened my grip. I wasn't ready to let her go.

"Tell me what you think you heard?"

"I heard why you want to marry me. Look, I'm not stupid. I knew from the beginning this was about business, but then you pretended to care for me, and I fell for it. And you know what? That's fine. I'm not mad at you. I'm not even mad at myself anymore. You just made me realize a few things."

"What's that?" I pulled her into my body. I needed to feel her. I needed to know she was back in my arms, safe where she belonged.

"It made me realize I'm not okay with a loveless marriage. I don't want my life to be part of some merger. I'm not the cherry on top of a bottom line, or a signing bonus."

The honesty in her eyes said her mind was made up, but I couldn't accept that.

"That's not—"

"Stop. You said you would never lie to me." She pulled away from my embrace. "I know why and how you stopped my wedding to Dubois, and frankly, I'm grateful. You saved me from a tedious existence that would no doubt eventually turn me into my mother. But blackmail isn't—"

"The blackmail is over. Harrison knows," I interrupted.

How was I fucking this up so badly?

"He had always known, and so had your father. Harrison is planning on going public with it, but even if he doesn't, I wouldn't use that information against your family."

"It doesn't matter." She stepped back.

"It does. I…"

Fuck, I had never done this before, and I didn't know what the right thing was to say.

How did I prove to this woman that I wanted her, not her family connections, not to screw over Dubois, but I just wanted her?

"What you overheard with my father, that was me letting him talk. I don't know what exactly you heard, but I don't agree with a thing he said. I just wanted him out of my house so I could climb back into my bed with you."

She merely looked at me, her emerald eyes big, bright, and filling with tears. Tears had to be a good sign. I prayed that it had to mean that she felt something for me. If she was indifferent, then she wouldn't have been about to cry. She was so beautiful, standing in the middle of the field, the lake behind her and the breeze blowing through her dark hair.

Even on the verge of tears, she was breathtakingly beautiful, and I knew without a shadow of a doubt she was the future I wanted. Whatever she wanted that to look like, I was in.

"Amelia, look, last night was the best night I have ever had. It was the first time I have ever done anything like that. I want more of that, more of us."

"I really liked it, too, but…" She gazed off to the side and pulled away from me.

"Then come home with me. Let me show you that every night can be like that. Come home, move in with me, and let's plan the wedding you want, that we want."

"Luc… I…"

"Amelia, baby, when we got engaged, I didn't ask for your hand. I blackmailed your mother. Now, I am asking. The blackmail is gone. It does not exist, and even if it did, I wouldn't use it. I am asking you."

I dropped to one knee in the grass and held her hand in mine.

259

"Amelia Mae Astrid, will you do me the honor of letting me love you, cherish, and provide for you? Will you be my wife?"

She looked at me for several long moments, tears streaming down her beautiful face, and looking directly into my eyes, she said the one word that destroyed me.

"No."

CHAPTER 34

AMELIA

ne Month Later

THE CRISP SEPTEMBER breeze finally displaced New York's August humidity.

Fall was pushing its way in, and the city seemed eager for summer to end.

In the evenings, the sidewalks were full of people walking hand in hand.

What was it about New York City and couples? The second someone became single, it was like every happy couple in New York got a text message to go outside and be in love around the miserable, lonely people. All I saw every single day were beautiful, happy couples in love.

It was just rude.

After I left Luc in the sculpture gardens, I took a cab back to the city and called my brother.

Harrison helped me secure my first, very own apartment in

Dumbo, a trendy Brooklyn neighborhood that was just far enough away that I would never see my mother.

He helped me set up everything and made himself available whenever I needed him, but also gave me the space I needed to figure out what I wanted to do.

Rose had even started coming over more and spending the night. She had also begun to distance herself from our mother. Something had happened that pushed her to rebel more, but she wouldn't talk about it, saying that she would when she was ready.

It was odd, but after only a week of having my own place, surrounded by color and life, I felt lighter. I no longer felt like every decision could make or break me.

The world wasn't out to get me, and I didn't have to impress anyone.

I started living for myself; it was new, and I loved it.

I also felt closer to my siblings. There was so much about Harrison that I didn't know, and Rose seemed like a different person when we weren't both under our mother's roof.

It only took a few days of ignoring my mother's calls while soul searching, missing Luc, and talking to Harrison for me to make a plan.

I needed to be useful.

Thankfully, Harrison also strong-armed our mother into making sure I got every single penny of my trust fund. He was overseeing all of it for me and managing the investments, so I had enough money to be comfortable.

It wasn't the lavish lifestyle I had in the mansion, not by a long shot, but I was adapting.

I had enough money that I didn't need to work, but I had no interest in squandering my days shopping and dining at cafés. I was convinced that was what turned women like my mother into bored, hateful shrews—women who had no real purpose and no drive, so they spent their time trying to outdo each other. Be it with self-serving "charity" work, becoming the new middle-aged "it girl," or outspending each other in the plastic surgeon's office.

That life seemed shallow, and I couldn't do it.

I just had no idea what I could do. My education had never been intended to be training for a career. I had no experience working, no marketable skills. Nothing.

"You love art," Harrison said, sitting on the dark green velvet couch I had bought at an amazing consignment shop a few blocks over. He and Rose were over that night to hang out for a dinner of Chinese takeout eaten straight from the paper boxes with disposable chopsticks.

"I do love art." I nodded, trying to hold on to a particularly slippery piece of orange chicken. "But sadly, I have no talent."

"That is ridiculous," Rose said with a wave of her hand that sent the piece of broccoli she was holding in her chopsticks flying through the air so that it hit Harrison in the face.

Rose and I fell into hysterics while he rolled his eyes and wiped his forehead with a napkin. Then he reached over to steal her container and handed her one with chow mein noodles.

"I was thinking more along the line of being a patron. Sponsoring indie artists, finding talent, then helping that artist break into the art world. Get their pieces shown, be their champion," he explained as soon as we calmed down. "You could even open your own small gallery. The family is known in the art community. We are on the board for the Met. Why not use those connections and do something similar while supporting up-and-coming artists?"

"Could I do that? I really don't want to compete for gallery space in Manhattan, and worse, Mother would try to sabotage anything I would do."

"I wasn't thinking of Manhattan. I was thinking of smaller, more modern art. Like small up-and-coming artists. Either here in Dumbo or even Williamsburg." Harrison sat back on the couch, and Rose leaned against him. They both looked tired, and I wondered what their lives would look like if they had broken away like I had.

It was tempting, but I wanted something more hands-on than cutting a check and attending the occasional party.

"That or you just give up and teach," Harrison joked. "Isn't that what they say, those that can't do, teach?"

His words struck a nerve.

Rose was quick to defend me, but it got me thinking.

He had a point. There was no way my passion could be a viable career option as an artist, but it wasn't really my art I was passionate about. It was the process. It was learning new mediums and playing with them. I had more enthusiasm and passion for the process of creating art than for the final product. Even when looking at the masters, I wanted to know what they were thinking, what they saw that they tried to convey in their work.

"Maybe my mission in life isn't to create the next great work of art, or even support someone else who does. Maybe I'm supposed to stoke that passion in others and help them find their passion," I said, interrupting an argument about chopstick etiquette.

Rose looked at me like I had lost my mind.

"Explain." Harrison set down his beer, took Rose's chopsticks out of her hand, and gave her a plastic fork.

"What if I'm supposed to teach art, maybe to kids? I know art programs are poorly funded in public schools. What if I could help fill that gap? I could create a school or an after-school program for children to learn and find their own passion."

"What would that look like?" Rose asked.

"I have no idea," I admitted. "I'd probably have to look at getting a teacher's certification. Then maybe a volunteer position or a part-time teacher's job to get some hands-on experience. Then look into what it would take to start programs or something."

Harrison had nodded then excused himself for a moment to make a call. It was weird, and he was cryptic when I asked him about the call.

It really didn't matter. Rose was even more excited about this idea than I was. With her as my personal cheerleader and Harrison's more practical help, I was enrolled in a teacher certification program within a week.

The classes were hard, and so was living on my own for the first time even if I was living in an upscale building with a doorman. But with the help of some college friends like Marco, I was acclimating to my new life of independence. I had only set the kitchen on fire twice… this week.

My life was suddenly my own. It was challenging, exciting, and sometimes a little unpredictable. The only thing I missed was him. Luc Manwarring.

Sometimes I thought I saw him or his assistant or one of his security goons out of the corner of my eye, but when I turned, they weren't there.

My days were spent full of life and new adventures.

Classes, new restaurants, the occasional club with friends, things I had not been permitted to do while under my parents' roof.

But at night, when everyone left for their own homes and I lay in bed, cold and alone, that was when loneliness and depression set in.

Most nights I dreamt about him, and I woke craving his touch.

I would also use my fingers to touch myself the way he'd touched me, thinking not just of the night he'd been gentle and adoring but also of the times he was rough and demanding.

More than once I had brought myself pleasure with my fingers clutched around my throat, applying just the right amount of pressure by squeezing the sides as I thought about his heavy breathing in my ear as he said the vilest things to me.

When he called me his whore, his desperate, needy slut, his good girl.

The more I thought about it, I wasn't sure if it was the honesty in the degradation—because for him then I had been all those things—or if it was being called his.

I missed feeling like I belonged to him, and he belonged to me.

I'd only had one night sleeping next to him in his bed, but it had changed me in a way I didn't know was possible.

Marco suggested I get over Luc by getting under a new guy. He told me to find someone with less damage and more soul, but I hadn't met a single man who could compare to Luc Manwarring, and I was afraid I never would.

It wasn't their fault. How could any normal man compare to someone so intense?

I had almost called him a few times, barely stopping myself, just wanting to know how he was, where he was, or what he was doing. I wanted to tell him about all the exciting things I was doing in my life. But I couldn't. We had never really been friends. We had been pushed together, and he probably had more important things to do than listen to me, a woman he was no longer engaged to, prattle on about her insignificant life.

He'd probably forgotten about the moment I turned him down. One call to one gossip in the clubs and society women everywhere would have their daughters dolled up and parading in front of him, ready to be chosen to take my place.

***

I was on my way back from classes, heading to my apartment and thinking about stopping to get some Mexican food so I didn't further infuriate my super by setting off the fire alarm again. I had been craving something greasy that my mother would have never let me eat in a million years. Tacos had been my current obsession. They were just the perfect food. I was focused on that when I got out of the subway and ran face-first into a very familiar suit-covered chest.

"Amelia." Just the sound of his voice was enough to make me ache for him.

"Mr. Manwarring." I jumped back. He raised an eyebrow. "Luc," I corrected. "What are you doing here?"

"I just left a meeting, and I was heading home. It's a lovely day, and I decided to walk."

"Oh, that's nice."

God, he smelled so good.

I didn't even question why he had an appointment on this side of the Manhattan Bridge, or why he would walk all the way back to the Financial District. I smiled as I laced my fingers together behind my back to stop myself from reaching out to touch him.

"How are you? I heard you moved out of your parents' house?"

"I did. How did you hear that?"

"Your father and brother saw the value in that business deal and held us to the contract," he explained, and my heart deflated a little. "I actually see your brother quite a bit now."

I'd hoped he had asked after me or was keeping tabs on me somehow, but that was silly. He may have been the first man in my bed, and therefore hard to replace, but he couldn't say the same about me.

Why hadn't Harrison mentioned anything?

"I'm glad it all worked out for you, in the end," I said.

"We'll see about that." He ran his fingers through his hair. "Where are you off to?"

"I'm meeting some friends for dinner," I said.

I didn't want him to know I was going home to an empty apartment with some takeout. The last thing I wanted was his pity, as he was no doubt on his way to an event or date or something.

Men like him didn't go home alone unless they wanted to, and he had no reason to.

"Some friends? Does that include a boyfriend?" He put his hands in his pockets and bounced on his toes a little.

If I didn't know better, I would have thought he was nervous.

I considered lying again, but my gut told me not to.

"No, no boyfriends. I am trying to figure out who I am, what I want. Besides, you aren't an easy act to follow."

I don't know why I said that. I really shouldn't have.

Heat rose to my cheeks. I wished I was smoother, more confident, or could at least figure out a way to run from this awkward situation with some of my dignity still intact.

"I hope you find what you are looking for, Amelia." He reached out to cup my cheek.

I wanted to lean into his touch, fall back into his arms, and never let go.

"I hope you do, too, Luc."

My eyes stung, and I swallowed the lump in my throat.

This was all my doing.

I had made my bed, and now I had to lie in it, alone. "I'll see you around."

He nodded and dropped his hand. He made to walk past me, then stopped.

I thought he was going to say something else, but he merely leaned down and placed a sweet, chaste kiss on my cheek.

I closed my eyes and held my breath, savoring the feel of his lips on my skin.

"Take care of yourself. I miss you," he whispered, the last part so low, I wasn't sure if I had heard him correctly, or if it was just in my head.

Before I could say anything else, he walked away from me.

I watched him disappear into the crowd before I turned and headed to my new home and the life I had chosen.

CHAPTER 35

LUC

*R*unning into Amelia earlier hadn't been part of the plan.

I should have known better than to tempt fate and walk around her neighborhood.

No, I wasn't on her normal path home, but I knew she took that route if she decided to pick up dinner on the way home.

There had been no avoiding it. I'd had to pick up the keys from the contractor, and I'd underestimated how much time it would take to finish going over everything.

It had required every ounce of my control not to say fuck the plan and beg her to take me back right then. Walking away from her was the hardest thing I had ever done, and I had no intention of ever doing it again.

But I had a plan, and I wanted to see it through.

I had to practically run from Amelia to get the keys to Rose so she could play her part. Harrison had given me the information I needed. Now Rose was helping with the execution.

I just hoped it was enough.

I stood in front of her door in a newer high-rise, a condo I had vetted and given Harrison the money to buy for Amelia.

It had taken a lot of convincing and several legal contracts stating that I was giving Amelia the money and expected nothing in return. Her mother had locked Amelia's trust fund up in miles of red tape, ensuring that she didn't get a cent until she was married.

So, with Harrison's help, I had given her what she was owed, which was a drop in the bucket compared to what she would have had access to as my wife. I made sure that she had the freedom to live her life and figure out her purpose.

Security was always watching her, not to spy but to make sure she was safe from muggers, rapists, and her mother.

Her mother was the largest threat. She had paid actors to pretend to mug Amelia and scare her into coming home.

Thanks to me, they never got close to her.

When that happened, I passed the information on to Harrison and let him handle his mother.

Once I knew Amelia was safe, I let her live her life while I moved to part two of my plan. With her sister's help, I built something just for her.

Now it was time to give it to her, hope she accepted my gift, and pray it was enough of a grand gesture to convince her I was worthy of a second chance.

I knocked again and heard some moving around in the apartment. I didn't think I had ever been this nervous. My heart raced as the chain lock jingled as she made sure it was in place before opening the door.

Good girl.

"Luc, what are you doing here?" she asked through the gap in the door.

Her hair was piled in a messy bun on her head, cute Michael Kors glasses on her nose, a book tucked under her arm.

She was still wearing the bright red, short-sleeved turtleneck, and her black dress pants. A gold necklace with a fractured fire opal sparkled around her neck. It was the same necklace she'd worn when she turned down my proposal. Somehow it suited her.

"I have something to show you. Can you come with me?"

"Where?"

"It's a surprise, just please?"

"Okay." Her agreement was hesitant, but that would have to be enough. She closed the door to slide open the chain and let me in. "Just give me a moment to get my shoes on."

Her apartment was neat, decorated in a mismatch of vintage designer furniture. It was the exact opposite of her room at her family's mansion, which had been all pretty pale pastels. This room was still chic, still feminine, but with bold colors and filled with life.

She disappeared into her bedroom for a moment, and I forced myself not to think about what was in that room and wonder if she had anyone else in that bed.

When she finally emerged, I was buzzing with energy.

I hated that she could be with another man, and it was none of my business. Harrison had given the order that my security was allowed to watch Amelia but never report back who she was with. I didn't like it, but I needed his help, so I'd agreed.

"What is this surprise?" she asked.

"You will see soon enough. I have it on good authority you will like it." I offered her my arm and guided her down to the waiting Town Car.

It wasn't a long drive. I was too nervous to say anything, so we sat for five minutes in a painfully awkward silence before we pulled up to a prewar brick building in Lenox Hill.

It was perfect—not too far from the park or the Met. She could take a cab or even walk to either. It was five stories and used to be a ballet school before it was turned into a family home, and now it was going to be hers.

When Harrison called me and told me she wanted to teach art, I had several real estate agents searching all five boroughs. One had found this beauty. It had been renovated in the past month, with no expenses spared.

I got out of the car and waved off the driver. I opened her door and offered my arm to her. She took it and stood. That little line between her brows was there again as she tried to figure out where we were.

"What is this place?" she asked as we headed up the little cobblestone sidewalk.

"Why don't you go find out?" I pointed to the brass plaque that was covered with a white cloth.

She pulled down the sheet and gasped as she read "The Amelia Mae Astrid Children's School of the Arts."

"What?" She looked back at me, eyes wide. God, I hoped it was just shock and not shock and outrage.

"Before you say anything. Let me give you the tour," I said, wiping the sweat on my palms off on my pants. Never, not in school, during multi-billion-dollar business deals, never had my palms sweated. But now, I was a terrified shaking mess.

She said nothing, her face frozen back in that mask of indifference I loathed. However, this was, in all likelihood, somewhere between a coping mechanism and habit. Still, it made my nerves worse and my stomach ache.

"The first floor has a reception area and a gallery. The basement actually has a top-of-the-line kiln. There are several studios, some big enough for full classes, others for private studios on the second and third floors. The fourth floor is mostly offices, and the fifth floor is your studio."

"My studio?" She took a few steps in and looked around. I still couldn't read her expression.

274

"Yes, your studio. You have the budget to hire a receptionist, as well as a few other art teachers and an event planner. Your operating costs will be covered for the first five years."

"Why?" She was walking around the polished wood floors, her heels clicking subtly with each step as she looked around. Then her eyes landed on a painting hanging on the wall—a beautiful garden landscape, one she had painted.

"Because I thought this would make you happy. Making you happy makes me happy, and Amelia, I haven't been happy since you left. In fact, the only time I have ever been happy was the night you and I spent eating s'mores and making love in front of the fire."

She turned to look at me, opening her mouth to say something, but I cut her off. If she was going to reject me, fine, I would accept it. Harrison had made damn sure I knew I had to respect her choices, but I had to explain first.

"This is not a bribe. This school, and the accounts associated with it, they're yours. My name no longer appears anywhere on the deed, the contracts, nothing. Everything is owned by the non-profit, and it is all yours."

She looked around some more, saw a few other paintings she had done, as well as a charcoal sketch Rose had insisted on framing and hanging by the door. I hoped eventually Amelia would draw another one without horns and hang it in her office.

"How did you get my paintings?"

"Rose. I came to her with this idea, and she has been an enormous help. She is the one who oversaw the decorators and the more cosmetic renovations to the building. Harrison has overlooked and approved all the legal paperwork to make sure that I can never take this from you, no matter what happens between us or doesn't."

"This is all mine?"

"Yes."

"Why?" She crossed the floor to where I was standing. "I don't understand."

"Because I'm a man who doesn't allow himself to make mistakes. I demand perfection in everything I do, and I achieved it. Until I met you. When it came to you, to us, I didn't know it at the time, but I was given the opportunity to have something far more valuable than money or power. I was given a chance at loving a woman who could see past my bullshit, a woman I wanted to be by my side in all ways. Then I fucked it up."

"Luc—"

"No, I fucked up. I want to be a better man for you. I will change, I'll be less controlling, less forceful, whatever you want…" I took a deep breath and looked into her beautiful eyes. "This is my way of apologizing, of trying to make up for the hell I put you through, and to show you I will always lo—"

She covered my mouth with her hand to stop me from talking.

Amelia stepped closer to me, her body almost touching mine. I immediately brought my hands around her waist and pulled her the last inch so she was against me. She was so soft, so warm, and I thought her curves may have filled out a bit.

"Can I ask you something and you give me a straight answer?" Her green eyes stared up at me, and I was lost in them.

Her hand was still pressed over my mouth, so I just nodded.

"What if I don't want you to change?"

My heart sank as those words left her perfect lips.

"What if I like it when you are forceful and controlling? What if I just want it in specific situations?" Her hand stayed over my mouth, and I merely nodded, refusing to get my hopes up that she was saying what I thought she was saying.

She drew a deep breath and closed her eyes for a moment before opening them again to look at me.

"In the sculpture garden, you asked me a question. Is it too late to change my mind?"

I pulled her hand away from my mouth and sealed my lips to hers in an all-consuming kiss.

CHAPTER 36

AMELIA

"**A**re you ready?" my father asked as he took my arm.

I gave him a big smile and nodded.

My cheeks and jaw ached.

I was smiling so much, and I didn't care. I didn't even care that I would get laugh lines. To be honest, I'd stopped caring about those perceived imperfections a while ago. I was excited and so happy.

The day was perfect.

The sun was out, but it wasn't hot; it was warm with a cool breeze. The last of the wisteria from the tunnel was about to die off, so the air smelled sweet, but not cloying or overpowering. Just the faintest floral hints mingling with the cut grass and fresh air.

The string quartet had set up on the lawn, and they were playing the most beautiful music I had ever heard. Everything was going right—even better than I could have imagined. I was so excited, that it could all go wrong and I probably wouldn't even notice. As long as he was still there waiting for me, it would all be wonderful.

"You seem different from when we did this last time." My father studied me while we waited for our turn.

"Last time I was supposed to marry a man I didn't know for a merger. This time, I'm marrying a man I know and love," I said as I watched my sister, the maid of honor, walk down the aisle in her pretty burnt orange dress.

"I'm glad this worked out in the end. I'm sorry your mother wasn't feeling up to coming."

"I know she chose not to come, and I'm okay with that. Today isn't supposed to be about her. It's about me and my husband and the life we are going to make together."

I had chosen not to tell my father about the long, ranting voicemail my mother had left, calling me a slew of names. Listening to it and discussing it was simply not worth my time. She had chosen not to darken this event with her presence, and I was going to respect that.

"You know, I brought you here when you were little. I don't know if you remember." He looked around the brilliant green garden area while we waited for the music to change to the bridal march.

"I know. I always loved this garden, and Luc and I couldn't think of a better place to get married. We come out here every weekend to have a picnic and just be together. He even leaves his phone in the car."

"Good." My father nodded. "You deserve a man who will do that."

"Thank you, Daddy." I blinked several times to stop the tears that were pricking at the backs of my eyes.

"This wedding is beautiful, and so are you," my father said, placing a kiss on my cheek as the music stopped. Then the small group of friends and family who supported Luc and me stood, and the opening notes of the bridal march played.

For the first time, I actually felt beautiful.

The dress I had chosen was perfect. It had a simple A-line silhouette made in a soft antique white with hand-embroidered red flowers starting at the skirt and twining down to the hem. I had kept my makeup light, and my hair was down and flowing.

It felt natural, beautiful, and like me.

The real me.

Not the doll my mother had made up, not the woman I had been expected to be, but just me.

With my arm linked with my father's, we walked down the makeshift aisle. It was sectioned off with small solar lights in soft reds and pinks. The flower girls had sprinkled the grass with orange and red rose petals. I wanted to commit every detail to memory.

The smiling faces of people I actually knew and loved looked back at me from rows of seats. The makeshift altar had been positioned just under the *First Love* statue that still made me think of that night with Luc when I realized we had a shot at happiness.

This was the spot where I had broken his heart and chosen myself.

Now that I had started finding myself, Luc had turned out to be the perfect partner.

He was patient when I asked him to let me make my own mistakes and take my own chances, like hiring a girl fresh from college with no experience as an event coordinator. He had been supportive when I wanted to take on more scholarship students. Even when I just needed to vent about the frustrations of starting such a large project, he sat and listened. Rose had told him to never offer help or solutions unless they were asked for.

The man hadn't even scoffed when I told him I wanted a small wedding and reception that was not covered by the press. When I told him I didn't want to wait a year or even a few months to get married, he had made the sweetest love to me, right there on the hardwood floors.

The justice of the peace stood, centered on that statue.

To his right were Rose, and Luc's sisters. Each wore simple dresses in muted shades of red that enhanced their complexions and complemented the red embroidery on my dress. On the other side stood my brother, as intimidating as ever, but with a soft smile as he gazed at me. Then, standing at the end, waiting to take my hand, was the most amazing man I had ever met.

Luc Manwarring, the man who in a few moments would be my husband.

He was incredibly handsome in his classic black suit with his red tie, his blue eyes wide as he looked at me in awe.

That look—I would never get sick of that look.

He looked at me like he saw me, all of me, every single flaw, and loved me all the more for it.

Most women I knew dreamed of a church wedding to a rich man. I had gotten something far greater—a garden wedding of my dreams to a man I loved more than anything.

"Dearly beloved, we are gathered here today to…" The justice of the peace went through his speech, and I barely heard a word of it.

I was lost in Luc's eyes, as he was lost in mine.

My world had imploded when he interrupted my first wedding.

It had set me on a path I hadn't known was possible.

Thanks to this man, I knew who I was and what I wanted out of life.

I supported him and his work and his goals like a good wife, but he also supported mine. In his eyes, at least, we were equals.

My school was close to being operational. We had decided that at least half of the spots would be for students on scholarships, and we had several qualified teachers coming in to teach classes. Then, at night, we had local artists to offer adult classes. The tuition for those would cover most of the operating costs.

Luc had even agreed to take a few pottery classes with me there.

For the time being, I had moved into his condo. We had found an older building we loved, a prewar brownstone, in which we got to design the new layout for. It combined the modern touches and conveniences he loved with the antique, old-world details and color I adored. It was perfect. As soon as it was ready, we'd be moving in there then figuring out the rest of our lives.

I didn't care what the world threw at us because now I knew, at the end of the day, I was his.

His wife, his lover, his equal, his obsession.

And when we were alone, his dirty little girl.

"I now pronounce you man and wife. You may kiss the bride."

EPILOGUE

MARKSEN

*W*ho held their wedding in a park during the New Jersey fall?

It was tacky.

No, worse than tacky, it was common. They hadn't even closed the entire park. I was able to just stand by a different sculpture and watch as Luc Manwarring stole what was supposed to be my future.

I couldn't believe he expected us to believe that they were "in love" now. They'd split up and then two months later they were married. That wasn't love. That was an unplanned pregnancy. Her brother had probably made some arrangement so his sister didn't embarrass him.

No one who knew Luc was ever going to believe he loved this girl. There were only two things Luc loved, and they were money and power. He loved thinking he was so far above the rest of us that he was untouchable. Everything he cared about was protected.

Soon, I was going to show him just how foolish that was.

Just like having an outdoor wedding in an unsecured location was foolish.

I sat back and watched their asinine little farce of a ceremony. His eyes were on his bride, but mine were behind her on my target. Olivia Eireann Manwarring, Luc's precious sister. Luc had stolen my bride, and the fortune that would have come with her. Fine, I'd steal his sister and take her as my own.

The ceremony was tedious, but the more I watched this girl with the sun shining red in her long dark curls, the more I realized that, despite the embarrassment of the first wedding, I might just have the better end of the bargain. Olivia was stunning, and she had been raised a Manwarring, so she'd know how to behave in society. There was no doubt in my mind that she was a brat who would need to be broken in. That was fine.

I would have fun showing her how to be a wife. I bet those pretty brown eyes would be even better with tears filling them as she sucked on my cock.

Finally, the crowd rose and cheered as Luc kissed his bride. He picked her up and carried her back down the aisle to everyone's adulation, and I couldn't help but bristle, my hands tightening into fists.

"Oh my, she looks so lovely," a woman in some hideous knit sweater said as she stood next to me. The wedding had drawn a crowd of peasants to watch the festivities.

So fucking common.

I moved away from the crowd and went to get into position.

The wedding guests would soon head to the reception in the little restaurant that was in the park. The Rats, which seemed appropriate, was on the other side of the park, and the guests would head there while the wedding party took a few pictures. It would be the entire wedding party for about twenty minutes, then some of just the bride and groom as the sun set.

Finally, the wedding party headed toward The Rats.

I would not be much longer.

I called my security team and told them to get the private plane ready.

Soon, the guests were leaving the restaurant to wander the grounds.

I watched as Olivia separated from the guests and made her way down the secluded forest path toward me.

This was, of course, by design. I had left nothing to chance.

A quick hundred-dollar bill in the right server's pocket had ensured that they dropped a few hints to Olivia about the more unique sculptures on the grounds that the tourists usually missed. Based on my research of her, I knew she wouldn't be able to resist.

When she rounded the final corner, I looked over my shoulder to ensure she wasn't followed, as the dense fall foliage swallowed her retreating form.

On silent feet, I stalked to within a few feet behind her.

I was so close, the scent of her perfume mixed with the rich, smoky scent of the woods.

The corner of my mouth lifted.

The sweet smell of revenge.

TO BE CONTINUED...

Then Hate Me
A Dark Billionaire Enemies to Lovers Romance
Gilded Decadence Series, Book Two

ABOUT BLAKE HENSLEY

**The sinfully decadent dream project
of best friends and USA TODAY Bestselling authors,
Zoe Blake and Alta Hensley.**

Alta Hensley, renowned for her hot, dark, and dirty romances, showcases her distinctive blend of alpha heroes, captivating love stories, and scorching eroticism.

Meanwhile, Zoe Blake brings a touch of darkness and glamour to the series, featuring her signature style of possessive billionaires, taboo scenes, and unexpected twists.

Together, as Blake Hensley, they combine their storytelling prowess to deliver "Twice the Darkness," promising sordid scandals, hidden secrets, and forbidden desires of New York's jaded high society in their new series,
Gilded Decadence.

ALSO BY BLAKE HENSLEY

THE GILDED DECADENCE SERIES

A Dark Enemies to Lovers Romance

The More I Hate

Gilded Decadence Series, Book One

His family dared to challenge mine, so I am going to ruin them... starting with stealing his bride.

Only a cold-hearted villain would destroy an innocent bride's special day over a business deal gone bad...

Which is why I choose this precise moment to disrupt New York High Society's most anticipated wedding of the season.

As I am Luc Manwarring, II, billionaire heir to one of the most powerful families in the country, no one is brave enough to stop me.

My revenge plan is deceptively simple: humiliate the groom, then blackmail the bride's family into coercing the bride into marrying me instead.

My ruthless calculations do not anticipate my reluctant bride having so much fight and fire in her.

At every opportunity, she resists my dominance and control, even going so far as trying to escape my dark plans for her.

She is only supposed to be a means to an end, an unwilling player in my game of revenge.

But the more she challenges me, the more I begin to wonder... who is playing who?

Then Hate Me

Gilded Decadence Series, Book Two

He dared to steal my bride, so it's only fair I respond by kidnapping his innocent sister.

Only a monster with no morals would kidnap a woman from her brother's wedding…

Which was precisely what I've become, a monster bent on revenge.

After all, as the billionaire Marksen DuBois, renowned for being a jilted groom, my reputation and business were in tatters.

There was nothing more dangerous than a man possessing power, boundless resources, and a vendetta.

I would torment him with increasingly degrading photos of his precious sister as I held her captive and under my complete control.

She'd have no option but to yield to my every command if she wished to shield herself and her family from further disgrace.

She was just a captured pawn to be dominated, exploited, and discarded.

Yet the more ensnared we become in my twisted game of revenge, the more my suspicions grow.

As she fiercely counters my every move, I begin to question whether I'm the true pawn… ensnared by my queen.

My Only Hate

Gilded Decadence Series, Book Three

From our very first fiery encounter, I was tempted to fire my beautiful new assistant.

Right after I punished her for that defiant slap she delivered in response to my undeniably inappropriate kiss.

As Harrison Astrid, New York's formidable District Attorney, distractions were a luxury I couldn't afford.

Forming a shaky alliance with the Manwarrings and the Dubois, I was ensnared in a dangerous cat-and-mouse game.

As I strive to thwart my mother's cunning manipulations and her deadly alliance with the Irish mob.

Yet, every time I cross paths with my assistant, our mutual animosity surges into a near-savage need to control and dominate her.

I am a man who demands obedience, especially from subordinates.

Her stubbornness fuels my urge to assert my dominance, my need to show her I'm not just her boss—I'm her master.

Unfortunately the fiancé I'm to accept to play high society's charade, complicates things.

So I rein in my desire and resist the attraction between us.

Until the Irish mob targets my pretty little assistant… targets what's mine.

Now there isn't a force on earth that will keep me from tearing the city apart to find her.

Fair Love of Hate

Gilded Decadence Series, Book Four

First rule of being a bodyguard, don't f*ck the woman you're protecting.

And I want to break that rule so damn bad I can practically taste her.

She's innocent, sheltered, and spoiled.

As Reid Taylor, former Army sergeant and head of security for the Manwarrings, the last thing I should be doing is babysitting my boss's little sister.

I definitely shouldn't be fantasizing about pinning her down, spreading her thighs and…

It should help that she fights my protection at every turn.

Disobeying my rules. Running away from me. Talking back with that sexy, smart mouth of hers.

But it doesn't. It just makes me want her more.

I want to bend her over and claim her, hard and rough, until she begs for mercy.

That is a dangerous line I cannot cross.

She is an heiress, the precious daughter of one of the most powerful, multi-billionaire families in New York.

And I'm just her bodyguard, an employee. It would be the ultimate societal taboo.

But now her family is forcing her into an arranged marriage, and I'm not sure I'll be able to contain my rising rage at the idea of another man touching her.

A Hate at First

Gilded Decadence Series, Book Five

The moment she slapped me, I knew I'd chosen the right bride.

To be fair, I had just stolen her entire inheritance.

As Lucian Manwarring, billionaire patriarch of the powerful Manwarring family, my word is law.

She's a beautiful and innocent heiress, raised to be the perfect society trophy wife.

Although far too young for me, that won't stop me from claiming her as my new prized possession.

What I hadn't planned on was her open defiance of me.

Far from submissive and obedient; she is stubborn, outspoken and headstrong.

She tries to escape my control and fights my plan to force her down the aisle.

I am not accustomed to being disobeyed.

While finding it mildly amusing at first, it is past time she accepts her fate.

She will be my bride even if I have to ruthlessly dominate and punish her to get what I want.

ABOUT ZOE BLAKE

Zoe Blake is the USA Today Bestselling Author of the romantic suspense saga *The Cavalieri Billionaire Legacy* inspired by her own heritage as well as her obsession with jewelry, travel, and the salacious gossip of history's most infamous families.

She delights in writing Dark Romance books filled with overly possessive billionaires, taboo scenes, and unexpected twists. She usually spends her ill-gotten gains on martinis, travels, and red lipstick. Since she can barely boil water, she's lucky enough to be married to a sexy Chef.

CAVALIERI BILLIONAIRE LEGACY

A Dark Enemies to Lovers Romance

Scandals of the Father

Cavalieri Billionaire Legacy, Book One

Being attracted to her wasn't wrong... but acting on it would be.

As the patriarch of the powerful and wealthy Cavalieri family, my choices came with consequences for everyone around me.

The roots of my ancestral, billionaire-dollar winery stretch deep into the rich, Italian soil, as does our legacy for ruthlessness and scandal.

It wasn't the fact she was half my age that made her off limits.

Nothing was off limits for me.

A wounded bird, caught in a trap not of her own making, she posed no risk to me.

My obsessive desire to possess her was the real problem.

For both of us.

But now that I've seen her, tasted her lips, I can't let her go.

Whether she likes it or not, she needs my protection.

I'm doing this for her own good, yet, she fights me at every turn.

Refusing the luxury I offer, desperately trying to escape my grasp.

I need to teach her to obey before the dark rumors of my past reach her.

Ruin her.

She cannot find out what I've done, not before I make her mine.

Sins of the Son

Cavalieri Billionaire Legacy, Book Two

She's hated me for years... now it's past time to give her a reason to.

When you are a son, and one of the heirs, to the legacy of the Cavalieri name, you need to be more vicious than your enemies.

And sometimes, the lines get blurred.

Years ago, they tried to use her as a pawn in a revenge scheme against me.

Even though I cared about her, I let them treat her as if she were nothing.

I was too arrogant and self-involved to protect her then.

But I'm here now. Ready to risk my life tracking down every single one of them.

They'll pay for what they've done as surely as I'll pay for my sins against her.

Too bad it won't be enough for her to let go of her hatred of me,

To get her to stop fighting me.

Because whether she likes it or not, I have the power, wealth, and connections to keep her by my side

And every intention of ruthlessly using all three to make her mine.

Secrets of the Brother

Cavalieri Billionaire Legacy, Book Three

We were not meant to be together... then a dark twist of fate stepped in, and we're the ones who will pay for it.

As the eldest son and heir of the Cavalieri name, I inherit a great deal more than a billion dollar empire.

I receive a legacy of secrets, lies, and scandal.

After enduring a childhood filled with malicious rumors about my father, I have fallen prey to his very same sin.

I married a woman I didn't love out of a false sense of family honor.

Now she has died under mysterious circumstances.

And I am left to play the widowed groom.

For no one can know the truth about my wife…

Especially her sister.

The only way to protect her from danger is to keep her close, and yet, her very nearness tortures me.

She is my sister in name only, but I have no right to desire her.

Not after what I have done.

It's too much to hope she would understand that it was all for her.

It's always been about her.

Only her.

I am, after all, my father's son.

And there is nothing on this earth more ruthless than a Cavalieri man in love.

Seduction of the Patriarch

Cavalieri Billionaire Legacy, Book Four

With a single gunshot, she brings the violent secrets of my buried past into the present.

She may not have pulled the trigger, but she still has blood on her hands.

And I know some very creative ways to make her pay for it.

I am as ruthless as my Cavalieri ancestors, who forged our powerful family legacy.

But no fortune is built without spilling blood.

I earn a reputation as a dangerous man to cross… and make enemies along the way.

So to protect those I love, I hand over the mantle of patriarch to my brother and move to northern Italy.

For years, I stay in the shadows…

Then a vengeful mafia syndicate attacks my family.

Now nothing will prevent me from seeking vengeance on those responsible.

And I don't give a damn who I hurt in the process… including her.

Whether it takes seduction, punishment, or both, I intend to manipulate her as a means to an end.

Yet, the more my little kitten shows her claws, the more I want to make her purr.

My plan is to coerce her into helping me topple the mafia syndicate, and then retreat into the shadows.

But if she keeps fighting me… I might just have to take her with me.

Scorn of the Betrothed

Cavalieri Billionaire Legacy, Book Five

A union forged in vengeance, bound by hate… and beneath it all, a twisted game of desire and deception.

In the heart of the Cavalieri family, I am the son destined for a loveless marriage.

The true legacy of my family, my birthright ties me to a woman I despise.

The daughter of the mafia boss who nearly ended my family.

She is my future wife, and I am her unwelcome groom.

The looming wedding is a beacon of hope for our families.

A promise of peace in a world fraught with danger and deception.

We were meant to be the bridge between two powerful legacies.

The only thing we share is a mutual hatred.

She is a prisoner to her families' ambitions, desperate for a way out.

My duty is to guard her, to ensure she doesn't escape her gilded cage.

But every moment spent with her, every spark of anger, adds fuel to the growing fire of desire between us.

We're trapped in a dangerous duel of passion and fury.

The more I try to tame her, the more she ignites me.

Hatred and desire become blurred.

Our impending marriage becomes a twisted game.

But as the wedding draws near, my suspicions grow.

My bride is not who she claims to be.

IVANOV CRIME FAMILY TRILOGY

A Dark Mafia Romance

Savage Vow

Ivanov Crime Family, Book One

Gregor & Samara's story

I took her innocence as payment.

She was far too young and naïve to be betrothed to a monster like me.

I would bring only pain and darkness into her sheltered world.

That's why she ran.

I should've just let her go…

She never asked to marry into a powerful Russian mafia family.

None of this was her choice.

Unfortunately for her, I don't care.

I own her… and after three years of searching… I've found her.

My runaway bride was about to learn disobedience has consequences…
punishing ones.

Having her in my arms and under my control had become an obsession.

Nothing was going to keep me from claiming her before the eyes of
God and man.

She's finally mine… and I'm never letting her go.

Vicious Oath

Ivanov Crime Family, Book One

Damien & Yelena's story

When I give an order, I expect it to be obeyed.

She's too smart for her own good, and it's going to get her killed.

Against my better judgement, I put her under the protection of my powerful Russian mafia family.

So imagine my anger when the little minx ran.

For three long years I've been on her trail, always one step behind.

Finding and claiming her had become an obsession.

It was getting harder to rein in my driving need to possess her… to own her.

But now the chase is over.

I've found her.

Soon she will be mine.

And I plan to make it official, even if I have to drag her kicking and screaming to the altar.

This time… there will be no escape from me.

Betrayed Honor

Ivanov Crime Family, Book One

Mikhail & Nadia's story

Her innocence was going to get her killed.

That was if I didn't get to her first.

She's the protected little sister of the powerful Ivanov Russian mafia family - the very definition of forbidden.

It's always been my job, as their Head of Security, to watch over her but never to touch.

That ends today.

She disobeyed me and put herself in danger.

It was time to take her in hand.

I'm the only one who can save her and I will fight anyone who tries to stop me, including her brothers.

Honor and loyalty be damned.

She's mine now.

RUTHLESS OBSESSION SERIES

A Dark Mafia Romance

Sweet Cruelty

Ruthless Obsession Series, Book One

Dimitri & Emma's story

It was an innocent mistake.

She knocked on the wrong door.

Mine.

If I were a better man, I would've just let her go.

But I'm not.

I'm a cruel bastard.

I ruthlessly claimed her virtue for my own.

It should have been enough.

But it wasn't.

I needed more.

Craved it.

She became my obsession.

Her sweetness and purity taunted my dark soul.

The need to possess her nearly drove me mad.

A Russian arms dealer had no business pursuing a naive librarian student.

She didn't belong in my world.

I would bring her only pain.

But it was too late…

She was mine and I was keeping her.

Sweet Depravity

Ruthless Obsession Series, Book Two

Vaska & Mary's story

The moment she opened those gorgeous red lips to tell me no, she was mine.

I was a powerful Russian arms dealer and she was an innocent schoolteacher.

If she had a choice, she'd run as far away from me as possible.

Unfortunately for her, I wasn't giving her one.

I wasn't just going to take her; I was going to take over her entire world.

Where she lived.

What she ate.

Where she worked.

All would be under my control.

Call it obsession.

Call it depravity.

I don't give a damn… as long as you call her mine.

Sweet Savagery

Ruthless Obsession Series, Book Three

Ivan & Dylan's Story

I was a savage bent on claiming her as punishment for her family's mistakes.

As a powerful Russian Arms dealer, no one steals from me and gets away with it.

She was an innocent pawn in a dangerous game.

She had no idea the package her uncle sent her from Russia contained my stolen money.

If I were a good man, I would let her return the money and leave.

If I were a gentleman, I might even let her keep some of it just for frightening her.

As I stared down at the beautiful living doll stretched out before me like a virgin sacrifice,

I thanked God for every sin and misdeed that had blackened my cold heart.

I was not a good man.

I sure as hell wasn't a gentleman… and I had no intention of letting her go.

She was mine now.

And no one takes what's mine.

Sweet Brutality

Ruthless Obsession Series, Book Four

Maxim & Carinna's story

The more she fights me, the more I want her.

It's that beautiful, sassy mouth of hers.

It makes me want to push her to her knees and dominate her, like the brutal savage I am.

As a Russian Arms dealer, I should not be ruthlessly pursuing an innocent college student like her, but that would not stop me.

A twist of fate may have brought us together, but it is my twisted obsession that will hold her captive as my own treasured possession.

She is mine now.

I dare you to try and take her from me.

Sweet Ferocity

Ruthless Obsession Series, Book Five

Luka & Katie's Story

I was a mafia mercenary only hired to find her, but now I'm going to keep her.

She is a Russian mafia princess, kidnapped to be used as a pawn in a dangerous territory war.

Saving her was my job. Keeping her safe had become my obsession.

Every move she makes, I am in the shadows, watching.

I was like a feral animal: cruel, violent, and selfishly out for my own needs. Until her.

Now, I will make her mine by any means necessary.

I am her protector, but no one is going to protect her from me.

Sweet Intensity

Ruthless Obsession Series, Book Six

Antonius & Brynn's Story

She couldn't possibly have known the danger she would be in the moment she innocently accepted the job.

She was too young for a man my age, barely in her twenties. Far too pure and untouched.

Too bad that wasn't going to stop me.

The moment I laid eyes on her, I claimed her.

She would be mine… by any means necessary.

I owned the most elite Gambling Club in Chicago, which was a secret front for my true business as a powerful crime boss for the Russian Mafia.

And she was a fragile little bird, who had just flown straight into my open jaws.

Naïve and sweet, she was a tasty morsel I couldn't resist biting.

My intense drive to dominate and control her had become an obsession.

I would ruthlessly use my superior strength and connections to take over her life.

The harder she resisted, the more feral and savage I would become.

She needed to understand… she was mine now.

Mine.

Sweet Severity

Ruthless Obsession Series, Book Seven

Macarius & Phoebe's Story

Had she crashed into any other man's car, she could have walked away—but she hit mine.

Upon seeing the bruises on her wrist, I struggled to contain my rage.

Despite her objections, I refused to allow her to leave.

Whoever hurt this innocent beauty would pay dearly.

As a Russian Mafia crime boss who owns Chicago's most elite gambling club, I have very creative and painful methods of exacting revenge.

She seems too young and naive to be out on her own in such a dangerous world.

Needing a nanny, I decided to claim her for the role.

She might resist my severe, domineering discipline, but I won't give her a choice in the matter.

She needs a protector, and I'd be damned if it were anyone but me.

Resisting the urge to claim her will test all my restraint.

It's a battle I'm bound to lose.

With each day, my obsession and jealousy intensify.

It's only a matter of time before my control snaps…and I make her mine.

Mine.

Sweet Animosity

Ruthless Obsession, Book Eight

Varlaam & Amber's Story

I never asked for an assistant, and if I had, I sure as hell wouldn't have chosen her.

With her sharp tongue and lack of discipline, what she needs is a firm hand, not a job.

The more she tests my limits, the more tempted I am to bend her over my knee.

As a Russian Mafia boss and owner of Chicago's most elite gambling club, I can't afford distractions from her antics.

Or her secrets.

For I suspect, my innocent new assistant is hiding something.

And I know just how to get to the truth.

It's high time she understands who holds the power in our relationship.

To ensure I get what I desire, I'll keep her close, controlling her every move.

Except I am no longer after information—I want her mind, body and soul.

She underestimated the stakes of our dangerous game and now owes a heavy price.

As payment I will take her freedom.

She's mine now.

Mine.

ABOUT ALTA HENSLEY

Alta Hensley is a USA TODAY Bestselling author of hot, dark and dirty romance. She is also an Amazon Top 10 bestselling author. Being a multi-published author in the romance genre, Alta is known for her dark, gritty alpha heroes, captivating love stories, hot eroticism, and engaging tales of the constant struggle between dominance and submission.

She lives in Astoria, Oregon with her husband, two daughters, and an Australian Shepherd. When she isn't walking the coastline, and drinking beer in her favorite breweries, she is writing about villains who always get their love story and happily ever after.

ALSO BY ALTA HENSLEY

HEATHENS HOLLOW SERIES

A Dark Stalker Billionaire Romance

Heathens

She invited the darkness in, so she'll have no one else to blame when I come for her.

The Hunt.

It is a sinister game of submission. She'll run. I'll chase.

And when I catch her, it will be savage. Untamed. Primal.

I will be the beast from her darkest fantasies.

I should be protecting her, but instead I've been watching her. Stalking her.

She's innocent. Forbidden. The daughter of my best friend.

But she chose this.

And even if she made a mistake, even if she wants to run, to escape, it's far too late.

She's mine now.

GODS AMONG MEN SERIES

A Dark Billionaire Romance

Villains Are Made

I know how villains are made.

I've watched their secrets rise from the ashes and emerge from the shadows.

As part of a family tree with roots so twisted, I'm strangled by their vine.

Imprisoned in a world of decadence and sin, I've seen Gods among men.

And he is one of them.

He is the villain.

He is the enemy who demands to be the lover.

He is the monster who has shown me pleasure but gives so much pain.

But something has changed…

He's different.

Darker.

Wildly possessive as his obsession with me grows to an inferno that can't be controlled.

Yes… he is the villain.

And he is the end of my beginning.

Monsters Are Hidden

The problem with secrets is they create powerful monsters.

And even more dangerous enemies.

He's the keeper of all his family's secrets, the watcher of all.

He knows what I've done, what I've risked… the deadly choice I made.

The tangled vines of his mighty family tree are strangling me.

There is no escape.

I am locked away, captive to his twisted obsession and demands.

If I run, my hell will never end.

If I stay, he will devour me.

My only choice is to dare the monster to come out into the light,

before his darkness destroys us both.

Yes… he is the monster in hiding.

And he is the end of my beginning.

Vipers Are Forbidden

It's impossible to enter a pit full of snakes and not get bit.

Until you meet me, that is.

My venom is far more toxic than the four men who have declared me
their enemy.

They seek vengeance and launch a twisted game of give and take.

I'll play in their dark world, because it's where I thrive.

I'll dance with their debauchery, for I surely know the steps.

But then I discover just how wrong I am. Their four, not only matches,
but beats, my one.

With each wicked move they make, they become my obsession.

I crave them until they consume all thought.

The temptation to give them everything they desire becomes too much.

I'm entering their world, and there is no light to guide my way. My
blindness full of lust will be my defeat.

Yes… I am the viper and am forbidden.

But they are the end of my beginning.

SPIKED ROSES BILLIONAIRE'S CLUB SERIES

A Dark Billionaires Romance

Bastards & Whiskey

I sit amongst the Presidents, Royalty, the Captains of Industry, and the wealthiest men in the world.

We own Spiked Roses—an exclusive, membership only establishment in New Orleans where money or lineage is the only way in. It is for the gentlemen who own everything and never hear the word no.

Sipping on whiskey, smoking cigars, and conducting multi-million dollar deals in our own personal playground of indulgence, there isn't anything I can't have… and that includes HER. I can also have HER if I want.

And I want.

Villains & Vodka

My life is one long fevered dream, balancing between being killed or killing.

The name Harley Crow is one to be feared.

I am an assassin.

A killer.

The villain.

I own it. I choose this life. Hell, I crave it. I hunger for it. The smell of fear makes me hard and is the very reason the blood runs through my veins.

Until I meet her…

Marlowe Masters.

Her darkness matches my own.

In my twisted world of dancing along the jagged edge of the blade…

She changes everything.

No weapon can protect me from the kind of death she will ultimately deliver.

Scoundrels & Scotch

I'll stop at nothing to own her.

I'm a collector of dolls.

All kinds of dolls.

So beautiful and sexy, they become my art.

So perfect and flawless, my art galleries are flooded by the wealthy to gaze upon my possessions with envy.

So fragile and delicate, I keep them tucked away for safety.

The dark and torrid tales of Drayton's Dolls run rampant through the rich and famous, and all but a few are true.

Normally I share my dolls for others to play with or watch on display.

But not my special doll.

No, not her.

Ivy is the most precious doll of all.

She's mine. All mine.

Devils & Rye

Forbidden fruit tastes the sweetest.

It had been years since I had seen her.

Years since I last saw those eyes with pure, raw innocence.

So much time had passed since I lusted after what I knew I should resist.

But she was so right.

And I was so wrong.

To claim her as mine was breaking the rules. Boundaries should not be broken. But temptation weakens my resolve.

With the pull of my dark desires…

I know that I can't hide from my sinful thoughts—and actions—forever.

Beasts & Bourbon

My royal blood flows black with twisted secrets.

I am a beast who wears a crown.

Heir to a modern kingdom cloaked in corruption and depravities.

The time has come to claim my princess.

An innocent hidden away from my dark world.

Till now.

Her initiation will require sacrifice and submission.

There is no escaping the chains which bind her to me.

Surrendering to my torment, as well as my protection, is her only path to survival.

In the end…

She will be forever mine.

Sinners & Gin

My power is absolute. My rules are law.

Structure.

Obedience.

Discipline.

I am in charge, and what I say goes. Black and white with no gray.

No one dares break the rules in my dark and twisted world… until her. Until she makes me cross my own jagged lines.

She's untouched. Perfection. Pure.

Forbidden.

She tests my limits in all ways.

There is only one option left.

I will claim her as mine no matter how many rules are broken.

THANK YOU

Stormy Night Publications would like to thank you for your interest in our books.

If you liked this book (or even if you didn't), we would really appreciate you leaving a review on the site where you purchased it. Reviews provide useful feedback for us and our authors, and this feedback (both positive comments and constructive criticism) allows us to work even harder to make sure we provide the content our customers want to read.

Printed in Great Britain
by Amazon

39742989R00185